DAALDER'S *Chocolates*

PHILIBERT SCHOGT

Translated from the Dutch by Sherry Marx

THUNDER'S MOUTH PRESS

NEW YORK

DAALDER'S CHOCOLATES

Published by
Thunder's Mouth Press
An Imprint of Avalon Publishing Group, Inc.
245 West 17th St., 11th Floor
New York, NY 10011

AVALON
publishing group incorporated

Copyright © 2005 by Philibert Schogt
Translation © 2005 by Sherry Marx

First printing October 2005

Library of Congress Cataloging-in-Publication Data is available.

ISBN: 1-56025-731-8
ISBN 13: 978-1-56025-731-8

9 8 7 6 5 4 3 2 1

Book design by Jamie McNeely
Printed in the United States of America
Distributed by Publishers Group West

For Astrid, David, and Nina

CONTENTS

Part 3

IN PARADISE

Part 4
SLAVERY

Part 5
SELF-EMPLOYED

Part 6
ONE LAST CHOCOLATE

Part 1

THE DEATH OF A CHOCOLATIER

Daalder's Chocolates

S top tormenting yourself, darling," cried Emma from the kitchen, but Joop already had his jacket on and now slammed the front door behind him even harder than he had intended.

Staring glumly ahead, he set off for St. Clair Avenue, the shopping street a five-minute walk from their house. It was all cheerfulness there. The concrete flower boxes placed along the sidewalk were already filled with daffodils, despite the forecast of snow. "Spring's here!" the silly fools yelled at him. "Spring's here!" When he walked past MegaDeli's interminably long shopfront, his expression darkened. As usual, he tried to ignore the decked-out windows and aggressive advertising, varying his pace to avoid walking to the beat of the cheery music that accompanied him along the way. Even the barrier at the parking-lot entrance contributed to the festive atmosphere, the way it kept flinging itself in the air to welcome every new driver. But some hundred yards or seven flower boxes farther on, the party was suddenly over.

Here, the parking lot ended and death row began, as Joop called the three shops that were about to be demolished. The outer two, Mr. and Mrs. Ho's grocery store and Tony Graziano's ice-cream parlor, had been boarded up for some time now in anticipation of the wrecker's ball. But you could still peer into the middle one. DAALDER'S CHOCOLATES it said in an arch across the window.

A workman was busy wrapping an iron chain around the flower box that stood in front of the door. Another workman was operating the control panels on a tow truck, letting the claw swing toward the flower box. When he noticed Joop, he signaled him to keep his distance.

Unbelievable.

The flower boxes were a gift to the neighborhood from MegaDeli, as were the fancy "Art Deco" streetlights with which they alternated along the north side of St. Clair Avenue. "An almost Parisian atmosphere," rejoiced a public relations assistant in a letter to the local residents. They had dumped such a flower box right in front of the chocolate shop, so that suppliers and elderly customers had to maneuver their trolleys and shopping carts in an awkward turn to get inside. When Emma finally got hold of the person in charge and asked him if the gift couldn't be moved a few yards to the side, she was told this would upset the rhythm of the street furniture.

But now that they needed room for the bulldozers, *whoosh!*—the unsightly monster was being hoisted up and whisked away just like that!

Stop tormenting yourself, darling.

As if he were imagining it all—everything that was happening here! As if it weren't so bad, as Emma kept suggesting. "You're sixty-two," she had said. "You would have stopped in two or three years anyhow." (Oh really?) Or: "Don't worry about money, we have more than enough of it nowadays." (As if that were the issue). And just think how much more dramatic this was for their neighbors on either side—the poor Hos, who had already suffered so much in

Vietnam, and Tony Graziano, an Italian whose entire family honor was at stake. Perhaps Emma meant well, but her soft talk made it all too clear how little she herself cared about the chocolate shop. Why else did she fall asleep instantly night after night, softly snoring away till morning? She hadn't lost a second's sleep or shed a single tear over the demise of Daalder's Chocolates.

No, it certainly wasn't his wife he should turn to for help in dealing with this blow, to say nothing of his son, Marcel.

"Well, Dad," was his reaction when he heard that the demolition decision was final, "that's the free market."

When they had emigrated to Toronto thirty years earlier, Joop and Emma had been amazed by all the dingy little shops along St. Clair Avenue and their motley collections of wares. Some tired old Latvian, Estonian, or Hungarian shopkeeper would be shuffling around between the shelves laden with yellowed greeting cards, notions, plastic toys, instant cake mix, and canned pineapple slices in heavy syrup. How did such shops manage to stay in business, they wondered. Time revealed that they often didn't. One day, the window would suddenly be obscured with FINAL SALE and EVERYTHING TO GO signs, sometimes the shop had already been boarded up. Where the shopkeeper had gone or even whether he was still alive no one knew for sure. No one cared. That was how cold and indifferent the free market could be, Joop would say to his wife and son. But at the same time he glowed with pride: Daalder's Chocolates was holding its ground.

He had encountered the same cold indifference in the wilderness north of Toronto. Endless though the forests were, the trees themselves were unimpressive. They jostled with one another for the few rays of sunlight, died slowly in one another's branches, or lay rotting away on the forest floor, where they served as nourishment for the hundreds of saplings that had begun their journey upward with naïve daring. Not a pretty forest, thought Joop.

By the same token, St. Clair Avenue with its endless flux of sprouting and withering shops was not a pretty street. But he had learned to live with it. He was a happy man as long as he could make chocolates the way he wanted. For twenty-nine years, Daalder's Chocolates had thrived in the harsh Canadian business climate—that is, until MegaDeli had appeared on the scene. That company's drive to expand had nothing to do with the natural laws of a Canadian forest. No, this was relentless clear-cutting, this was downright deforestation.

The New Neighbors

MegaDeli was a new American supermarket chain. After opening branches in several cities in the United States, the directors had set their sights on Toronto. The only thing they had to wait for was a suitable location. A site had presented itself on St. Clair Avenue, when the Pereiras could no longer scrape together the rent for the vast low-rise building complex that housed their grocery business.

The death throes of the Portuguese family business had lasted for years. When you entered the shop, it smelled more of compost than of fruit or vegetables, and there were always more Pereiras than customers—three generations strong, identifiable through their big doleful eyes and fatigued manner. Even the youngest grandson on his tricycle didn't seem to advance more than an inch at a time. Out of pity, Emma occasionally bought a drooping bunch of carrots there for her granddaughter's rabbit or a basketful of mealy apples that she could use in a pie. It was to no avail. Early one morning, six workmen in blue overalls showed up to empty the shop and cart everything away in two trucks. The family itself seemed to have disappeared off the face of the earth. Until, a few months later, Emma spotted Grandfather Pereira working as a cleaner on a subway platform.

In the meantime, the grimy interior of the premises had

been transformed into an ultramodern sparkling-clean super-market. The undeveloped plot of land next to it—where local residents had been walking their dogs since time immemorial and kids braved the highest mounds and deepest pits with their mountain bikes—had been smoothed over and paved, to serve as a parking lot for prospective customers.

Long before the opening, passersby were already being enticed with advertising slogans.

"Coming to this theater: the biggest selection of French cheeses in all of Toronto!"

"Fish sticks or oysters? Hot dogs or venison? The choice is yours!"

"That lemon grass sure smells good, but how do you use it? Soon you can ask our friendly stir-fry specialist, Chong Li!"

MegaDeli wasn't just another supermarket. No, "We com-bine the ease and low prices of the supermarket with the refinement and personal touch of the deli."

That didn't auger well, thought Joop, when such texts caught his eye as he walked to the chocolate shop. Refined eating was "in," so commerce had started to meddle with it—with all the consequences. He thought of what had happened to the crois-sant, which had first become the symbol of the romantic French breakfast, before deteriorating into the world's umpteenth quick snack, available in ten varieties. He thought of olive oil, which had recently been "discovered" by the Northern European and North American consumer, causing the market to be flooded with dirt-cheap, dark-green sludge. The first pressing, no less, because the second just wouldn't do. But when Emma drove to the Italian specialty shop for a new bottle of Oro di Altobelli, a golden-yellow oil so smooth and aromatic that Joop sometimes walked to the kitchen cupboard just to sneak a teaspoonful of it, the shopkeeper reported that the age-old family concern had just gone bankrupt, pressed out of the market by the big guys.

Joop was so upset that he wrote something resembling a letter of condolence to the Altobellis. An all-too-appropriate gesture: from Mrs. Altobelli's touching thank-you note, it became clear that her husband had recently taken his life.

The modern consumer demanded quality, it was said, but fulfilling that demand was precisely how true quality was being destroyed.

Still, Marcel often reminded his father, he was making a damned good living off the modern consumer.

Joop couldn't deny that Daalder's Chocolates was earning money like water. But the people who visited his shop these days were no cause for joy. The main reason they bought chocolates was to impress each other. Just the sort of public the planned supermarket was aiming at.

Then one day, the flower boxes and lampposts were placed along St. Clair Avenue. Like a guard of honor they heralded MegaDeli's final publicity offensive prior to the festive opening.

"Is this Paris? Is this New York? No, darling, this is Toronto!" The slogan took clever advantage of the Canadian double inferiority complex, which looked up to both a refined Europe and a dominant America. And the good souls loved every minute of it. "The arrival of MegaDeli is more proof again that Toronto has started to make its mark on the international culinary stage," drooled one critic in the *Toronto Star.* And what an improvement those gorgeous flower boxes and elegant lampposts made to St. Clair Avenue!

A short time later, Joop and Emma received another of the countless flyers—in the shop as well as at home. On behalf of all the employees, the splinter-new branch manager was "MegaDelighted" to invite all the local residents to a sneak preview. Or should that be "snack preview"?

Very funny. But Joop tore the "strictly personal" invitations in half and threw them in the wastebasket.

The Daalders' demonstrative absence didn't stop the preview from being a smashing success. And when MegaDeli opened its doors to the general public the following Saturday, the police had to be called in to keep the traffic under control on St. Clair Avenue.

Even Emma seemed to be infected by the hype. Never before had she complained of having to scour the city in search of the fine foods needed to meet Joop's high standards. But now, in a meek voice, she suggested that MegaDeli might save her a lot of time and money. Joop gave her a scathing look: she had to solemnly swear never, absolutely never, to buy anything there, not even dish detergent or toilet paper.

The Three Chocolateers

Shortly after the opening of MegaDeli, Joop's revenue started to decline. His shop assistant, Martha Simmons, was the first to notice, when she found time between customers to wipe the greasy fingerprints off the glass plates. That same evening, for the first time in years, Joop had to throw away a handful of unsold chocolates. The next evening, it was a few more. And a week later, a whole trayful slipped into the garbage bin just like in the early days of the chocolate shop. Orders he could set the clock by didn't come in, like that of Gérard, a French restaurateur he had being doing business with for more than a decade and whom he had almost come to regard as a friend. When Joop phoned him for an explanation, the cat came out of the bag. A serious competitor—or perhaps it was better to say three, seeing as they called themselves The Three Chocolateers—had appeared on the scene. That wasn't all. They turned out to have set up shop somewhere within the walls of the MegaDeli complex.

"And people nowadays are always looking for something new, aren't they?" Gérard had proffered apologetically.

Toronto was a vast city, one and a half times the size of the province of Utrecht, Joop's cousin Nico had once claimed. But now, three unscrupulous fellow craftsmen had set up camp less than two hundred yards from Daalder's Chocolates—to steal his customers.

An article about "The Three" had appeared in *The Art of Living*, of all places, the same glossy lifestyle magazine that had featured Joop a few years before. A full-page photograph showed two boys and a girl, all under thirty. For people devoted to preparing food, Joop certainly thought they looked unsavory. One of the boys had three silver rings dangling from his eyebrow, the girl also had a piercing, a silver ball that clung to her lower lip like a pimple, and the other fellow had an arty wisp of reddish hair hanging from his chin.

As if Joop had never existed, the article opened with the same refrain they had used for him. For a metropolis like Toronto, it was a sad state of affairs where the availability of good chocolate was concerned. But that was about to change with the arrival of The Three Chocolateers.

The boy with the mutilated eyebrow talked about his new "line." He had chocolates filled with morsels of chicken breast. For whoever dared, he also had whole chicken legs, bone and all, ensconced in a layer of chocolate. And he even had wishbones doused in chocolate (Joop had first encountered the barbarian custom of making a wish and then pulling on the wishbone to break it at the home of Canadian friends). The line was called *mole con pollo*—a play on *pollo con mole*, chicken in chocolate sauce, a famous Mayan dish—and could be seen as a tribute to the Mayans' fascinating culture, in which chocolate had originated. Hence the handsome rectangular Mayan motifs in gold leaf that he had embossed on the chicken-breast chocolates. Not that the cultural-historical message was to be taken too seriously. It was also just "nice and kinky" to combine meat and candy: the guiltiest food, so to speak, clad in the most innocent.

The girl with the silver pimple on her lip made chocolate

replicas of the Venus of Willendorf, the famous fertility figure dating from prehistoric times. The idea had come to her when she was visiting a museum while attending a chocolate competition in Vienna. She had recognized the figure from photographs and been startled by how small it was in reality: only four and a half inches tall, an ideal size to duplicate in chocolate. Because she had always felt cheated as a child when the chocolate Easter bunny turned out to be hollow inside, she filled every last corner of her little Venuses with chocolate. They were real calorie bombs, and therefore the ultimate statement against the modern ideal of slenderness: nice fat wenches that made you nice and fat, too.

The boy with the stray wisp of pubic hair on his chin specialized in abstract shapes, which, according to the author of the article, would not be out of place in a museum of modern art. *My my,* thought Joop, *never heard that one before.* This fellow detested the introvert designs of traditional chocolates; chocolate was meant to be fun! The grand gesture, the enchanting story, that's what it was all about, like in his Sleeping Beauty, a prickly tangle of caramel strands dipped in chocolate and concealing a fresh raspberry. You had to eat your way through the spines like a brave prince (or princess). Caution was recommended though, otherwise you might get a nasty cut on your lip. The reward for a hero's courage was the delicate raspberry, to which, so to speak, you could give the kiss of life.

Ideas and gestures flew in all directions. But not a word was said by The Three about the chocolate they used or the methods they employed. There wasn't the slightest hint of a vision about the combining of tastes and textures. As long as the results were "fun" and "exciting." For their aim was to make their product—the better chocolate—attractive to a younger public, a public that all too often preferred Mars bars and other such junk not worthy of the name chocolate. And why? Were chocolates too expensive? Nonsense! Nowadays everyone had money to burn. No, according to The Three Chocolateers it was because chocolates had something stuffy about them—they were still associated with little old ladies. And that was a downright shame for such a mysterious and spiritual substance as chocolate. A substance with such a complex nature that scientists never stopped talking about it. Apparently, chocolate was good for the concentration and effective as an antidepressant. And a recent study had shown it contained a substance that made you horny as hell. Well, The Three could have told the researchers that themselves!

Sure enough, there it was again, the alleged erotic effect of chocolate. That story had already been around when those little upstarts were still in diapers.

Enraged, Joop had tossed the magazine aside.

From then on, in protest against the empty words of The Three, Joop left even the most functional decorations off his chocolates. What did they mean, stuffy or introvert! The real adventure took place inside the mouth, and you didn't need caramel spines, prehistoric women, or chicken legs for that.

Meanwhile, his income continued to dwindle, even to the level of the early frugal years. Since the arrival of The Three, Joop's clientele did indeed seem to consist only of little old ladies. The young trendy Canadians who until recently had flooded into his shop had converted en masse to the daring creations of his youthful competitors.

People nowadays were always looking for something new, weren't they?

MegaDeli's True Colors

T he deathblow came in winter.

The row of three shops that included Daalder's Chocolates had always belonged to Dario Graziano, the uncle of his neighbor Tony. He used to come and announce the annual rent increase in person with such a tearful face that it had become a tradition for Joop to offer him a chocolate by way of consolation. Joop knew full well that Dario's remorse was mostly staged, but he couldn't help liking him. As a businessman Dario moved in the ultraconservative circles of Toronto's Wasp establishment, where he survived by playing the role of the clownish and thus harmless Southern European. By now, the poor soul couldn't behave in any other way. What's more, the rent increases were minimal—because the chocolate shop was given the same special treatment as Tony's ice-cream parlor. "Any friend of Tony's is a friend of mine!" Dario would cry emotionally. It was doubtful whether Joop's other neighbors, Mr. and Mrs. Ho from Vietnam, paid as reasonable a price. A grim expression would appear on Dario's otherwise so friendly face whenever he talked about the unique bond that existed between "we Europeans." Joop preferred not to think about it too much.

Another thing he preferred not to think about too much was

that after twenty-five years, the premises were badly in need of a facelift. He never mentioned the rotting window frames or patches of mold on the wall above the kitchen counter, partly for fear of jeopardizing the good rapport he had with Dario, but mostly because he dreaded having workmen underfoot. Once, when Emma had persuaded him to mention the plumbing, Dario responded most charmingly: "Of course, Giuseppe, of course. We'll have a look at it as soon as possible." To Joop's great relief, nothing ever happened.

As Emma suspected, Dario didn't have the money to maintain the premises. His three little children, as he affectionately called them, slowly became a millstone around his neck. Meanwhile, the real-estate market in Toronto had reached a boiling point. With increasing frequency, agents phoned to ask if he wasn't interested in selling the premises. Naturally he refused—he had promised on his brother's deathbed always to take care of his nephew Tony—naturally. But when a MegaDeli representative contacted him and almost doubled his previous offer, Dario could no longer resist.

"But have no fear, my dear friends," he assured Tony and Joop. "They've given me rock-hard guarantees that nothing will change for you people."

From the sale of the three shops, Dario could realize his long-cherished dream and return to his birthplace with his wife.

"The Canadian soil is too cold for a Sicilian to be buried in," he confided to Joop.

One freezing day in December, Dario came into the chocolate shop dressed in a thick fur coat, to say good-bye. Never in all his life would he forget Joop and his charming wife, Emma. When Joop handed him a box of chocolates, it all became too much for him. "Oh, Giuseppe, my friend," he sniffed. "You're much too good to me."

A moment later, Joop was standing at the window waving

good-bye. Holding the chocolates awkwardly in front of him, Dario edged his way through the snowy slush on the sidewalk. He didn't look back, probably for fear of slipping. No, Canada was no country for an old Sicilian. He was meant to spend his last years on a sleepy village square nursing a bottle of wine with his cronies of yesteryear.

Some time later, the Hos, Joop, and Tony each received a registered letter from MegaDeli. The tone of the letter was totally different from that of the chummy "dear neighbor" flyers they were still receiving every week. MegaDeli had been granted a demolition license so they could expand the parking lot. The premises had to be vacated within three months. If they weren't, the owner would take immediate legal action in the form of a penalty for each day the tenant failed to comply. Although there was no contractual obligation whatsoever to do so, MegaDeli was willing to make a contribution to the moving costs, according to a formula that stated that the earlier the premises were vacated the higher the contribution would be.

Could MegaDeli get away with this?

Donald Wilson, a lawyer friend of Joop's, read the letter with growing indignation. Typically American, to threaten like that. And the good-riddance premium was downright insulting. But, unfortunately—and that's why this sort of company had an army of legal advisers on the payroll—MegaDeli was entirely within its rights. The rental agreement Dario had entered into with his friends was full of loopholes, and the new owner was simply taking advantage of the "rock-hard guarantees" that said nothing would change. Specifically, the term of notice was nowhere clearly stated.

According to Donald, their only hope was to lodge an appeal against the demolition at the office of the municipal zoning committee. They could argue that the unique, diverse, multicultural character of St. Clair Avenue, so typical of Toronto, was being jeopardized by an anonymous megasupermarket. That, yet again, three little tiles of the mosaic known as Canada were being pulverized by an American company's drive to expand. Donald became so impassioned he offered to act on their behalf.

Joop hesitated. Given the fees lawyers normally charged, even the discount Donald might offer as a friend could prove to be a rude awakening. But when he broached the delicate subject, Donald looked surprised.

"Don't be silly."

"You mean . . ." Joop blushed. "Thank you, Donald."

"No problem."

Joop heaved a deep sigh. No problem. There it was again, that quintessential Canadian blessing. It expressed such a wholesome tranquility—a tranquility and generosity of spirit in keeping with the size of the country. You could say what you liked about Canadians (and Joop had done that to his heart's content over the years), but they *were* helpful. No problem. It sounded so much better in English than in Dutch. *"Geen probleem"* seemed such a mouthful, and, what's more, it didn't tally with the Dutch mercantile spirit. No, it was much easier to get your tongue around *"Voor wat hoort wat"*—"You owe me." But a Canadian was genuinely glad to help with absolutely no strings attached. Perhaps it was a remnant of the pioneer days, when the nearest neighbors lived eight miles away and people were happy for any opportunity to see each other.

When Joop dropped into the ice-cream parlor to mention the possibility of an appeal, Tony, who had been on the verge of a nervous breakdown ever since the eviction notice, hugged him passionately. But when he went to see his other neighbors, he found a half-dismantled shop.

"MegaDeli," said Lok, sitting on the floor surrounded by boxes and garbage bags. He shrugged his shoulders and giggled nervously. Through his broken English, Joop could decipher that they were moving to Mississauga, a Toronto suburb, where they could work for a while in the kitchen of the restaurant of Lok's second cousin.

"But MegaDeli's only bluffing," bluffed Joop. "We can fight the eviction. United we stand!"

"Yes, yes. MegaDeli!"

Lok looked at his wife, Lin, who had just appeared from behind an empty shelf cradling a sleeping baby in her arms. She too gave a friendly nod and started giggling.

No matter what Joop did to change their minds, Lok and Lin just kept shouting "MegaDeli!" and "Mississauga!," laughing harder by the minute.

In the end, he had stalked off angrily.

Cowardly traitors, the Hos, wooed by a miserly good-riddance premium.

Emma came to their defense, of course. They had been through so much already, she said, referring to the war in Vietnam. And besides, it wasn't as much part of their culture to defy authority.

A few days later, Joop came out of his shop to watch as the Hos' jam-packed minivan headed off for Mississauga. Lok and Lin waved to him, but he kept his hands stuffed deeply in his apron pockets. The van had no sooner been swallowed up by the St. Clair Avenue traffic than a small team of workmen arrived to board up the premises. During the last few months of the chocolate shop's operations, the wall on the Hos' side felt cold like the skin of a corpse.

Without the Hos but under the passionate guidance of Donald Wilson, Joop and Tony launched the offensive against MegaDeli. To strengthen their position, Emma and Donald's wife, Margaret, canvassed the neighborhood with a petition. They must have told the same story at least a hundred times—

of two friendly neighborhood stores being threatened by an anonymous multinational. Unfortunately, the petition failed miserably. Most of the local residents were quite pleased with the arrival of MegaDeli. It had given St. Clair Avenue a great boost. And, yes, of course it was too bad for those two shops, but you couldn't deny that they were rather dilapidated and that the parking lot really was getting too small. There was another reason why the petition failed, which Emma didn't dare to confess to Joop: from several reactions, it became clear that the chocolate shop wasn't exactly loved in the area. One old grouch, who reeked of whisky, was willing to sign for "good old Tony," but as far as he was concerned, that Daalder could stuff his yuppie chocolates up his ass.

"I'm so sorry," said Margaret to Emma, after the door was slammed in their faces.

"And that, when he hates yuppies so much himself!" said Emma, dumbfounded.

We'll manage without signatures, was Donald's reaction. No problem.

On the day of the hearing, he argued his case as calmly and confidently as always, but his political arguments didn't sit well with the members of the committee. If he objected to the free-trade agreement with the United States, then he had come to the wrong place, said the chairman. He would just have to go to Ottawa and apply to Parliament.

While Donald did his best to portray the interests of the small man in a broader perspective, his opponent reduced MegaDeli's large-scale plans to human proportions. Thanks to the expansion of the parking lot, the side streets of St. Clair Avenue would be relieved of traffic, so that children could once again ride around safely on their bicycles and play soccer out on the street. The local merchants would benefit too. If MegaDeli's customers could leave their cars somewhere safely, they would have more time to wander around the neighborhood and discover the other shops.

"What other shops?" shouted Donald.

But the chairman ordered him to calm down. And when MegaDeli's spokesman conjured a petition of enthusiastic local residents from his inside pocket, Joop and Tony's fate was sealed.

After a short recess, the chairman announced that the Daalder-Graziano appeal had been dismissed and the demolition of the three premises could go ahead on the set date.

"Oh, papa!" sobbed Tony. "Yes, dear Papa . . . go ahead, turn in your grave. Because this is the blackest day in the history of the Graziano family! And it's all my fault, Papa, all my fault!"

It was embarrassing for friend and foe alike. The consoling arm that his wife, Angela, put around him also served as a vice with which to usher him out of the room as quickly as possible.

"I'm so sorry," mumbled Donald meanwhile to a stony-faced Joop.

Emma stroked his rigid back, while anxiously studying his profile.

"I'm so sorry," whispered Margaret into her ear.

During the last weeks that the chocolate shop was open, Joop could no longer concentrate on the chocolates. He had always hated listening to customers, but now he kept coming out of his kitchen, ready to tell any little old lady about the injustice that had been done to him. They too were "so sorry." Not knowing how to deal with the painful situation, they hurried to place their order.

"Oh, and I'll take a few of those too," they would add at the end to buy off their guilt.

Meanwhile, he sold some of his kitchen equipment and supplies to a chef friend, who wanted to pay more than Joop asked but who eventually agreed to the lower price so as not to humiliate Joop—which made the humiliation all the greater.

But rock bottom was reached when one of The Three Chocolateers—the fellow with the goatee—walked into the shop. Joop had sent Martha home early that day because there was nothing to do, and he was already busy removing the chocolates from the showcase. Without flinching a muscle, the boy asked if Joop had any kitchen equipment he might want to sell.

In his fantasy, Joop had ranted and raved at those three windbags—about cheap gimmicks, about a devil's pact with commerce, about the moral responsibility of a true chocolatier. But now that he stood face-to-face with the enemy, he forgot his lines.

"Fuck off, you MegaDeli bastard!" he shrieked.

The boy was startled for a moment, then began to snigger.

"Take it easy, buddy. It's not my fault they're pulling down your shop!"

Joop gasped for breath. Had today's youth lost all respect? Where was his decency? Where were his manners? But he didn't voice these thoughts; they would only be dismissed by such a snot-nose as the grumblings of an old fogy. He uttered a quivery sigh. Then he thought of something.

"Style," he said. "Where's your sense of style?" Yes, surely style was a concept that today's youth could relate to.

"Everything's style," commented the boy, thoughtfully scratching his goatee. "It's no big thing, man. If you don't want to sell me that stuff, you don't have to, okay?"

He spun round and walked toward the door.

Tears sprang to Joop's eyes, but his throat constricted and stopped him from crying.

If only he could cry the way his neighbor Tony Graziano had done that day. If only he could call upon his father to turn in his grave. But his father, and his mother, too, for that matter, would only shrug their shoulders in their graves; they had always found his fussing with food overdone and decadent. If only he could get rid of all his pain and grief with Southern European theatrics at one go, and then without a qualm start working at MegaDeli a few weeks later, like Tony, who had accepted a job at the Cappuccino Corner ("Yes, Giuseppe, I had to do something, didn't I?").

If only he could laugh like Lok and Lin Ho, and slink away to Mississauga with oriental resignation and a measly good-riddance premium in his pocket. Those Hos had been right after all. They weren't cowardly, they had seen it was point-less to resist such a superior power right from the start. It was better just to pack your bags and start a new life elsewhere. Joop should have waved good-bye to them after all and wished them all the best.

There was Dario, sitting in some Sicilian village square with his old cronies, savoring his wine. And there were Lok and Lin, having fun cooking egg rolls with their second cousin in Mississauga. And, over there, somewhere in the bowels of the MegaDeli complex, was Tony, frothing warm milk for weary shoppers.

Only he had stayed behind on St. Clair Avenue. And there he stood, in front of the empty window of Daalder's Choco-lates, tormenting himself in the early-spring cold.

Winners and Losers

On the thirty-fourth floor of the office tower, Marcel Daalder—or Mark Daalder, as he had insisted on being called since the age of twelve—was studying a client's file with a contented smile. The news that he was to go to the United States for a few days the following week had made his day. Looking out across the steel-gray water of Lake Ontario, he could see an even darker gray strip of the promised land.

He was always relieved to cross the border. Everything around you made it clear that you had left spineless Canada behind and set foot in the most powerful country in the world. You knew right away from the greater number of losers hanging around on the streets, that there would also be more winners.

The client he had to visit was a pharmaceutical company near Austin, Texas, which had been accused of dumping poison in the municipal garbage dump for years on end. It was the same old story: the vats had started to leak, the ground had to be cleaned, and who was going to foot the bill. Several family doctors in the area believed the increase in the number of cases of leukemia in their practices was attributable to the poison. Well, just let them prove it! No, the most difficult part of this case was to convince the director they could play it tough. He was one of those young fellows who had inherited the company when Dad had retired, one of those naïve idealists who still wanted to be liked by everyone and was thus aiming for a settlement, for creating a special environmental fund—that kind of stuff. Totally uncalled for.

The telephone rang.

"Your mother on line two," said Linda, the secretary.

His mother on line two, with her daily portion of trivialities, this time about Tyler, whom she was about to take to the family doctor. The last cream—how long had they been using it? And had the spots in the hollows of his knees grown bigger or just brighter?

"Is Susan coming to pick up the children?" she went on. "At six-thirty? Oh, after her fitness training?"

A silent reproach to her daughter-in-law. A mother should come home early.

"But they can have a bite to eat here, if it's easier for you."

In other words, children should eat on time. Maybe it was time to start looking for a nanny again. He was fed up with his mother's phone calls.

"Is that all?" he asked.

"Well, yes, I think so. Except I'm a bit worried about your father."

"Oh, yes?"

"He's gone to look at the demolition site again. That's not healthy, is it?"

"Ah, maybe it's his way of coming to terms with everything."

"I don't know, Mark, I just don't know."

"Sorry, Mom, but I really have to get back to work now. We'll talk about it some other time, okay?"

A touch of the button and the connection was broken.

So Pa went to the demolition site again.

Good riddance—the demise of Daalder's Chocolates was long overdue. It was painful to the point of neurotic how his mother had always protected his father. The chocolate shop had been suffering losses for months, and had only kept its head above water thanks to the substantial financial reserves his parents had at their disposal. Potentially, his father's expensive hobby could have dragged on for years, using his intended inheritance for fuel. Thank goodness MegaDeli was putting an end to that.

But apart from that . . .

A smirk appeared on Marcel's face.

Apart from that, he always enjoyed it when a weaker party was beaten by a stronger one. At home, he liked watching nature films about predatory animals; the crueler it got, the better. And, fortunately, in the same way as sex scenes in feature films were becoming increasingly explicit, so today the killing of prey could be shown in all its gory detail. Last night he had watched how a female killer whale kept throwing a baby seal up out of the waves, high up into the air, just for the fun of it — until finally she got bored and bit it to death. People who saw themselves as having a delicate disposition looked away from such shots, traditionally women more than men. But today's better bitches watched every bit as eagerly. Like Susan last night. And why shouldn't they? It was a fascinating and exciting spectacle.

What applied to nature also applied to man. Why did you always have to choose the side of the underdog? Why was it necessarily sad if a powerful concern ruined a helpless family business with playful abandon? Why weren't you allowed to see the beauty of it?

It hurt his mother that he hadn't been more loyal in the struggle of Daalder's Chocolates against MegaDeli. By now, she knew what he thought of winners and losers. But couldn't he just this once make an exception for his own dad's business? Sorry, mom, but no way. And as for loyalty . . . he didn't owe that bastard a thing.

With a dark glimmer in his eye, Marcel returned to his client's file. But a moment later, when a subtle legal detail made him gaze pensively out of the window, his expression cleared again.

America was still smiling at him from the other side of the lake.

A Visit to the Family Doctor

The doctor examined Tyler's patches of eczema, listened to his breathing just to be sure, and wrote out a prescription for a potent hormone cream. Apply sparingly twice daily. While Emma took Tyler on her knee to get him dressed, the doctor asked how Joop was doing. At the last appointment, he had seemed rather tense and downcast.

"Well, what can I say?" said Emma.

But once she started, she couldn't stop. She told him the shop had closed definitively the week before and that Joop walked to the site of the disaster every day, returning home more somber than ever. She told him about the hours he sat silently in his chair, and that sometimes, halfway through dinner, he would push his plate away and leave the table (and if Joop didn't eat, something was really wrong). And in the middle of the night, she could tell from the creaking floorboards that he was pacing back and forth downstairs.

The doctor nodded understandingly. "If you ask me, what we have here is depression."

"Depression?" asked Emma, just managing to stop Tyler from grabbing the letter opener off the doctor's desk.

"It's very normal," said the doctor, "that a man—or a woman, of course, but in my experience it's mostly men who have this problem—suffers an enormous blow when he suddenly ends up sitting at home after working all his life. You could almost call it a grieving process, and you can count on it lasting at least a year."

"A year . . . Oh no!"

The doctor smiled. "For a wife who's used to having the house all to herself, it can be quite an adjustment too. Am I right, or not?"

Emma nodded.

"May I ask you a personal question?"

"Yes, all right."

"Are you still intimate? I mean on a sexual level?"

On a sexual level, on a sexual level . . . was this really necessary? Perhaps it was old-fashioned, but she found it embarrassing to discuss her married life with a man young enough to be her son. Tyler, forever trying to squirm off her lap, didn't make it any easier.

The doctor opened a drawer and handed him a toy car to play with.

"Oh, the need diminishes of its own accord as you get older," Emma heard herself say, by which she already revealed more than she cared to. "I think we both feel the same about that."

"Yes, yes. But do you still sometimes—?"

"Yes, oh yes."

"And does he ever have a problem, I mean, with an erection? I'm asking this because sometimes it makes a difference if a man can still . . ."

So that was it. The doctor couldn't wait to write a prescription for the new potency pill. Emma knew exactly the last time she and Joop had . . . It was the day the zoning committee had rejected the appeal against the demolition. She had wanted to be extra sweet to him in bed that night. He had lain on his back and stared at the ceiling with huge, terrified eyes. She had unbuttoned his pajama top, stroked his chest softly, and let a shower of tiny kisses follow. Suddenly he had grabbed her like a madman and pushed her against the mattress. His face contorted with pain, he had . . . taken her—she couldn't think of a better word for it. Once she had abandoned herself to it, it hadn't even been that unpleasant, in spite of how little time it had lasted and Joop's falling asleep right after the climax. Poor Joop. But there was certainly no talk of impotence.

"No," she said definitively. "That's no problem at all."

"Fine then," said the doctor, a bit disappointed.

Meanwhile, Tyler had let the little toy car crash to the floor and was grabbing at a picture frame on the desk.

"No, little fellow," said Emma. "Give me that."

She gently took the picture frame from his hands, pulled out the support, and placed the photo back on the desk. Three laughing children's faces. It crossed her mind that on a sexual level, the doctor and his wife had been active at least three times.

"Let's stick to depression," said the doctor. "There is good medication on the market nowadays . . ."

"I don't think he'll accept this diagnosis. 'First MegaDeli destroys my life,' he said the other day, 'then you come along and blame me for how I feel.'"

"That's a common misunderstanding, Emma. Recognizing depression is not a confession of guilt . . . nor can problems that are also partly social or economical be solved with pills. But medication can help reduce those problems to manageable proportions. I had a top executive in here not long ago who had to radically reorganize his company and dreaded it so much that he called in sick. The mild antidepressant I prescribed gave him just the little push that he needed to hold the bad-news talks with his employees. And this is only one case out of many."

"Well," said Emma. "I just don't know, doctor."

"At least see if you can get Joop to drop by. You could say I want to check his blood pressure and cholesterol again — which isn't such a bad idea anyway, under the circumstances."

"Don't count on it, but I'll do my best. Come along, Tyler, we're going."

The Death of a Chocolatier

When Joop came home, he found a note on the kitchen table. Emma had gone to the doctor with Tyler, was picking Jessica up from school afterward, then was going shopping, et cetera, et cetera. She would be home around five o'clock. The children were staying for dinner.

Oh, no!

Joop did have a soft spot for six-year-old Jessica. She was a quiet, dreamy girl who reminded him a lot of himself when he was a child. Tyler, on the other hand, was as clumsy a specimen as Marcel had been as a baby, with his ever-dripping nose, his ever-gaping mouth, and that lifeless expression in his eyes. ("Come on," Emma would say, "the little fellow can't help it.") He was three years old now, but Joop still hadn't noticed the slightest trace of intelligence or sensitivity in him.

He crumpled up Emma's note and threw it in the pedal-bin under the sink.

Now what?

Sit down in his armchair and brood.

But the question remained, now what? What was he going to do with his time now that he wasn't making chocolates anymore? He had always violently resisted the question. In the heat of the battle against MegaDeli, it would have been a sign of weakness to contemplate life after an eventual defeat. Even in better times, though, he had disliked looking beyond the bounds of his artistry.

Emma saw this differently. She thought he had become too fanatic about his chocolate making over the years. There had once been a time when he would read a book or newspaper, or they would go to the theater or movies together, a time when he was still interested in other people (in her, she probably meant). Wouldn't it be better to start looking further afield in preparation for retirement?

Joop reacted grumpily to her unsolicited advice. Thinking of the future was for sissies. A chocolatier lived in the here-and-now.

If he had his way, he would die on the job like his master, Jérôme Sorel. He had had a heart attack at the age of sixty-eight while berating a customer. Boom. Dead. Too young, perhaps, but what a wonderful way to go.

Joop wasn't quite sixty-eight yet, but a strange glimmer had appeared in his eyes the last time he had visited the family doctor when he heard that his blood pressure and cholesterol were too high. Not yet alarmingly high, but just to be safe, the doctor had tried to talk him into more physical exercise and a low-fat diet.

That? Never! Joop wanted nothing to do with the sickly modern obsession with personal health. He had never felt the need to "work on himself," either physically or mentally. That was for people who had nothing better to do with their lives. He preferred to work on his chocolates. Was he avoiding himself? Quite possibly. Did overweight grouches live shorter lives than cheerful sports lovers? He would leap at the chance for a death like his teacher's. Whenever he launched into a tirade against MegaDeli or The Three Chocolateers, he always hoped Emma would say, "Take it easy, Joop, remember what happened to Monsieur Sorel." And whenever she did, he was as happy as a child. But deep down, in his much-too-healthy heart, he knew he wasn't worthy of the comparison. His tantrums were no match for those of his master. A heart attack just wasn't in the cards.

When the demise of the chocolate shop became inescapable, Joop had toyed with the idea of committing suicide. He didn't know how the bankrupt olive farmer had done it, but he imagined him dangling from a branch of his favorite olive tree. For a chocolatier, poison was the most obvious choice. He would make one last chocolate—a perfect, soberly designed specimen of the finest cacao filled with a deadly toxin, preferably a very bitter one; he wanted to taste his own death; that much he owed his palate. It would be a beautiful dramatic ending intended, for starters, as revenge on Emma. What did she mean, that the MegaDeli disaster was "worse for the Hos" or "worse for Tony Graziano"? He reveled in the thought of his wife in tears, in tears at last—until he felt the urge to comfort her, whereupon he realized he loved her too much to do such a thing to her. Moreover, it was intolerable to think that the directors of MegaDeli wouldn't lose a second's sleep over his death, or even worse, that the fellow with the goatee might laugh about it. And so the poison chocolate never got beyond the mental drawing board.

There was no way around it: for dying on the job it was too late.

Part 2

THE BIRTH OF A CHOCOLATIER

Milk

He was born just before the war. He wasn't very welcome.

"I had had my fill of motherhood," his mother, Françoise, often sighed, "and then he came along."

His parents' fatigue was even reflected in the name they gave him. While his eldest sister, seven years his senior, went through life as Charlotte Penelope and his other sister, six years his senior, as Rosalinde Antoinette, all they could come up with for him was a single one-syllable name: Joop. It wasn't even an abbreviation. That was how his father Laurens had registered him at the town hall.

Françoise hated breast-feeding her baby boy. "Come on, you little runt, drink!" she would say, when her nipple popped out of his mouth for the umpteenth time. "I've got better things to do."

Impatiently she would stuff her breast back into his mouth as deep as she could. He would suckle for a while, but then out popped the nipple yet again.

"Hey, damn it!"

It was as if Joop could taste his mother's aversion in the milk and therefore didn't want to get too much of it inside. The little that he finally did drink often came back out again with the proverbial burp—as a sour whitish gob. Sooner than with her daughters, Françoise buttoned up her blouse once and for all. Joop would simply have to make do with cow's milk and solid food.

Though his parents and sisters were tall, he would always stay short. Outsiders tended to attribute it to the war, but Françoise scoffed at this explanation. The Daalders lived on their estate, Swaanendal, a portion of which they leased to a farmer, so that right into the Starvation Winter of 1945 they had ample access to milk, eggs, vegetables, and meat. Was it the war? Hogwash! The child just ate poorly . . . and didn't drink his milk.

With a deep ladle, the lukewarm, creamy cow's milk was scooped out of a bucket that his sisters had just fetched from Farmer Evert and was poured into five large mugs standing on the counter. You couldn't get it fresher than that. "Delicious!" the others would cry, almost menacingly. While they downed their milk in a single go and wiped away their white mustaches, Joop had yet to take his first sip.

"And you're staying here till you finish every last drop," Françoise would say to him. "We're off to make sick."

"To make sick" had become a coined expression at Swaanendal, ever since Joop had first used it as a toddler in reference to the others making music together. The love of music had flourished for generations in the Daalder family. Laurens's great-grandparents had fitted up the most beautiful room of the estate as a music room. Laurens and Françoise had met each other in the student orchestra and were overjoyed when, at an early age, their daughters Lotte and Rosa proved to be "fiendishly musical," as Françoise put it. That they called themselves the Daalder Quartet was only half in jest. Their playing was certainly not without merit, and house concerts were organized regularly at the estate, even during the war. No, especially during the war, for only by staunchly persevering with their music did the Daalders and their friends manage to keep up their spirits. Years later, at Laurens's funeral, Swaanendal was lauded by an emotional friend as a bastion of civilization in the fathomless darkness of the war years.

But world history passed Joop by unnoticed. A far more imminent danger was the fathomless whiteness in front of him on the kitchen table, as the zealous sounds of the Daalder Quartet emanated from the music room. A yellowish-white depth, with a few whiter flakes floating on top. That was the cream, his sisters said. Best of all!

Later, when he looked back on this scene, which must have been a daily ritual, he wanted to call out to that little boy: Look behind you! There's the sink! But such a subversive thought doesn't occur to an obedient child. He had no choice but to drink the milk, preferably in one single go and as quickly as possible. He brought the mug to his lips, held his breath so he wouldn't smell or taste anything, and *glug-glug-glug* let the slimy fluid stream in. Joop felt his eyes grow larger and more terrified by the moment, even larger than those of the poor orphan boy in the painting above the mantelpiece at the house of Farmer Evert and his wife, Riet, the orphan boy he felt so sorry for but who made his sisters and his parents laugh so mockingly. Things were running smoothly, though—he was already halfway, the bottom of the mug had come into view. But then he felt a blob of cream stick in the back of his throat.

Between the Andante and the Allegro ma non troppo, his mother came into the kitchen to see how things were going.

"Ugh, Joop! Not again!"

Holland was liberated, and the war was over. As a six-year-old, Joop walked through the woods with his sisters into the village to watch the arrival of the Canadians. He was frightened by all the grown-ups screaming and weeping with joy, but once he was safely positioned between his two sisters along the main street, he enjoyed the passing tanks, which made the ground tremble under his feet, and waved as happily as everybody else at the infantry who brought up the rear.

One of them separated himself from the group and headed straight for the Daalder children.

"Here you go, sonny," he said, bending down on one knee to hand Joop a small flat object wrapped in paper. After giving the sisters a big wink, he took off to catch up with his buddies.

Joop tore off the wrapper, sniffed suspiciously at the gray-brown bar that emerged from it, and took a cautious bite. It was hard and grainy, and had a stale taste that reminded him of the cigar breath of Uncle Albert, his father's brother. He made a face, and, lips spluttering, spat the stuff out onto the street.

"Give me that chocolate!" said Charlotte, snatching the bar from him and smacking the back of his head so hard that he saw stars. "Ungrateful wretch!"

The First Supper

Joop not only ate poorly as a child, he was also forever complaining of stomachaches. Theatrics, suspected the others, but just to be sure, Françoise took him to the doctor. Doctor Westland poked and pinched his belly, listened to his heart, and put him on the scales, but he couldn't find anything out of the ordinary.

"Hmm," he said. "We see this kind of stomachache more often in young schoolchildren, especially the quieter ones. It could be pent-up tension. How's he doing at school? Is he having a hard time? Is he being bullied perhaps?"

"Not that I know of. No, eh, Joop? You like school, don't you?"

Joop nodded obediently.

The doctor maintained that stomachaches were silent cries for attention that could probably be set right through some fun, relaxing activity. A sport, for example. Or a hobby. Did "our little patient" perhaps have an idea of his own?

Françoise sighed. That was precisely the problem. So damn little came out of him. They had stopped his music lessons recently. Their roles had briefly been reversed: while the Daalder Quartet sat in the kitchen drinking tea, Joop was in the music room practicing his scales.

"What a clumsy touch that kid has," Charlotte had remarked.

"Come, come," her mother laughed. "We all had to learn."

"I don't know, Frannie, I just don't know," said Laurens, grimacing painfully. "With the girls it sounded different right from the beginning."

The piano teacher (a delightful person; the girls just loved her!) threw in the sponge after about seven lessons. Joop just didn't have it in him.

But what did he have in him, then?

"What about scouts or carpentry?" Françoise volunteered, as they drove home from the doctor. As a token of good faith, she listed things that she hated.

"I don't know, Mom."

She sighed and patted him on the shoulder. "Well, then, Joop. Just sleep on it."

Later, it was as clear as day to Joop what the real problem was. He ate so badly and got stomachaches because their food was so terrible.

Though there was little to spoil in Dutch cooking, his mother managed it. She burned the kale, the mashed potatoes had the consistency of wallpaper glue, and the meatballs were black outside and raw inside. As if that weren't bad enough, more and more American products appeared on their table: soup from a package and corn from a tin, ready-made salads mixed with sweet mayonnaise, and peach halves in heavy syrup. All wonderfully handy, thought his mother. The claim that fresh produce was healthier she dismissed as Calvinist gumpf meant to keep women slaving away in the kitchen for as long as possible.

She even seemed proud of how badly she cooked, just as she hated housekeeping. "I'm probably not a good housewife," she said, "but I prefer to read Proust than to make apple pies or scrub toilets."

Laurens totally understood—"Quite possibly Françoise is

more intelligent than I am," he confided once to an old college friend—and so he gladly paid for domestic help to come and clean the enormous house every two weeks. More wasn't necessary. At Swaanendal, cleanliness was scoffed at as a petty bourgeois ideal. Nor should the standards be too high for meals. After all, eating was just a bothersome interruption, an animal need on the same level as urination and defecation. While Joop shifted his food glumly from one side of the plate to the other, the Daalder Quartet wolfed everything down indiscriminately, so that they could return as quickly as possible to the finer pleasures of life—like poetry and literature and, especially, music.

At the time, there was a boy in Joop's class called Pascal Vandenbroucke. Pascal was teased very badly—about his hair, which was neatly combed to one side and pasted down with brilliantine, about his pink shirts with their strange frilled collars, about his mother, a stylish woman who reeked of perfume and kissed him on the lips when she said good-bye to him in the school yard. But mostly about the fact that he came from Belgium. One day Pascal found himself in such a tight spot that he wet his pants. Aldo de Vries, one of the worst bullies, called out, "Hey, there's Little Mister Piss Pot!" alluding to the famous statue in Brussels of a boy passing water. The teacher had difficulty suppressing a smile. That brief moment when she forgot her role was gratefully registered by the rest of the class, and destroyed in one stroke the painstaking progress she had made with her many anti-bullying sermons. From then on it went from bad to worse. Pascal wet his pants more and more often, and one day Little Mister Piss Pot even became Little Mister Poop Pot.

Mrs. Vandenbroucke had a long talk with the teacher, who, among other things, advised her to get in touch with the mother of Joop Daalder, a quiet boy who didn't take part in the bullying and could use a friend of his own.

The two mothers agreed that Joop would come and play with Pascal that Saturday afternoon. He could even stay for dinner, despite Françoise's warnings that he barely ate anything.

"Oh, children are like that," said Mrs. Vandenbroucke, in a conciliatory tone.

The playing didn't go smoothly. Pascal turned out to be a little tyrant in his own territory. When they went upstairs to his room to play with the electric train, all Joop was allowed to do was flick the switch, and then only according to Pascal's very precise instructions. Meanwhile, he was bombarded with all manner of difficult sums. "Don't you even know what square roots are? You're a dummy!" When Joop accidentally knocked the tracks with his foot and one of the cars derailed, he was sent out of the room.

He wandered around the upstairs floor of the house for a while until he gathered the courage to go to Pascal's mother, who was busy downstairs in the kitchen.

It smelled very different and much better than at home.

"Hey, Joop, what are you doing here? You two aren't fighting, are you?"

Without replying, he came and stood beside her, next to the stove.

"What's that?" he asked, as she sprinkled little green snippets from a jar onto the simmering meat.

"That's thyme. Don't you know it? It makes food taste and smell so good."

She sprinkled a few leaves into his hand. "Rub it gently between your fingers, then you can smell it better."

Joop sniffed the aroma. And kept sniffing.

Mrs. Vandenbroucke had to laugh. "Come along, and we'll see if Pascal can't be a bit nicer to you."

They didn't get farther than the hallway because at that very moment the front door opened. Mr. Vandenbroucke had come home from work, an impressive figure in a three-piece gray suit who put a trim black attaché case down on the floor. Very different from Joop's own father, with his baggy sweaters and worn-out leather briefcase.

"Papa!" Pascal raced down the stairs and jumped into his arms.

Mr. Vandenbroucke took off his jacket and began horsing around with his son. He tried to include Joop in the tussle but Pascal resisted. Besides, Joop preferred to watch from a distance and sniff at his fingers now and again.

After they sat down at the table and Pascal's mother had served, the father asked for a moment's silence for grace. It was a mysterious, solemn ritual during which Joop automatically closed his eyes. According to his parents, God had been invented by ignorant people who otherwise couldn't cope with life. But someone like Mrs. Vandenbroucke, who put thyme in her cooking, couldn't possibly be ignorant, and if someone like her thanked God for the good food, then perhaps He did exist after all. Joop's theological reflections were interrupted by the Vandenbrouckes' "Amen." It was time to eat.

The meat was so tender and succulent, the sauce so flavorful, each French fry so perfect that Joop went mad with greed. He would have liked to stuff everything into his mouth all at the same time.

"You seem to like it, don't you, Joop?" asked Mrs. Vandenbroucke, amused.

"Watch out you don't get a stomachache," said Mr. Vandenbroucke.

Stomachache? For the first time in his life he didn't get a stomachache!

"You're eating like a pig," said Pascal.

"Pascal! Don't talk to your guest like that."

After dinner, the boys went and played with the electric train again.

Drowsy and content, Joop let his host shower him with abuses.

The other Daalders, who had taken full advantage of Joop's absence to enjoy a day of culture over in Amsterdam, drove past the Vandenbrouckes' on their way home to pick him up.

Proudly, Mrs. Vandenbroucke told them how well Joop had eaten.

"Well, what do you know!" said Françoise dryly.

But on the way home in the car, the whole Daalder Quarter lit into him.

"Eating well all of a sudden while you're out . . . yes, sure! We know what you're up to, buddy! From now on you'll eat everything on your plate. The show's over!"

Joop endured it all, meanwhile resolving to stay friends with Pascal so he could eat there more often.

Unfortunately, there would never be another meal at the Vandenbrouckes'. Joop was unable to protect his friend from the bullying, which took on such vicious forms that the Vandenbrouckes decided to withdraw their son from school and move back to Belgium with him.

By this time, Joop was eating better at home. The others congratulated themselves. Their four-part tirade in the car had cured him of his childish antics once and for all.

In reality, he found the food at home as bad as it had always been, but he could stand it better now because he knew it could be different. He modeled himself after noble Pascal, holy Pascal — the way he would stand in the middle of the school yard surrounded by jeering children, and, despite his wet pants, keep his dignity by not shedding a single tear. Now Joop, too, suffered in silence, chewing on a piece of poorly cooked bacon while dreaming of a better world.

That summer, as he looked at a painting called *The Last Supper* with his family in a museum in Italy, he was once again reminded of the memorable meal at the Vandenbrouckes', which from that point on he called "The First Supper."

Father Tells a Story

Laurens Daalder never occupied himself with the "toilet, tummy, and teething" business of little children. He was the first to admit he wasn't cut out for it. He spent all the more time on their general education as soon as they were a bit older. As a professor of classical languages he had a vast repertory of wonderful stories at his disposal. Charlotte and Rosalinde nurtured the most wonderful memories of Odysseus' adventures, which he recounted in vivid detail, and of the chilly nights when they stood in the middle of a field gazing up at the starry sky and he would not only point out all the constellations but bring them to life with the corresponding myths.

One Wednesday afternoon, when Joop, who now was nine years old, was free from school, Laurens thought the time was ripe to initiate him into Homer's world. He came down from Olympus—as his study had been called since that marvelous poem Charlotte had written for him on the occasion of Saint Nicholas's Eve—summoned his son into the living room, and ordered him to sit on the couch beside him.

Françoise was sitting at close range in her armchair, ostensibly absorbed in a book of poetry, but over the rim of her bifocals she kept a vigilant eye on Joop. Did he have any idea how lucky he was to have such an amazing father?

Lips curling slightly at the corners—the way eloquent

people warn their audience that something beautiful is about to be said—Laurens began his story.

As his father talked, Joop couldn't sit still and kept banging his heels against the bottom of the couch.

"Hey, will you stop that?" asked his father.

They managed to keep it up for a few Wednesday afternoons. But when Odysseus and his comrades were imprisoned in the cave of the one-eyed Cyclops, things went wrong. Laurens carefully worked up to the climax, recounting how the men were devoured by the giant one by one, but that Odysseus outsmarted him by introducing himself with the odd name of Nobody. How clever his choice had been became clear when Odysseus pierced the eye of the sleeping giant with a stake of olive wood and the unlucky one cried out for help.

"What's all that racket in the middle of the night?" shouted the other giants, amused. "If Nobody has attacked you, then nothing can be wrong!"

Laurens left a moment's silence, looking at his son expectantly.

"Do you get it?" he asked, when there was no reaction. Homer's joke was one of the oldest known puns. Laurens had once given a lecture on it at a conference in Florence.

Françoise eyed her son severely from her armchair. Laugh, or I'll shoot.

Joop quickly conjured a smile. Of course he got the joke, but he thought it was rather corny.

"Incomprehensible," said Laurens. "Lotte and Rosa were always all ears. But this . . . There's simply no point." Shaking his head, he left the room to return to his study.

"You should listen to your father, you know, Joop," said his mother.

"I did, Mom."

"Oh well, never mind. Go and play outside or something."

A strange suggestion. It was pouring with rain.

A Chocolate *J*

Now that he was eating rather well, and now that his father saw no point in devoting any more time to his general education, Joop was mostly ignored. In his memories, he was always alone, surrounded by an immeasurable space in which the nearest people seemed endlessly far away. The Daalder Quartet emphasized this distance by being only audible, not visible, from behind the closed doors of the music room. And whenever he roamed around the estate, Farmer Evert's tractor always seemed to be chugging along in the most remote corner of the wheat field.

Because his sisters were in high school and doing homework all the time now, he was the one sent to the farm to fetch the hated bucket of milk. But these expeditions were not solely a punishment—for Auntie Riet always slipped him a treat. One time she gave him a handful of cherries. On his way home he put the bucket of milk carefully on the ground. Sitting with his back against a tree, he savored one cherry after another as he gazed out over Farmer Evert's wheat field. The fun thing about cherries was that they all tasted different. Sometimes, even a single cherry concealed a world of different tastes. A white moldy patch tasted earthy, the brown patch around it bitter at first, then watery. Then there was the lightly fermenting zone that made his tongue tingle, and finally he reached the other side of the cherry, which was simply sweet. With another cherry, he would start with the unripe part and nibble his way from hard and bitter to sour to sweet. The best specimens, which were dark red on all sides, he saved for the last. But you were never quite sure with cherries. Sometimes they looked delicious but were absolutely tasteless.

In the peace and quiet of parental neglect, Joop was free to develop his sense of taste. He still would have been surprised, though, if someone had said he would later become a chocolatier. He didn't like sweets very much to begin with, but after that unfortunate incident with the Canadian soldier, it was chocolate in particular that remained a problematic product. He hardly ever ate chocolate spread, and chocolate milk made him nauseous. Nor was the first filled chocolate that he tasted a success—his teeth had suddenly sunk through the outer layer and his mouth was filled with a sickly-sweet goo.

But then Joop became acquainted with the chocolate of Otto Vermeulen, "the famous chocolatier from Baarn." It was on the eve of Saint Nicholas's Day, December the fifth, the time they celebrated it with Uncle Albert, Aunt Gerda, and Nico, his cousin, who was three years older than Joop.

Relations between Laurens and his younger brother were strained. Albert still thought their parents' inheritance had been unfairly divided, whereas Laurens insisted he had taken on the responsibility of the estate purely for noble reasons. Only if it was administered as a whole could Swaanendal and its rich history be preserved for future generations. Nor did the women get along well. Gerda thought Françoise was arrogant and Françoise found Gerda vulgar. Normally the two families would never have celebrated Saint Nicholas together, but Albert had just been through a rough patch. He had been forced to cancel a three-year contract with an oil refinery in the Antilles after only six months because of a conflict with his boss.

Françoise regretted her gesture the minute she saw the three platinum-blond, deeply tanned figures step out of the Mercedes, and as if by tacit understanding, she and Gerda only offered each other a hand instead of kissing.

The visitors had brought beautiful chocolate initials for each of the children, as was the tradition on Saint Nicholas's Eve, from no one less than Otto Vermeulen, the fanciest chocolatier in all of Holland. Each initial was wrapped in a gold box, decorated with little sugar violets and swirls of softer chocolate, and filled with whole hazelnuts.

Joop and Nico were given milk-chocolate initials, while Rosalinde and Charlotte received "extra bitter, for the real connoisseur," according to the golden sticker on the box.

"You girls do like bitter chocolate, don't you?" asked Aunt Gerda, when she thought she noticed a flash of disappointment on Rosalinde's face.

"Yes, delicious, Aunt Gerda," cried Charlotte.

"Now we're in for something," Françoise whispered to Laurens. "Those chocolate letters alone are more expensive than all the gifts we bought for them."

"Oh come on, that's not what it's all about."

As Françoise feared, the gifts Albert and Gerda had bought for everyone were obscenely expensive. What's more, they had been wrapped without the slightest imagination, and, worse still, they weren't accompanied by poems. Such poems, often poking fun at the recipient and to be read out loud before unwrapping the present, were considered by the Daalders of Swaanendal to be the highlight of a Saint Nicholas celebration. This made it all the more painful for Laurens, who as a classicist attached great importance to getting the meter just right, to hear his brother mangle his wonderful poem while Gerda was already noisily rummaging through the bag of presents to fish out yet another gigantic one for her son.

Never again, said Françoise and Laurens to each other when it was over, as they stood in the kitchen washing the dishes.

A similar conclusion was drawn in the Mercedes as it left the estate.

Rosalinde, who did indeed prefer milk chocolate to bitter, had thrown jealous glances at Joop's *J* all evening. When Charlotte withdrew to the music room with the book of Beethoven sonatas that the good Saint Nicholas had given her, she grabbed her chance. She explained to Joop that there was more chocolate in an *R* than in a *J*, and moreover, that it contained no milk, which he hated so much.

Joop didn't mind one way or the other. He would have given her his initial even if she hadn't given him hers.

The serene smile that Charlotte wore upon returning from her first encounter with Beethoven faded the moment she saw her younger sister greedily gnawing on the wrong initial.

Rosalinde calmly finished her mouthful before explaining herself. "Joop wanted to swap initials too. Didn't you, Joop?"

He nodded.

"You can be such a child, Rosa." Shaking her head, Charlotte went back to the piano, where she vented all her wrath in the opening chords of the "Pathétique" sonata. She too preferred milk chocolate to bitter.

Joop withdrew to his bedroom. He opened the box and took out the letter, which felt bumpy on the bottom because of the hazelnuts. He picked off one of the little violets and took a bite. The perfume taste reminded him of soap. The swirls of soft milk chocolate that he shaved off the letter with his front teeth made him feel sick to his stomach. But when he sank his teeth into the actual letter, and the taste of "extra bitter, for the real connoisseur" was released, he sighed deeply. So that was how chocolate was meant to taste. He quickly bit off another piece. Too bad about the whole hazelnuts though. Their woody texture and relatively weak flavor detracted from, rather than enhanced, the intense experience.

In no time, he had eaten the slanted leg of the *R*, leaving a *P*. After he had nibbled off the upper serif, the most difficult challenge presented itself: to take just the right bite out of the curve of the *P* so that, if he turned the letter upside down, he would have his *J* back again. Saliva dripping out of his mouth, he tried to position his jaws in the right place on the letter, but when he bit, the letter broke in two at the wrong place. So much for *J*.

Suddenly he broke out into a cold sweat. He stumbled to his bed, where, head spinning and heart pounding wildly, he lay motionless for some time. It was Joop's first choco-shock, as his later master, Jérôme Sorel, would call this state of overstimulation.

Cousin Nico

Occasionally Nico would come and play for a day. He was very wild and unmanageable. According to Françoise, that was often the case with only children.

"Come on, man," he kept saying to Joop, who would then obediently trundle along behind him into some new adventure.

Joop wasn't very experienced or lithe, and constantly ran into difficulty.

Nico wormed his way effortlessly under the barbed wire after they had pelted the cows with hard apples; Joop tore his pants. Nico climbed right up to the top of the tree; Joop got no farther than the second branch, egged on by his tough cousin, and then didn't dare to come down again. Nico pole-vaulted over the ditch; Joop, dripping with duckweed, had to go inside to get dry clothes.

One day they went to the vegetable garden by the farm, where, at Nico's suggestion, they slipped through the bird nets and raided the raspberries. When the farmer's wife came running over, Nico just managed to escape, but Joop, arms thrashing, became entangled in the nets.

"Oh, oh, oh," said Auntie Riet. "What a disappointment this is."

His parents were told, and by way of punishment Joop had

to help pick raspberries one morning without eating a single one himself.

"And they have to go to market, so don't squish them, will you?"

After an hour or so, Auntie Riet took pity on him. "That's all right, my boy. Go on home now."

But even though she had forgiven him, he was never given anything special to eat again when he came to fetch the bucket of milk.

A Bag of Madeleines

As an academic, Laurens was privileged with long
summer holidays, and as soon as school was out,
the Daalders headed off in their fully packed
Renault, roof rack and all, for France or Italy (Greece was
too hot and too far away, and Spain was out of the question
because of Franco). Laurens and Françoise always prepared these trips down to the finest detail. A route was
mapped out according to a specific theme—Romanesque
churches in Languedoc, frescoes in Umbria, mosaics in and
around Ravenna—and as avid hikers, they always made
sure to visit the most scenic areas en route. The children
were thus exposed to a well-thought-out mixture of culture
and nature that would stand them in good stead for the rest
of their lives.

The girls cherished the fondest memories of their holidays,
whereas Joop developed an aversion toward both culture and
nature.

Later when he thought of cathedrals, he saw himself
standing in the burning sun while the others searched in a
thick book for the carved figures above the portal, then discussed them one by one. He longed for the coolness inside,
but when they finally entered the cathedral, his father would
pull out his collapsible reading glasses from his breast pocket

at every new niche and every new decorated column. As the women clustered closely around him, he would read out of the thick book, whispering, so as not to disturb the other visitors, and in German, because the book was written by one Eberhart Kaufmann, who, apart from being *the* authority in God-knows-what field, was apparently also a gifted stylist. In the dank, dark coolness, with dozens of columns and niches still to go, Joop soon found himself longing for the sunny square.

For the rest of his life, he would associate museums—where if possible the tempo of the quartet was even slower—with leaden legs and a terrible thirst that was in no way quenched by the puny glasses of drink on offer in the cafeteria.

The tempo of the Daalder Quartet on hikes in the mountains was as brisk as the shuffling through the cultural attractions was slow. Sweating and wheezing, with the taste of iron in the back of his throat, Joop constantly had to catch up to the four waiting figures higher up on the hill, their pose one of utter annoyance. Whatever possessed these people to punish themselves, and especially him, in this way? They didn't even want to reach the peak. Mountains weren't there to be conquered, they said, but to be enjoyed. The moment climbing aids like ropes and pickaxes were employed, which Joop thought would be pretty exciting, you were lapsing into contemptible alpinism. Then you were little better than the lazy bums who let themselves be hoisted to the top in cable cars, which Joop thought would be pretty nice. True pleasure primarily entailed covering great distances, but without being too proud of it. One or two comments were permitted, but a third was one too many—and it was usually Joop who made it.

"Have we really climbed more than a thousand meters?"

"For God's sake, Joop," Charlotte would say, "that's not the point."

What the point was—the so-called "pleasure"—remained a

mystery to him. But one thing was certain. When he grew up and could make his own decisions, he wouldn't take one step more than necessary.

In the rich blend of culture and nature that the Daalder children were exposed to every summer, one striking ingredient was missing. Whether they were in the heart of France or deep in Italy, their parents managed to steer almost totally clear of the culinary riches of these countries. Because Françoise was prone to constipation, they avoided the fresh baguettes. Instead, they bought the gray whole-wheat loaves that every baker always had lying around somewhere, had them sliced "just like in Holland," and put the very cheapest cheese spreads or sausage meats on them. They managed to avoid the sweetest peaches and reddest tomatoes by doing their shopping in dingy, out-of-the-way grocery shops. Occasionally, on days when they had to cover great distances by car, they were forced to eat in real restaurants. Even then, they tried everything within their power to avoid the good food by ordering a sandwich or an omelet, if possible accompanied by a glass of milk (only very rarely did they drink wine). If the waiter objected to their skimpy order, they sometimes stalked out angrily (take it or leave it, fellow!), and continued their journey with rumbling stomachs. But Joop always hoped his parents would be too tired to get on their high horses, and that just this once, they would order the cheapest menu, which, especially in the smaller villages, often proved to be a wonderful meal.

Joop thus caught a glimpse, a whiff, a tinge of that better world that he had first encountered at the Vandenbrouckes' dinner table. But those moments were so scarce that he didn't connect them, and he had no idea that France and Italy were blessed with such rich cuisines. The food he came to associate with these countries was certainly different from the food at home, but definitely not better: ravioli from a tin, little jars of lumpy yogurt with cloudy puddles of whey floating on top, thin bars of chocolate that never broke along the lines and had no taste. And always those huge bags of madeleines that were stuffed into the shopping basket, those stale, dry little cakes that sent the others into ecstasy because their great hero, Marcel Proust, had written about them so beautifully. With great aplomb, the cakes were dunked in the tea that they drank in front of the tent, late in the afternoon upon returning from a long hike.

But even Joop cherished some beautiful memories from these holidays. Sometimes Rosalinde was in a funny mood, especially if she had argued with Charlotte. She would take him along to the local market, for instance, to the sweet peaches and red tomatoes and to all the other fruit and vegetables their parents ignored. But this vegetarian profusion was only a prelude to the real stuff. After the cheese stalls, which they ran past with their noses plugged and snorting with laughter, they arrived at the fish stalls, where the stench was even worse. There, they peered into a basin of lobsters crawling slowly over each other, and his sister would tell him of the horrible death that awaited them. At the next stall, they watched as a cheerfully babbling woman relieved one frowning fish after another of its earthly body with a single blow of her chopping knife — or sometimes not quite. Farther along was the "scary meat." Rosalinde would point out the liver, kidneys, and brains, and explain what tripe was. There were also buckets full of blubber and protrusions she couldn't identify. They passed a wicker basket filled with goat heads with milky-blue eyes, and bunches of skinned hares and rabbits hanging from a rack, some with little bags tied around their heads so that they would marinate in their own blood. And at each of these horror stalls stood prim and proper Mrs.

Vandenbroucke–like women with their shopping baskets, as if nothing at all were the matter. In fact, they sniffed and poked at everything without the slightest fear or embarrassment.

Giggly and lightheaded, Rosalinde and Joop would walk back to the campsite, where the other three members of the family were lying on the picnic blanket in front of the tent reading their books.

But the girls always made up again quickly, and by the afternoon, Rosalinde would have rejoined the others as they shuffled through the local archaeology museum, opened especially for them by some shaky old man. Bending over the display cases, the four of them furnished even the tiniest, dullest little shard with commentary. Joop stood at a distance, with leaden legs and a parched throat.

A Vague Longing

When Charlotte did her final high school exams, it rained straight A's, but the best news was that she was accepted at the conservatory in Amsterdam. Despite the long traveling time, she preferred to continue living at Swaanendal. She found student life in the city superficial, and at home she had access to both a piano and a harpsichord, which she could play to her heart's content at any time of day without having to consider neighbors. On the odd occasion that she wanted to stay in town to attend a concert, she could sleep at a girlfriend's.

Sometimes on the weekends a group of students armed with all manner of musical instruments would come to Swaanendal to practice in the calm of the rural environment. Laurens and Françoise would discreetly withdraw, only reappearing to serve the "real" musicians coffee and cakes or, at the end of a long workday, to act as audience. Once, they even had the privilege to welcome Manfred Scholl, a renowned harpsichordist from Stuttgart who was a visiting lecturer at the conservatory and saw great promise in Charlotte. After curtly greeting the radiant parents, he withdrew into the music room with his students. Later that day, Joop and Rosalinde were in the kitchen with their parents eating a sandwich when Manfred barged in and slammed his empty coffee mug down on the counter.

"Bitte, noch einen Kaffee."

To Joop and Rosalinde's amazement, their mother jumped up to put the kettle on.

When the Daalders made music *en famille* as of old, it was now Charlotte who gave the instructions. She was stricter and more impatient than her father. Now that she was accustomed to higher standards, she found it difficult to put up with the hobbyistic approach of the other three. Lately, Rosalinde in particular had been making only a halfhearted effort.

"For God's sake, what's the matter with you?" Charlotte asked her one day, noticing how she was sawing away on her viola like a robot while something in the garden seemed to draw her attention.

Rosalinde began to sob softly. "I think it's so sad, the way he just hangs around out there."

Bewildered, the others glanced outside, where Joop was listlessly tugging at the branches of a bush.

"Gee," said Charlotte. "Is that all?"

Françoise came and stood beside her youngest daughter, placing her hand on her shoulder. "Ah, Rosie, you have to keep in mind that he himself isn't aware of anything. Not everyone is as sensitive as you and your sister."

But Rosalinde put her instrument on the floor and ran out the door and upstairs to her room, where she threw herself onto her bed and cried her eyes out, not only about her poor little brother but about all the ignorance and injustice in the world, and her own ugliness and boring character, which doomed her to going through life as an old maid.

Back in the music room, the three other members of the quartet looked at each other questioningly.

"I think she's having a hard time because Lotte's at the conservatory," offered Laurens. "Perhaps more difficult than we realize."

Meanwhile, Joop had left his branch pulling and had wandered farther away from home, past the wheat field, toward the woods. Although his situation was perhaps less dramatic than his sister imagined, at the age of twelve he had begun to feel a bit lonely for the first time in his life. Over the years, he had always done his best not to be noticed and to be left alone, with reasonable success at home as well as at school. But sometimes, when he sat next to a pretty girl in the classroom, he felt shy; a thrilling yet uncomfortable sensation that required just the opposite sort of approach on his part, inciting him to attract attention. Having no idea how, he withdrew even more, a strategy he had to pay for with bouts of melancholy—of the kind Rosalinde had just caught him in.

One day Joop was forced to face some facts of life.

His cousin Nico, now sixteen, had left school as soon as he could and was about to embark on a fantastic adventure. Through a business friend, his father had arranged for him to work on a tobacco farm in Ontario for a year, in faraway Canada!

Just before leaving, he dropped in at Swaanendal to say good-bye. Up in the bedroom with his cousin, he pulled out a magazine with dirty pictures—literally dirty, because he had fished it out of the garbage bin at home. Every time Nico turned a page to show the next "gorgeous broad," Joop smelled coffee grounds and moldy orange peels.

"Hubba, hubba!" his cousin kept shouting, the way he had seen a man do in an American movie.

Joop was so intensely shocked by all the nudity parading so shamelessly before him that he couldn't get a word out of his mouth.

After they had looked at all the pictures, Nico ordered his cousin to keep the magazine for him until his return. It was much too dangerous to take it on the plane with him to

Canada. If customs caught him, there was no telling what would happen! In the best case, he would get off with fifty lashes; in the worst, he would have to spend a few years in jail.

On Nico's advice, Joop stashed the magazine under his mattress.

It was discovered there a few days later by the cleaning lady when she was changing the sheets. Unfortunately, she felt obliged to inform Professor Daalder of her shocking find.

As with all the earlier pranks, here too Nico got off scot-free. While he was high above the Atlantic, being served Coca-Cola by a gorgeous stewardess, Joop was in his father's study, where he had to give a full explanation for the filth spread out on the desk.

After Laurens had thrown the magazine into the waste-basket, he took a thick art book out of the bookcase and began to show Joop how the theme of the "female nude" could be dealt with in a respectful way. Where his cousin had spoken of "gorgeous broads," his father spoke of "pose" and "use of light," of "voluptuous cloudscapes" and "sexual symbolism."

Joop was equally uncomfortable with this respectable nudity, especially in the presence of his father. If only he could flee outdoors and wander quietly through the fields alone. But Laurens took all the time in the world to leaf through the history of art with his son, and they never had to look for long before the next nude presented itself. Joop gradually became used to it, so that by the time they arrived in the nineteenth century, his heartbeat remained almost normal, even when he looked at a picture a bit longer, like the one with the two clothed men and the naked woman sitting in the woods picnicking. The painting was called *Le Déjeuner sur l'herbe* and it was by a certain Edouard Manet. The scene would begin to lead a life of its own in Joop's imagination, in which it was unclear what captivated him more — the woman or the picnic basket.

The Apricot

S hortly after her crying fit, a miracle happened. Rosalinde got a boyfriend. His name was Wouter. A decent lad, although to her parents' taste, and especially to Charlotte's, he was a bit too science-oriented.

They became an inseparable duo. Like Rosalinde, Wouter was an avid bird lover, and if they weren't up in her room or at his house cramming for the final exams, they were out walking or cycling with the binoculars and bird guide always close at hand. To her sister's displeasure, Rosalinde barely practiced on her viola anymore, which was painfully obvious on those rare occasions when the family still made music together.

After graduating from high school with a decent series of A's and B's ("Just fine, dear!"), Rosalinde announced she didn't want to go on holiday with her family that summer. She and Wouter had other plans.

"Who wants to go cycling?" said Charlotte contemptuously. "In Denmark, of all places!"

That first holiday without Rosa felt strange for the other members of the family. As Laurens put it, a middle voice had been cut out of the Daalder chord, so that the remaining tones still harmonized but sounded rather thin.

The Danish adventure was only a foretaste of the inevitable. In September, Rosalinde left the parental home to live with Wouter in Utrecht, where he was going to study biology and she, French language and literature.

Meanwhile, Françoise was worried about Charlotte. Since starting at the conservatory, she considered herself quite the lady, perhaps too much so. She always knew everything better and was scathing in her opinion of others, including her fellow students, whom she found "juvenile" or "immature." The old-fashioned skirts and jewelry she wore even made her look like a middle-aged lady rather than like a young student who ought to be in the prime of her life.

"Perhaps it would do Lotte good if she met a person of the opposite sex," sighed Françoise one evening.

"Hmm," echoed Laurens from behind his book.

A few days later, Françoise made the cardinal error of voicing this wish again, but now at the breakfast table in the presence of Charlotte herself, who responded furiously. It was the lowest of the low to reduce her completely legitimate way of doing things to a question of hormones. And by the way, there was no reason at all for mother dear to worry about her love life. Her needs in that area were amply met.

A deathly silence.

Yes, that surprised them, didn't it?

Bursting with pride, she told them she had been the mistress of her harpsichord teacher, Manfred Scholl, for more than a year now. Those nights when she stayed at her girlfriend's in town? Three guesses whom she had really spent them with. That pretty skirt she was wearing? That brooch? Three guesses who had given them to her.

Her parents looked at each other in bafflement, and Joop too, could hardly believe it. That ugly old asshole who had slammed his coffee mug down on the counter? Was that who his sister was screwing?

Françoise asked just how old the fellow was.

"Fifty-eight? He's old enough to be your father!"

"Yes. So what?"

There was no stopping Charlotte now. She had known her parents would react like this; that's why she had kept the relationship a secret for so long. Oh sure, they liked to present themselves as free-thinking intellectuals, but when it came down to it, they were every bit as narrow-minded as the people in the village. While true love had nothing to do with age, and her relationship with Manfred was a hell of a lot more mature than that mommy-and-daddy business between Rosalinde and Wouter, with their identical windbreakers and their identical backpacks and their lovely little cycling holidays . . .

"And sure as hell more exciting than your boringly predictable bourgeois marriage!" she added.

"Good lord!" said Laurens.

The next summer holiday was planned more tightly than usual. This wasn't because of the unfavorable location of the cultural sites in relation to the beauty spots en route, but because of the poste-restante addresses Charlotte had given Manfred before he joined his wife, Hannelore, at their summer residence on Lake Constance. If there turned out to be no letter at the post office, Charlotte was unbearable for the rest of the day, but if there was one, she was equally unbearable. She would go and sit away from the tent to read it, but always so that the others could still see her. Manfred had beautiful, firm handwriting, she informed them, and he wrote in the most exquisite German you could imagine. Dutch was so stiff and clunky in comparison!

"Shall I read some of it aloud?"

"I don't think that's such a good idea," said Françoise.

"But it's about Mahler."

"No, I'd really rather you didn't."

"All right then, I won't."

Rosalinde had gone to Wales with Wouter, Charlotte had her love letters from Manfred, his parents had each other and their poetry collections. More than ever that summer, Joop was left to his own devices.

The space he had felt around him since childhood, in which he used to love losing himself, now raised questions, pressing philosophical questions. Who am I? Why am I? Does the world exist around me or am I just imagining it? Or am I being imagined, too? Joop didn't know. It was making him unhappy.

The simple answer to all his questions came unexpectedly during a walk in Provence. Their goal that day was a little twelfth-century chapel at the top of a mountain, but after climbing for two hours in the burning sun, they ran into a military site cordoned off by high fences. Laurens, whose sense of direction usually never failed him, studied his ordnance map till he went cross-eyed, but still he couldn't figure out where they were. In the hope of being able to continue their ascent farther on, they walked for some time alongside the NO TRESPASSING site, but a sharp bend in the fence forced them down the hill and eventually deposited them on the shoulder of a busy highway.

Laurens consulted the map again. "Damn it! How is this possible? This is the *route nationale!*"

To return to the campsite, they now had to walk for four kilometers along this road in the scorching heat. After they had marched silently in single file for half an hour, the shoulder widened out into a dusty parking lot. A small delivery truck was parked there, and in the shade of the open tailgate sat an old man in a folding chair, selling apricots.

Normally, the Daalders never bought from roadside fruit stands, but the demoralized party badly needed something to perk themselves up. The apricots didn't look bad and, what's more, they weren't too expensive.

Joop had eaten apricots occasionally in the past. A mediocre experience: if they weren't hard or sour, they were as sticky and sweet as jam. But this one . . . this one melted on his tongue and yet had a wonderfully fresh flavor. Despite the heat, shivers ran down his back. This is what it was all about, this kind of moment . . . a moment that made all others fade into oblivion. And that's when he knew it: I taste, therefore I am.

With these words, everything fell into place. This was the answer to all his doubts. His life consisted of moments of tasting. They formed the lowest points, like the awful mugs of milk, the highest points, like The First Supper at the Vandenbrouckes, and all the everyday, in-between points, like the leaves of sorrel that he chewed on when wandering around the estate. At these moments, Joop knew he was alive, that he was part of the world around him. No matter how dreamlike the rest of his existence might seem, no matter how much he was at the mercy of his family and his school, no one could deprive him of this certainty. I taste, therefore I am.

And if he was ever so lucky as to have a picnic in the woods with a girl, like in the painting *Le Déjeuner sur l'herbe,* if nothing else there would have to be an apricot like this one in the picnic basket — so that the woman of his dreams could taste that she really existed too.

After the ecstasy came the inevitable disenchantment.

When the exhausted party finally reached the campsite, Charlotte secluded herself with a pile of letters from Manfred. Laurens set to work at the camp stove, putting on a pot of water for tea. And Joop asked if he could have another apricot. But his mother wanted to keep them for the next day and stored them in the tent. In their stead, she pulled out the bag of madeleines.

The next morning, after sweltering against each other all night long, the apricots were covered with brown patches.

Françoise removed their pips, threw the apricots into the plastic salad bowl, and mashed them to a pulp. Then she added a few scoops of oatmeal and poured yogurt into the mixture: solid sustenance for their second attempt to reach the ruins at the top of the mountain.

Joop Decides
What to Study

After repeating his final exam in French, Joop graduated from high school by the skin of his teeth. To everyone's astonishment, he chose to study art history. Was there some hope for the little barbarian after all? For that little boy who stood picking his nose in front of the world's greatest masterpieces? They had their doubts.

For Joop, it had been a question of elimination. He had no ear at all for languages, he found history boring, and psychology got on his nerves. In the end, only art history and philosophy were left, and Joop discarded the latter because the word was too much of a mouthful.

With little ado (Françoise was glad to be done at last with her mother role), Joop moved to Amsterdam. Through friends of his parents', he could stay in the attic of the house of Mrs. Verstege, an elderly widow.

The nondescript schoolboy became a nondescript student, who seldom opened his mouth and silently navigated his way through the first year with C's and the occasional B. Outside the lecture rooms, he had little contact with his fellow students, with the exception of Peter, the only other boy among fourteen girls in his year. They would meet in the pub now and again. But whenever Peter became involved in another one of his romantic adventures, weeks could go by without their seeing each other.

Joop spent most of his time in his attic, in the tiny back-room that served as a little kitchen. He bought his first cook-book, *French Cuisine*, by Hugo van Driel, and studied it more meticulously and critically than his university textbooks. His first doubts arose as he tried out the recipes in chapter one, "Basic Techniques." Halfway through "Sauces," when van Driel's béarnaise sauce turned out too sour, Joop took to improvising. He tried four different types of wine and three types of vinegar until he found a ratio that satisfied him. He began to work like this with every recipe, and only noticed that his experiments were costing him handfuls of money when he didn't have enough money left to pay the rent. He asked his father if he could advance his study allowance for the next month.

"I just don't understand it," said Laurens. "The girls never ran short."

For the next sauce in the cookbook, the real French chef preferred to start with a *fond*, the viscous liquid left after a bouillon, made from bones and offal, had boiled for a few days. "But for our modest purposes, a shot of ordinary bouillon will do just fine," van Driel assured his readers. Joop didn't settle for that. He jumped on his bicycle and cycled to the slaughter-house, where he bought a large bag of "leftovers," some still covered with skin and hair. Back in the attic, the meat that came out of the bag didn't smell very wholesome, and when he put it in a pan of water on the stove, an unmistakable slaugh-terhouse stench began to spread through the kitchen. A smell that a thin wall of gypsum couldn't hold back and that soon had the whole attic in its grip. Joop opened all the windows as far as he could, then left for classes. It was a good thing his landlady was staying at her sister's in Groningen for a few days, because when he returned home a few hours later, the awful smell already greeted him at the bottom of the attic stairs. Still he refused to take the pan off the burner. Those who want to be beautiful must endure pain, as the Dutch saying went. And apparently so did those who wanted to eat well. As he sat at his desk studying, he had to keep sucking on peppermints to drive the worst stench out of his nose. He left the brew on the burner for two days and two nights. On Sunday morning, he sieved the remaining liquid out of the pan and took a cautious lick. The suffering had not been in vain, for the fond tasted sublime.

When Mrs. Verstege opened the front door on Sunday evening and sniffed around, an anxious foreboding took possession of her. Her fear seemed confirmed when the smell of decay worsened on the second floor. You occasionally read such notices in the newspaper, and Joop was such a quiet, lonely boy.

"Hello?" she shouted from the bottom of the attic stairs, not daring to climb them. "Is someone there?"

After some stumbling, the trapdoor opened and Joop's head appeared. "Is something the matter, Mrs. Verstege?"

In April, the first-year students went on an excursion to Tuscany and Umbria. Joop returned to all the places he had visited with his parents and sisters, but the works of art looked totally different now they were being looked at by fourteen fiercely competitive girls instead of by a diffident scholar and his family. "Division of space" was the watchword that year, Giotto the big hero. Joop remembered how his father had stood with his nose almost against the frescoes in the basilica of Assisi, searching for every minute detail discussed in the thick German book he was holding in his hand. Joop's fellow students did just the opposite, standing as far back as they could. With one hand on their hips, they used the other to draw all kinds of sweeping lines in the air to clarify Giotto's intentions to each other. When one of the frescoes prompted Daphne to accuse the old master of having had an off day, Mathilde reacted with scornful laughter. How could she be so presumptuous! There was a sharp exchange of words between the two students that resounded throughout the cathedral and led to indignant whispers among a tour group of American nuns standing a few frescoes away. Professor Donkers, who had watched the dispute with some amusement, decided to intervene. This fresco was indeed the subject of heated debate among art historians, he explained, because it seemed so out of line with the others. Daphne therefore deserved a compliment. It was essential in this field to maintain a certain freshness and naiveté, and not to drool automatically like Pavlov's dog in front of every work by a great artist.

They continued their tour through the cathedral without further incident, but as soon as they came outside, Mathilde burst into tears. She had felt so humiliated just now. She had felt so cruelly exposed with that remark about Pavlov's dog that . . . that the startled professor sent the others back to the hotel so that he could go to a café with his deeply aggrieved student to set things right.

They were gone for a long time, a very long time.

The group was complete again by evening as they walked through the narrow streets of the village toward what Professor Donkers called "the best little restaurant in all of Italy," which, thank goodness, was not mentioned yet in any of the travel guides. The whole time, Daphne kept a close eye on Mathilde, who walked separately from the others and was noticeably quiet.

When they entered the restaurant, Donkers was enthusiastically embraced by Luciano, the owner.

"Ah, professor," he cried. "What a life you have! They get more beautiful every year!"

They sat down at a long table, little baskets of bread were

served and five bottles of wine were opened, and Luciano's outrageous flirting made for much merriment.

When dinner was served, everyone vied to make the loudest compliment about how delicious it all was, everyone but Joop. He would believe anything they said about the division of space, but the pasta here was nothing but sticky, the slices of aubergine were drenched in an oil that left a rancid aftertaste, and the leg of lamb, charcoal-grilled in the "authentic Umbrian way," was tough and dry and tasted, with its overly pungent flavor, more like an old sheep.

The dessert was cassata, served so hard and cold that it was impossible to tell where the cake ended and the ice cream began. Only the shredded almonds, serving as decoration, were soft, so soft you could even bend them in half without breaking them.

"Libidonoso, Luciano!" cried Professor Donkers. "You can't get it better than this!"

Joop looked at him disapprovingly. It wasn't a question of tasting here, it was a question of staging a show, the I-know-the-owner show.

After coffee and a liqueur on the house, it was time to pay the bill. Babbling excitedly, they left the restaurant. Luciano stationed himself by the doorway and showed each of the giggling girls out with a kiss on the hand and a little compliment. Outside, in front of the restaurant, a lively discussion arose on what to do next, when Professor Donkers abruptly wished the group a pleasant evening.

"Are you coming?" he then said to Mathilde.

They walked away together through the alleyway. Just before they disappeared from sight, he put his arm around her.

"Holy Mary," was how Peter gave vent to the amazement among those left behind. "I'd say this calls for some more alcohol."

But most of the others were now too tired, and trickled

back to the hotel in small groups. In the end, a party of five, including Joop, went to one of the cafés on the square. They ordered a carafe of red wine and were served an unsolicited bowl of green olives. Joop sampled one but unfortunately it had a chemical taste.

"It seems Donkers chooses a new one every year," Vera was saying in the meantime. "I don't understand why his wife keeps taking it."

Daphne was particularly incensed about Mathilde's tears, the cheapest trick on earth.

"I think it's disappointing that he falls for it."

"Sour grapes, Daphie?"

"Yes, sure, Pete. If that's what you want." She took an olive, then offered the bowl to Joop, but he declined.

"Oh, don't you like olives?"

"Not these ones, no."

Daphne didn't hear this extra qualification. She had already gone back to squabbling with Peter.

Joop couldn't care less which seduction techniques had or hadn't been used. It had all happened too quickly for him anyway, and he had little to add to the discussion. But with Daphne's "Oh, don't you like olives?" his pride had been wounded. First the professor in the restaurant, and now this. The wrong people drawing the wrong boundaries around the wrong food. Culinary snobs they were, worse than ordinary barbarians. With an icy gaze, he watched as another third-class olive disappeared into Daphne's first-class little mouth.

The atmosphere at the table became increasingly grim as the drinking became more excessive. Peter in particular couldn't stop, and kept insisting that Daphne would have been only too glad to go to bed with Donkers herself. She and Vera retorted that Peter was too oversexed to see the difference between flirting and wanting to go to bed with someone.

It seemed there was no end to the downward spiral, until two Italian boys at a neighboring table, who had been watching the group for some time, grabbed their chairs and joined them uninvited, one next to Daphne, the other next to Vera. "Are all Dutch girls as beautiful as you are?" they wanted to know. "Your eyes are as blue as the bay of Naples," said one. "Your hair is as golden as a wheat field in September," said the other. And did they maybe want to go for a ride on the scooter? Vera and Daphne looked at each other. Sure, they would like that.

"Incredible," muttered Peter, as the girls allowed themselves to be helped out of their chairs, and then tripped along behind their newfound friends.

"Ciao, bambini!" cried Daphne from the back of the scooter, and off they went, her blond hair blowing in the wind.

After a few false starts and the appropriate expletives, the other boy and Vera set off in pursuit.

"Do you understand that?" Peter asked Joop. "Daphie just takes off with that creep! My Daphie! And did you see how it worked? Those bastards acted as if we weren't here. They looked straight through us. Yes, man, here in Italy we Dutch guys just don't count. Here, we're the invisible men."

"Then I must be the invisible woman."

"Eh? What?" Peter took a sip of wine and looked around. Only then did it dawn on him that their fellow student Corinne was still sitting at the table. "Yes, babe. You just happen to have dark hair and brown eyes. That's bad luck for you."

"Or good luck, maybe."

"Ah! Sour grapes again?" He grabbed the carafe and squeezed the last drop into his glass.

"Speaking of sour grapes, let's order another one."

When he stood up to catch the waiter's attention, his chair crashed backward onto the ground. Confused, he looked over his shoulder. Joop shot up and just managed to keep Peter from losing his balance and taking the table and all its glassware with him.

"My Daphie, damn it!" he shouted. "That bloody Italian has taken off with my Daphie!"

One of the waiters gestured for them to leave.

"So, what's the problem, man?" said Peter, his chin jutting into the air.

Corinne and Joop had to pull him away before he got into a fight with the waiter.

They dragged him, ranting and raving, back to the hotel. After they had laid him on the bed and pried off his shoes, he fell into a deep sleep.

"Well, Joop," said Corinne, smiling. "Good-night to you too, then."

But Joop couldn't fall asleep. Not because of the wet snoring of his roommate but because of the shy smile Corinne had given him just now as she wished him good-night. And it wasn't the first time that evening she had looked at him that way. She was sweet, and she was pretty. Not the life-of-the-party à la Daphne, not the dazzling (because blond) center of Italian attention, but, as the invisible woman, eminently suitable for the invisible man, as Joop had always felt himself to be, and not just here in Italy. It was dumb of him to have been fretting about the olives when a girl had been looking at him so sweetly all evening, very dumb. He was still lying there wide awake when the clock of the little thirteenth-century affair opposite the hotel struck three. Dumb, dumb, dumb.

More Naked
Than Naked

Back in Holland, Joop wanted to make up for lost time by letting Corinne know he had feelings for her, too. But how? With flowers? An evening out? Then he knew. He would cook for her. Before extending the invitation, he composed a menu comprising his most successful experiments of the past year. He was awestruck; too exquisite, too expensive, too much of a good thing. But instead of cooking less extravagantly for her, he decided to dampen the shock effect of his culinary tour de force by inviting more people.

Peter was allowed to come, and Daphne, too. Their eternal squabbling always brought life to the party, and who knows, perhaps something would finally happen between them. To avoid the impression of a double date, he asked Vera to join the party. Only after she pulled her chair up to the table did he realize that it was the same five people who had sat at the outdoor café in Assisi.

As he had expected, it was one surprise after another for his guests. But Joop wasn't happy. Peter, who had eaten at his place before, monopolized the attention by acting as the master of ceremonies: "Yes, dear ladies, this boy really can cook." Nor did the girls' enthusiasm give him any satisfaction. But what had he expected? Obviously, they couldn't keep saying how delicious it all was. The topic of the table conversation soon shifted. Encouraged by Peter and, to Joop's horror, by Corinne, and after a lot of giggles and protests, Vera and Daphne finally revealed just how far they had gone with their scooter boyfriends. And it was far, very far.

After coffee, Vera and Daphne helped with the dishes. They showered him with compliments again, but these meant nothing to him now. He hadn't made the slightest progress with the dinner. Not once during the meal had Corinne looked at him with her sweet smile. He felt more naked than naked, standing in his kitchen obediently answering all kinds of questions about his "hobby," which he didn't want to talk about at all, at least not like this, and not with these two.

In the middle of his exposé on how to sear different kinds of meat, he noticed the girls looking at each other with a mischievous smile.

"It sure is quiet in there," said Daphne. "Do you guys dare to go and look?"

When they peered around the corner, Peter and Corinne were lying on his couch bed in a passionate embrace.

Joop remembered Assisi, and everything became clear. Corinne had indeed looked at him all evening with her moonstruck smile, but it had only been to share with him her deeply felt feelings for Peter, who at that moment only had eyes for Daphne, was highly incensed about the Italian boys, and at any rate was too drunk to notice a thing. But what better place for the spark to jump over than the cozy little attic of a mutual friend, after a heavenly meal, and having been put in the mood by the erotic adventures of two girl-friends? It became so horribly and painfully clear to him that all he could do was laugh.

So his disappointment in love lasted only briefly, and when Peter and Corinne asked him to go for a walk with them in the dunes one beautiful summer afternoon, he didn't hesitate for a moment. After a while, they found shelter in a hollow in the dunes and spread out a tablecloth. Peter and Corinne took sandwiches and raisin buns out of their bag and Joop a potato salad and a bottle of white wine out of his. Two men, a woman, and a picnic. Although Corinne didn't take off her clothes, the scene approached that of *Le Déjeuner sur l'herbe* in his imagination. Languid from the wine and sun, Corinne snuggled up to Peter, who gently massaged her neck and shoulders while talking to Joop. The circles he was making became bolder, until finally he dove under her blouse with both hands. She froze for a moment, then heaved a sigh, and wriggled even closer. Joop blushed and looked down at the ground. To keep himself occupied, he picked up a handful of sand and let it run slowly through his fingers.

"Hey, Joop," said Peter. "Why don't you go for a little walk?"

"Oh, come on!" cried Corinne, wrenching herself out from under Peter's hands and sitting up straight. "You can't do that, Petie."

"Okay, okay." He leaned over to her and whispered something in her ear that made her burst out laughing. "Sorry, Joop," he said. "I guess it's us going for a little walk."

Giggling, they scrambled up the dune and disappeared out of sight.

Joop cleaned up the picnic stuff. Chewing on a sprig of chives, he lay down on the blanket and watched a few little clouds as they drifted past.

He had just dozed off when Peter announced their return with a "Hey there, Joop!" Not a word or knowing look in reference to what had just happened. But Joop did notice that the two lovers focused their attention on him now, as if wanting to make amends for something.

On the way back to the train station, Corinne even slipped her arm through his, while Peter walked a few yards behind

them with all the picnic gear. Had he ever been in love, she
wanted to know.

"No, not really."

Joop could have said, "Yes, not long ago, with you." But
that would have sounded so tragic, and it didn't suit the lightness of that summer day.

"You know, Joop," said Corinne tenderly. "Not long ago,
Peter and I talked about how the love lives of everyone in our
year would turn out. We concluded maybe you would be
alone the longest, but that in the end, you would meet the
woman of your dreams and be the happiest of us all."

She looked back over her shoulder, "Right, Petie?"

"Huh? What? Oh yes, right."

Chocolates and Cathedrals

The horniness that Joop had sensed all around him during his first year at university gave way in the second year to a certain apathy. The die was cast, the students knew where they stood with each other. Daphne, one of the trendsetters in the first year, didn't come back after the summer. Peter and Corinne had become a respectable couple, sitting next to each other in every class and cycling straight home as soon as classes were over.

The yearly excursion was also much tamer than the one the year before. They went to Burgundy for four days to look at cathedrals, and instead of the flamboyant Professor Donkers, who had left for Italy together with a fresh batch of first-year students, this time they were accompanied by two teachers, a man and a woman, inspired scholars perhaps, but dull as doornails. The lines Joop's fellow students drew in the air when they stood in front of a work of art had become more cautious, more hesitant. A few more years and they would be standing there just like his father, whispering aloud from a thick German book—humility personified. They stayed in the town of Avallon, where there was little to do after sundown. The teachers went to bed early, as did Peter and Corinne. Downstairs in the hotel bar, Joop listened to the bored comments the girls made about the three French boys who were hanging out at the pinball machines. Less handsome than the Italians, was the consensus.

The next morning, they had a few hours off. Joop was wandering through the town on his own when the window of a chocolate shop caught his eye. That was strange. It was usually the meat, fish, or cheese shops that drew his attention. Bakeries didn't interest him as much, not to speak of pastry or chocolate shops.

It was especially the plainness of the window that appealed to him. No frills and trimmings, no cute little boxes with shiny pink ribbons—just chocolate. But when he looked back on it many years later, it was a plainness very different from the modern, stylish variant that he abhorred, the cold, over-wrought design business that seemed bent on making food look as inedible as possible. No. These chocolates lay there composed and casual. They didn't have to prove themselves, their quality was so obvious that even Joop's mouth started to water, although he still wasn't much of a chocolate lover.

After hesitating for a moment, he went inside.

There was a wonderful smell of chocolate, which of course wasn't so strange for a chocolate shop. But when he took a deeper breath, it still smelled of chocolate, unlike in Dutch shops, where you could smell the sweet gooey fillings right through the chocolate.

He wasn't able to enjoy it for long. The salesgirl, a haughty, wasp-waisted beauty in a black dress, asked what "monsieur" wanted, eyeing him with obvious distaste. His eyes shot nervously to the chocolates in the glass display case. Here, too, there were strikingly few chocolates; many of them were the same and most of them were bitter. There were no prices anywhere—with quality like this, of course, money didn't matter—nor names nor descriptions, only a sign on the wall behind the salesgirl that said you could order coffee, tea, or a drink with two chocolates of your choice. They could be consumed at one of the three little tables in the far corner of the shop. Again, monsieur was asked what he wanted.

Joop poked at the glass with his finger, and inquired about the contents of the chocolates at the top right there.

Routinely, she rattled off the ingredients, probably intentionally so he couldn't understand a word of it.

"How many would you like?"

Joop gestured that he wanted to continue looking.

"Of course, monsieur. Take all the time in the world."

"No, sorry. Give me two of those after all, with coffee, please."

"Two of the same?"

"Isn't that possible?"

"Whatever you want, monsieur."

Joop went and sat down at one of the tables.

While the salesgirl operated the loudly gurgling espresso machine, a door opened behind her. A man wearing a cook's apron came out of the kitchen with a fresh batch of chocolates. He held the tray with both arms and looked around suspiciously, as if reluctant to give up his creations to the world. Joop gave him a friendly nod, but the man had just turned away to slip the chocolates into the display case.

The salesgirl brought his coffee and chocolates, announced the price, and waited for him to pay. Engulfed by her perfume and with the threat of her cleavage at eye level, Joop groped in his wallet with trembling fingers. She snatched the first bill that he hesitantly pulled out and took it to the cash register. A saucer with change was returned to his table with a lilting *"Merci!"* The words *"service non compris"* were printed on the bill. So he had to tip her too. But he would worry about that later. For the time being, he was rid of her.

The chocolates had a beautiful dark color, a near-black that reminded him of Rosalinde's extra-bitter *R*. He took the first chocolate from the saucer. An agreeable weight, which he would have preferred to hold a bit longer between his thumb and index finger, but his hands were so warm from his encounter with the salesgirl that the chocolate began to slip away between his fingers. He quickly took a bite. As his teeth sank through the outer layer, they happily met not a sticky goo but a firm interior, finely structured and even more bitter than the outer layer. Occasionally he encountered tiny pieces of roasted almond coated in a layer of crispy caramel, sweet glimmers in the chocolate darkness. Very remotely, he now tasted alcohol, but almost as an absence, the way a warm breeze on a summer evening calls to mind the sun that disappeared behind the horizon hours before. Sighing with satisfaction, Joop popped the rest of the chocolate into his mouth.

Only when he opened his eyes again did he realize that he must have shut them while tasting, for without his noticing, the man had come out from behind the counter and approached his table to within several feet.

Joop remained surprisingly calm under his penetrating gaze. Completely out of character, he took the initiative to say something, so powerful was the drive to express his admiration.

"This is . . ." he began, gesturing to the remaining chocolate on the saucer. That damn French! If only he had tried harder at school. "This is . . . a cathedral!"

"Pardon me? What's that you said?"

Joop blushed. He had said something ridiculous. Too lofty. Too pubescently poetic. Or was he being stared at because it should have been *une cathédrale* instead of *un*?

The man turned to the salesgirl.

"Did you hear that, Frédérique? Did you hear what this young man said? A cathedral. A chocolate is a cathedral!"

He came over and offered Joop his hand.

"My name is Jérôme Sorel. And you must be no less than an angel, sent to earth by the Good Lord to cheer up a sad old chocolatier!"

"Joop Daalder," said Joop bewildered, adding, with an apologetic laugh, that he was an art history student from Holland.

Sorel's enthusiasm didn't wane. "I knew it," he said, as he sat down next to Joop. "I knew it the moment I saw two of the same chocolates on your saucer. Only a real connoisseur does that. If something is good, why not try it twice? We reread a good novel, don't we? Frédérique, could you pour us two marcs, please?"

"But monsieur, you know what madame says about that."

"Don't nag! Two marcs, I said."

Frédérique came to their table with two well-filled cognac glasses.

Sorel proposed a toast to the divine providence that had led their paths to cross.

The stuff was so strong that it made Joop's eyes water.

Marc de Bourgogne," said Sorel proudly. "A real man's drink."

They came to discuss the chocolate Joop had chosen, which happened to be one of the chocolatier's absolute favorites.

Joop could only partly follow his detailed explanation and constantly apologized for his bad French.

"It doesn't matter, my boy, because you and I, we speak *la langue de la langue.*"

La langue de la langue. The language of the palate. How beautiful and profound everything sounded in French. And, indeed, although he understood only a fraction of what Sorel said, he felt a connection on a level that he had never known could be shared with another human being. They ended up talking about chocolate with nuts, a brilliant combination as far as taste was concerned but problematic texture-wise. While chocolate revealed its flavor almost instantly upon contact with the tongue, and kept revealing its flavor until the moment it was swallowed, nuts had to be chewed for some time before their flavor was released, and then that flavor disappeared again and a lot of junk was left behind on your tongue and between your teeth. How could you still enjoy the velvety-soft texture and pure flavor of the chocolate when there was all that rough, tasteless grit mixed through it? A problem. In the chocolate Joop had chosen, Sorel had managed to minimize the roughness by chopping the almond slivers very fine, and he had compensated for the reticence of their flavor by coating them with sweet caramel. In his ongoing struggle to mediate between nuts and chocolate, he had enlisted the help of liqueur—liquid, of course, just like melted chocolate, but with the taste of almonds. Incidentally, Sorel believed the role of alcohol in chocolates should remain a modest one—to build bridges, as in this chocolate, or perhaps to accentuate. His face clouded over. Or did our little Dutchman fancy cherry brandy chocolates and other such alcohol bombs?

Joop winced.

"I knew it! I knew it! Because you're a civilized person, and civilized people drink from glasses, not from chocolates. To your health, my boy, to your health!"

The chocolatier couldn't believe how much they agreed with each other on everything, and on so many different issues. It had to be more than just a coincidence that Joop had come in here.

"And that, when I don't even like sweets," Joop wanted to add. But because of his poor French, it came out as "And I don't like sugar."

"Yes, you see? That's exactly what I mean! Oh, my boy, I could kiss you! Of course you and I don't like sugar. Sugar may be needed to draw out the finer flavors, but in itself, it's vulgar obnoxious filth. Sugar is like the dumb American, without whom, unfortunately, you can't win the war. The trick is to use the loudmouth without being bothered by him too much. Did you hear that, Frédérique? He doesn't like sugar!"

"That's wonderful, monsieur."

Every time Frédérique—and along with her the customers who occasionally entered the shop—looked in their direction, Joop saw them thinking, "What is Monsieur Sorel doing with a dumb foreigner who doesn't even speak decent French?" Their almost hostile glances didn't faze him. What these people didn't understand was that here at this table a completely different language was being spoken: *la langue de la langue.*

Time slipped by, and Sorel asked him if he wanted another drink. Joop glanced at his watch and froze. It was already a quarter to twelve, and they were supposed to have gathered at the hotel entrance at eleven o'clock. Squirming awkwardly in his chair, he told Sorel he should have been sitting in a bus long ago with his fellow students en route to Fontenay Abbey.

"Have you already forgotten what you said?" With a quick nod, Sorel drew his attention to the other chocolate still on his saucer. "Here. Here's your Fontenay."

He gestured to Frédérique, who came around with the bottle to fill their glasses again.

Joop took a hefty sip and grinned. It was the first time in his life he had played truant and he loved it.

But then, unexpectedly, Sorel reprimanded him—wondering what in heaven's name could have possessed him to study art history. You can't taste paint and stone, can you? A crying shame, to waste his real talents like that. Oh, so he was fiddling around in his attic kitchen in his free time? Well, bravo, but that was the sort of halfhearted hobbyism that really got his ire up. If you were blessed with a talent, you had the key to paradise in your hands! Surely, then, you should do everything within your power to find the gate? Or did Joop prefer to go through life sleepwalking, like most of the human race? He should come and do an apprenticeship with him right away, before it was too late. Art history! It was too disgusting for words!

While Sorel had to pay for his outburst with a coughing fit, Joop wondered if the chocolatier hadn't rattled on in his enthusiasm or if he had really meant it—what he had said about an apprenticeship. Had he in fact understood it correctly at all, or was it another one of those bizarre conditional verb forms—"were one to have come here for an apprenticeship, it may have been so that . . ." His French wasn't improving any with the alcohol, but he was getting bolder. When Sorel finished coughing, Joop asked when he could start with the apprenticeship.

"Why not tomorrow? Or this afternoon, as far as I'm concerned. Actually, haven't we already started?"

"So you're serious, then?"

"Of course, my dear boy, why shouldn't I be?"

This was no longer playing truant, this was turning the world upside down. Joop could no longer visualize the consequences. Tears of excitement sprang into his eyes. He had a strong urge to run out of the chocolate shop and skip through the streets of Avallon like some happy madman. To keep himself under control, he put on the emergency brake: "There are still a few things I have to take care of in Holland."

"Of course, my dear boy. Then why don't you start next week? It's up to you. In any case, you are most welcome."

Joop Burns
His Bridges

The students were sitting in the train on their way back to Holland, drinking cheap wine and having heated discussions. Only Joop sat with his forehead pressed to the window for most of the journey, watching as the hilly landscape gradually collapsed until it breathed its last just north of Brussels, where the flat countryside began. How dead and ugly it was here compared to Burgundy!

"God, Joop," cried Corinne. "You look like you're in love."

"Huh?" he said, looking over his shoulder.

"That's what I mean."

The others in the compartment had to laugh.

Smiling vaguely, he turned away from his traveling companions once more. His mysterious absence during the outing to Fontenay (a real shame, he had missed the highlight of the whole trip!) had given rise to the wildest of speculations. No one believed his explanation, that he had lost his way on a walk outside the city walls. Peter insisted he had disappeared into a broom closet with one of the Portuguese chambermaids.

For now, he kept his encounter with the chocolatier a secret. He didn't know whether he would dare to accept the invitation for an apprenticeship, and he was afraid other people's skepticism might be enough to prevent him from doing so. First, he wanted to ensure that his decision was irreversible by giving notice on his room and officially withdrawing from the university.

Back in Holland, everything was taken care of in a single morning, although it did entail a nasty financial blow. Mrs. Verstege asked for an extra month's rent, after having first had to explain what giving notice was. It was doubtful whether the money that was left would cover a one-way ticket to France. He would once again have to approach his father.

Money or no money, there was no going back now. When Peter came around later that day to ask why he hadn't been at class, Joop was finally able to tell him what had really happened during Fontenay.

"Gosh," said his friend, after he heard the whole story. "Aren't you worried those chocolates will bore you after a while?"

"What do you mean?" Joop asked irritably.

It was an enormous step to quit university just like that, and to move to another country on the basis of a vague invitation possibly offered in a fit of drunkenness. He really could have used his good friend's blessing. Although they had a lot of fun that evening and although on parting, Peter called out tearfully and thick-tongued that he would miss him terribly, it was his first reaction that continued to haunt Joop during the night. So making chocolates was boring. It was doubly painful coming from someone as self-assured and popular as Peter. Now Joop understood why he had kept his plans secret for so long, and he resolved to keep listening to his inner voice even without the approval of his environment.

The next morning, he handed in his keys and a thick envelope to his landlady, who now, all smiles, wished him the very best and made him promise to come and visit her after his apprenticeship was finished. With a box of homemade chocolates, mind you! The night before, with an aching heart, he had put some of his kitchen supplies out with the garbage, and given some to

Peter, who accepted them grudgingly ("Sorry, but what use are three kinds of vinegar to me?"). With only a shoulder bag and a suitcase full of textbooks, he set off for Swaanendal. The following morning, he would take the train to France.

He could have phoned his parents from the phone booth in the village square to ask if they would come and pick him up. But, as if to prove his independence, he walked the half mile from the bus stop to the estate despite the heavy suitcase he had to lug along with him.

When he finally reached the driveway, he allowed himself to put the suitcase down after every third beech tree to catch his breath. The stately house he now haltingly approached had always been the self-evident center of civilization, where the last judgment was passed over his comings and goings. But today it was different. Today his parental home was no longer the center but just a stopover, an oversized storage depot for the suitcase with textbooks that were no longer of any use to him now.

Panting, he opened the front door and put down his luggage in the front hallway. A terribly complicated fugue by Bach emanated from the music room. Charlotte, by now almost thirty, still lived at home. Her playing sounded more virtuoso than ever—but also more feverish, more dogged.

Not very nice to listen to, actually. The sweat on his forehead turned cold at the thought. It was the first time he had ever dared to judge the music. Until now it had been the music that had judged him. The playing of the Daalder Quartet had always sounded like a reproach—that he was a dumb, unmusical little boy. No. As a matter of fact he couldn't stand that neurotic *pita-pat* on the harpsichord. Grinning broadly, he walked to the living room.

His parents were sitting in their armchairs reading, exactly as he had left them on his last visit. As if they had never left their chairs. At most they sat a bit more hunched over the pages and their fingers were a bit more gnarled.

"So, Joop," said Françoise, peering out over her bifocals. "Come to do another laundry?"

"No, I'm about to leave for France."

"What do you mean? You just came back from France, didn't you?"

Against his better judgment, he began to tell his parents about his encounter with Jérôme Sorel. They had never taken him seriously. As a toddler, he had already wisely resigned himself to that and had retreated into his own world. So whatever possessed him at that moment, he would later ask himself, to want to share his innermost feelings with them after all? He probably couldn't help it. Since his encounter with the chocolatier, he had been bubbling over with enthusiasm.

His parents barely appeared to listen, their attention distracted by a difficult run Charlotte had stumbled over and was now repeating ad infinitum.

"Shouldn't you go to her for a moment, Laurens?" asked Françoise, right in the middle of Joop's story.

"No, it's probably better if I don't."

Joop fell silent and looked from one parent to the other. He had the same awkward, naked feeling as on the evening he had cooked too extravagantly for Corinne and the others.

"Yes, sorry, Joop," said his mother, when she noticed he had stopped talking. "But your sister is having a very difficult time right now."

Her lover, Manfred, turned out to have had a second mistress for some time now, a lovely young thing who was barely twenty and who, like Lotte at the time, apparently showed great promise at the harpsichord. Everything indicated that this was deeply hurtful to Lotte, but the dirty old man had indoctrinated her so much with his talk of free love that she had actually defended his behavior with a twisted smile. And it came at such a bad moment, too, just when she was auditioning at the Overijssel Chamber Ensemble, where there was finally the chance of a permanent position.

"So, as I'm sure you understand, Joop, we all feel terribly for her. But, listen, what's that nonsense you were going on about just now? You're dropping out of university to go and make chocolates in France?"

"It isn't nonsense, Mother."

His father slammed his book shut and joined the conversation. "What kind of a fellow is he, this Soreau?"

"Sorel, father. A real craftsman. An artist."

"Yes, sure. Everyone calls himself an artist these days. But is he a member of a professional organization? Is it an officially recognized apprenticeship he's offering you?"

"Not that I know of. Should it be, then?"

By this time Charlotte had abandoned the difficult run and returned to the beginning of the fugue.

Joop's parents looked at each other.

"Reculer pour mieux sauter?" offered Laurens.

"Let's hope so," sighed Françoise.

"No, Joop," said his father, resuming the conversation about Sorel. "It sounds much too vague to me. If you ask me, all the man is looking for is a cheap, foreign kitchen boy. Have you made any concrete financial arrangements?"

Joop swallowed. "Well, actually, I wanted to ask if you could deposit my monthly allowance to an account in France—as soon as I open it, of course."

"Wait a minute, my boy. It's not as easy as that."

Joop's cheeks became flushed. "Why not? You're always saying that children should study what they want and that parents shouldn't make an issue of it!"

"Correct, but with the emphasis on 'study.' Now if this

were a trustworthy, officially recognized training, *une école de pâtissier* or whatever they call it in France, that would be different. But to finance this crazy whim of yours . . . No, Joop. For your own sake, no."

"To be perfectly honest, I find that whole culinary business really quite distasteful," threw in Françoise. "Do you ever read the newspaper? At this moment there's a terrible famine in Chad. When you think of those poor people and then of that finicky fiddling around with food . . . I think it's simply decadent!"

The flushes on Joop's cheeks deepened, but before he could respond to his mother's objections, she raised her hand.

"Quiet for a moment, fellows."

Charlotte had reached the difficult run again. And again it went wrong. After a brief silence, Joop and his parents were jolted by a series of horrible discords, as if the harpsichord was being smashed to pieces with a sledgehammer.

Joop's parents jumped up and rushed to the music room.

The din stopped, and through the open doors, Joop could hear his sister's long primitive howls, and occasionally, his father's voice: "There's a girl, there's a girl."

Alone in the living room, Joop looked around. Books on all sides, walls full of learned books. *You know what,* he said to himself, *they can all go to hell here. I'm off.*

He left his suitcase with textbooks standing in the hallway. His parents could lug it up to the attic themselves. Less than half an hour after arriving at Swaanendal, he was walking down the beech-lined driveway toward the road with the firm resolve to never return.

Young Man with Traveling Bag

Joop was no adventurer. As a child, the second branch of the tree was as high as he would climb—and only when his tough cousin, Nico, had goaded him into it. And when camping with his parents and sisters, he would break out into a sweat at the first rumblings of an approaching thunderstorm. But his parents' reaction to his plan for an apprenticeship made him so angry—and now that he was free of the textbook-laden suitcase he felt so light-footed—that he far transcended his own fearful nature. No money for the train? Then hitchhiking it would be!

He took a bus from the village and got out at the viaduct, where he clambered up the embankment, climbed over the railing, and, without the slightest hesitation, stuck his thumb in the air. Young man with traveling bag. At that moment, he felt invincible. And he grew in his role: the countless cars and trucks that shot past him added their horsepower to his anger and determination. Small-minded assholes they were, just like his parents—except, of course, the office-machine salesman who stopped for him after half an hour and took him to Utrecht.

As it turned out, he was let out on the outskirts of the new housing development to which Rosalinde and Wouter and their two-year-old son and newborn daughter had moved. He had promised to drop in on them some time. For a moment he was tempted. All he had to do was climb over a fence, make his way across a sandy area, and find the Zonnebloemstraat, where a cup of tea and cake would await him. And Rosa would be prepared to lend him money. He could sleep there, then take the train the next day. But the prospect of stilted conversation and a baby crying all night dissuaded him.

Besides, at that same moment, a Citroën Deux Chevaux stopped with three tall boys crouched inside, who could take him as far as Tilburg. They were studying economics at the university there, and found Joop a bit of an eccentric, with his French plans.

"Can you make any dough with chocolates?" asked one of them.

They were nice enough to make a detour and dropped him off on the southward road out of Tilburg. There, at the edge of a pasture with grazing cows, Joop unexpectedly got a lump in his throat when, in his thoughts, he said farewell to Holland—to the bright sun, the harsh wind, the glaring-white cumulus clouds that drifted by, their dark shadows sweeping across the countryside. But the wave of sentimentality changed to annoyance when one of the clouds passed over him in the form of a cold downpour.

From then on, Joop made a series of wrong decisions by accepting rides from well-meaning local residents, who, with shorter and shorter rides on smaller and smaller roads, kept dropping him off at worse and worse places for hitchhiking. His heroic flight thus threatened to come to an inglorious end in farmlands in the southern province of Brabant. When no one had stopped after forty-five minutes, Joop started walking down the road in utter desperation. There was little left of the proud young man with traveling bag of a few hours earlier. If he ever reached the village on the horizon, he would take the bus there and then the train back north, where, tail between his legs, he would knock on his parents' door in the dead of night.

Still, all the minirides hadn't been in vain, for the concrete posts on either side of the road turned out to mark the border with Belgium. Joop heaved a sigh of relief. His flight was no longer a childish, runaway prank that ended on the corner of his own street. It was dead serious now. As always, whenever he passed through Belgium he was reminded of his elementary school friend Pascal Vandenbroucke. What had become of him? Full of longing and with a rumbling stomach, Joop remembered The First Supper he had eaten at Pascal's house. How stupid to have given those Tilburg students the last three raisin buns that he had bought in the village bakery at the start of the trip. Now he was dying of hunger. No, of course not like those poor people in Chad. What a mean trick of his mother to bring in the suffering of the world to bear against his dream of becoming a chocolatier. As if harpsichord music would make the lives of those people any better!

It was turning dark. Because the village was still in the distance, and he didn't dare knock on the door of any of the farmhouses, he had no choice but to spend the night beside the road. He put on all the warm clothing he had and wrapped himself in a piece of plastic sheeting that he found in the ditch next to the road. He spent the whole night shivering from the cold and in a state of semislumber. Whenever he did manage to doze off, the headlights of a passing car would awaken him. At the first glimmer of dawn, he crawled out of the ditch chilled to the bone. He managed to reanimate his numb limbs with stretching exercises—enough to be able to walk—but his neck was painfully stiff.

It would remain a weak spot for the rest of his life. If he slept in a draft or worked too hard on a chocolate, the strained neck muscle would suddenly seize up. But the pain always became bearable again when he recalled its noble origins. It was a pilgrim's injury, incurred on the way to the promised land.

Just before sunrise, he got a ride from a friendly, taciturn truck driver. In no time, they reached the village that the evening before had seemed glued to the horizon. They parked in front of a café, where the driver treated him to a sour coffee and a snotty fried egg with limp bacon. A few miles later, they turned onto the big highway that Joop had lost sight of the day before. After the horrible night in the ditch, he again felt invincible, high up in the cabin of the truck, above all the decent little men and women in their dinky little cars. And he could ride with this driver until deep into France.

When he climbed out of the truck a few miles south of Reims, he found himself on a road as straight as an arrow that ran endlessly through gently rolling farmland. It was still hundreds of miles to Avallon, and there was almost no traffic here. After a gleaming black Citroën DS rushed past, and two enormous army trucks made the earth tremble under his feet, it took another fifteen minutes before the next car appeared on the horizon. Already from afar he could hear from the familiar purring of the engine that it was a Deux Chevaux, the proud possession of many a student and bohemian in Holland, the kind of people who tended to pick up hitchhikers. Joop already started to beam, but its occupants turned out to be a surly old farmer and his wife who, left indicator flashing, let their little car screech past him with the widest possible berth.

After standing in the icy wind for an hour and a half, he had no choice but to start walking down the road. France, too, could be deathly monotonous, and here there weren't even church steeples on which to focus his hope or despair. With his ear pressed against his increasingly hunched up shoulder, he stumbled ahead. During his night in the ditch, a piece of gravel had become lodged in his shoe, but he hadn't bothered to take it out, so that by this time it had translated itself into a blister. Now, he no longer dared to take off his shoe for fear of what he might find. He tried to use his stiff neck to forget the blister and vice versa—until, with every step, they were linked by a nasty stab of pain.

Doubts arose in the emptiness and the cold. Had the invitation from Sorel really been an invitation, or had they just been words? Was that why Joop hadn't called him to say he was coming, because he was afraid the bubble might burst? To quote his father, what kind of a fellow was he, this Soreau?

The sun was ever so low again, and his doubts turned into despair. That was his destiny in life—to trudge along in this godforsaken agrarian wasteland. Forever alone. He kept thinking about the picnic with Peter and Corinne in the sun-baked hollow in the dunes, and about the fate that had determined that Peter's hands could slip so brazenly down Corinne's blouse, while he walked here, suffering, in the freezing cold—forever alone.

When at long last another car approached, he didn't even take the trouble to face it, his raised thumb already changing into a dismissive wave before the car passed by. It took a while before he realized that the car had stopped a hundred yards down the road. He hobbled as fast as his blister would allow him toward his redeeming angel, who was backing up to meet him with the door already open. The driver was a boy his own age who was the spitting image of the movie star Alain Delon—until he smiled and revealed his bad teeth. What little he said was incomprehensible and drowned out by the roar of the engine. But from the duffel bag on the backseat, it was clear that he was a soldier on weekend leave. Joop was constantly offered cigarettes, which he gratefully accepted for want of food and things to talk about. Silent and smoking, the two boys tore through the desolate landscape, angry young men ready to take on the world. Effortlessly, they passed slower traffic, if need be just below the top of a hill where there was no visibility at all of any oncoming traffic. The shot of adrenaline Joop got during these death-defying maneuvers made him forget all his pain and fatigue.

The wild ride ended at a crossroads in the middle of a little village. The soldier had to turn left here to drive to the even smaller village where his mother lived.

When Joop saw a hotel on the other side of the street, he was tempted to call it a day. But the soldier's bravura had infected him and, encouraged by the signpost on which Avallon was mentioned for the first time, he decided to continue hitchhiking. Outside the village, though, the beet fields stretched out endlessly again, and when two crows flew up off the road where they had been pecking at what turned out to be a dead hare, he decided to return to the village.

Joop was the only guest in the hotel. When he asked the owner if he could get something to eat, the response was a grumpy "Non." Not even a sandwich? *Non.* Perhaps somewhere else in the village then? *Non.* So he just went to bed — after first mustering all his courage to put his foot in the bidet and pop his blister. Though he hadn't slept a wink the night before, he lay wide awake again. His neck hurt, a spring in the mattress jabbed into his back, and a dog barked incessantly. What had he got himself into? He kept seeing the dead hare, haplessly run over in blind flight.

So deeply had he sunk into his loneliness that the next morning, when the hotelier put a basket with pieces of baguette and a pot of coffee on the table in front of him, he almost burst into tears. He was a disagreeable man, the bread was stale, and the coffee had stewed, but none of that mattered. What mattered was that a fellow human being had taken the trouble to prepare this bread and this coffee especially and only for him, Joop Daalder.

The wind had died down, and now, with the warm morning sun shining in his face and his stomach filled with bread and coffee, the world looked like a much friendlier place. Even the dead hare lay there peacefully. As he walked past it, an odor greeted him that reminded him of the time Rosalinde had taken him to a French market. What a waste it was, this tasty creature lying here in vain rather than dangling from a hook awaiting a casserole.

Fortune smiled on him that day. The very first car that drove past stopped for him, and what's more, was on its way to Avallon. The driver was a history teacher and an enthusiastic member of the Communist party. For sixty long miles, he went on about the current political situation in France. But Joop didn't mind, as long as the man kept his hands on the steering wheel.

And then it was over. As suddenly as the trip had begun, and as interminably long as it had seemed to take, now it was suddenly over. He stepped out of the car and found himself bathed in the warm spring sun in the heart of Avallon. There he stood, Joop Daalder, young hero, pilgrim of good taste. And there, on the other side of the square, was his destination, the chocolate shop of Jérôme Sorel. Beaming, his face taut from the sun, wind, and grime, Joop completed the final stretch of his noble journey.

He pushed against the door, which opened to the cheery tinkle of a bell. He closed his eyes and sniffed up the wonderful scent of cacao.

"Oh lá lá!" cried Frédérique. "You look like a gypsy!"

She knocked three times on the kitchen door, which apparently was a warning signal because a moment later, the door flew open.

Where Joop had expected a warm welcome, he now found

himself being thrown out of the shop by a furiously gesticu-
lating Sorel.

"But it's me," he tried. "Joop Daalder, the Dutch student
from not long ago!"

"I know damn well who you are," said Sorel, following him
outside. "How dare you come into my shop like that! You're
unshaven! You're dirty! You stink!"

"I couldn't afford the train," peeped Joop. "I hitchhiked all
the way."

"Hitchhiked? What kind of masochistic behavior is that?
You should have phoned me! I would gladly have paid for
your train ticket!"

Slowly it dawned on him that Sorel's fit of anger was anything but rejection.

"Stupid idiot," said the chocolatier. "Wait here for a moment."

He went into the shop to instruct Frédérique, then came
outside again.

"Come with me."

He was about to put an arm around Joop but then thought
better of it.

They walked—that is to say, Sorel walked and Joop stumbled—through the arch underneath the clock tower, and followed the road that ran along the outside of the city wall
down to the lower part of town, which was built, from the
riverbank up, against the slope

When Sorel opened the front door of his house, Joop was
attacked in the hallway by a dull-white lap dog.

A woman came rushing out from another room. She had a
wrinkled, heavily made-up face and her hair was done up in a
stern bun.

"No, Ronnie-Boy Johnjohn, down!" she shrieked, just
managing to pull the growling dog away by the collar. "What's
all this about?" she asked her husband meanwhile.

"Isabelle, this is Joop, the Dutchman I was telling you about."

"Yes? And?"

"My, aren't we friendly today! You had better run a bath for the poor fellow and prepare the guest room."

"The guest room? You can't be serious."

Shortly afterward, Joop was undressing in the Sorels' bathroom. Everywhere he looked, there were little rugs and pieces of perfumed soap. When he took off his socks, such a penetrating stench of ammonia was released that he quickly stuffed them as far as he could into his shoes and covered them with his clothes. As the water flowed out of the tap in a sluggish braid, he climbed over the edge of the tub and lowered his exhausted body into the steaming water. When he turned off the tap, he heard a violent exchange of words downstairs, accompanied by the shrill barking of Ronnie-Boy Johnjohn.

It wouldn't be about him, would it?

And what to do now, with no money and no house?

No, don't think about that yet. He sank deeper into the warm water. For the first time, he dared to relax his right shoulder and turn his neck a bit, even though he heard a frightening creak from inside his body. Closing his eyes, he saw beet fields and trucks hurtling past. And the dead hare and the laughing soldier, and all the other images of the last few days. And he saw himself standing in the living room of his parental house, where his journey had begun. It seemed like a very long time ago now. He sank deeper into the tub, until only his knees and nose protruded out of the water. But then he smelled something that made him sit up straight. From under the bathroom door came more than just a streak of sunlight. Through the perfume of the soap and the stench of the socks, he smelled garlic being fried in olive oil, and rosemary and thyme and meat—roast lamb. It all smelled so delicious, and the bath was so wonderfully relaxing, that he

was overwhelmed. For the first time since his earliest childhood, he felt tears streaming down his cheeks.

Later, he liked to say that he wasn't born in Holland, and
that he wasn't born as a baby but at the age of twenty, in the
bathtub of Monsieur and Madame Sorel.

Part 3

In Paradise

Hyperharmony

What, ultimately, did his childhood in Holland signify? Not much more than the curtain in the Sorels' guest room, which he pushed aside that first morning with one firm tug. It was only here that his life really began, he thought, as he looked out over the vegetable gardens and blossoming fruit trees down in the valley toward the wooded hills beyond.

At six-thirty, he was already sitting at the breakfast table with monsieur and madame. As in the hotel when he was hitchhiking, the coffee tasted as if it had stewed for hours, a striking flaw in French cuisine. And to his horror, the Sorels filled their cups right to the brim with lukewarm milk. But everything was set right again by the fresh baguette that madame had picked up at the bakery during her early-morning stroll with Ronnie-Boy Johnjohn. Joop could have eaten endless amounts of it, with butter and a generous dollop of apricot jam.

"What delicious jam!" he cried. "Did you make it yourself?"

Madame Sorel sneered.

Joop looked at her questioningly, but no explanation followed.

Monsieur Sorel threw down his piece of baguette and stood up.

"Come on, Joop. Let's go."

The apricot jam was a sore point, he explained, as they walked up the road along the city walls. Not that Joop should be bothered by it, because for a frustrated woman like his wife the whole universe was made up of sore points. The jam was made by her younger sister, Marie-Claire. Who *did* have a good life. Who *was* married to a rich, charming, athletic man. And *did* have children. And lived on the Côte d'Azur, where the weather was always gorgeous. And had an apricot tree in her garden. Her enormous garden. With a view of the Mediterranean.

"Et cetera, et cetera," he said, making a churning motion with his arm.

It was a steep climb, and where the road made a hairpin turn, they stopped for a moment for Sorel to catch his breath.

"But it's beautiful here, too, isn't it?" said Joop, gesturing to the hills of the Morvan.

"Oh, people like Isabelle will never be satisfied, whereas I would feel at home anywhere as long as I could make chocolates. Even in the middle of the desert."

They continued their walk past the church and under the clock tower, into town. They had to stop a few times when Sorel had a coughing fit. By the time they reached the chocolate shop, he was wheezing and his face had turned purple. They walked straight through to the kitchen, where Sorel went to the counter and splashed his face with cold water. With one last rattle, he deposited a gob of mucus into the sink. After he dabbed his face with a towel, the day could begin.

Molds and mills were pulled out of cupboards, an array of little knives and shredders laid out on the counter, a thick slab of chocolate taken out of its wrapper and placed in a bain-marie. It was a small kitchen, and no matter how inconspicuously Joop tried to position himself, he kept getting in the way.

Sorel was a chocolatier of the old school, a real craftsman, who was proud of his handiwork and took the time for everything. He detested modern appliances, which were only meant to let you do ten times as much in half the time. That more-more-more and faster-faster-faster was a mentality that had blown over from America, and in his view represented a serious threat to French cuisine.

Slow but precise and elegant. That was Jérôme Sorel's style of working. Like the way he cut open a bag of almonds that first morning, shook a little pile of them out onto a board, arranged them so that all the pointed ends lay in the same direction, and then chopped them into equal-sized pieces—Joop could have watched him for hours.

But to his horror, he was now handed the knife.

"Will you finish it? I have to keep an eye on that little pan over there."

In his attic in Amsterdam, Joop had sometimes imagined himself a master chef, doing everything with great flair, even when he was adding a pinch of salt to a dish. But now that it was for real, he tensed up. When he tried to imitate Sorel's chopping technique, the pieces of almond flew in all directions. It was mostly flakes and grit that stayed on the board, not shapes that could easily be roasted "golden-brown on all sides," as the next instruction put it.

Sorel gave him a gentle tap on the shoulder in passing. "You'll be just fine, you know."

At about eight-thirty, the front-door bell tinkled. It was Frédérique, who had come to open up the shop. She popped her head around the corner and greeted her boss with a girlish *"Bonjour, Monsieur Sorel!"* only acknowledging Joop's presence with a minimal nod. Sorel gave her the first trays of chocolate to take out front. After that, she was to stay in the shop. He and his apprentice were to be disturbed as little as possible.

The filling he was working on was ready only by the end of

the morning. He gestured to Joop to come closer, stirred the pan one last time, and held up the spoon so his pupil could suck off the frothy layer of chocolate sauce.

Though he kept his eyes shut to concentrate fully on the taste in his mouth, Joop could tell he was being watched — while judging the sauce, he too was being judged. What was expected of him? Was he supposed to find this delicious or just the opposite, to make a critical remark?

"Just right," he finally gambled.

"I totally agree with you. Especially with your lack of enthusiasm."

Sorel beamed when he saw the perplexed look on Joop's face.

"Don't get me wrong. 'Just right' isn't bad at all. Many colleagues don't even reach that level. But for the true chocolatier, 'just right' isn't good enough. This is where the real work begins, my dear boy. From this moment on, we enter the forbidden kingdom of the gods. From here on, we're going to be doing something that really isn't possible."

Sorel let one drop at a time of rich cream dribble from a little jug into the pan, which Joop then had to "caress" into the sauce with a spatula. The chocolate wanted nothing better than to reject the cream but was forced to absorb an unnatural amount of it, thanks to the smooth stirring technique and the gradual increasing of the temperature. What was happening here was quite like what happened with geese, who were force-fed through a funnel in their throats in order to turn their earthly livers into heavenly foie gras.

"Scrape the chocolate from the sides of the pan as well," said Sorel. "Otherwise it will thicken. And from the bottom too. No, no, Joop, you have to stir more smoothly. Loosen up those shoulders. No, with more spirit. Not so feeble. And stop that panting."

Sorel put the jug of cream down on the counter, and came

and stood behind him, then grabbed his shoulders and started to massage him. It may have been well intended, but instead of relaxing, Joop stiffened—especially when Sorel pinched him in the spot that had been painful since the night he spent beside the road in Belgium.

"Damn it, boy! You're going to ruin it like this." Sorel grabbed the spatula from his hands. "Look. This is the way to do it."

Joop felt deeply hurt by the brusque way he was literally pushed aside. Head flushed and legs trembling, he watched as Sorel stirred the sauce vigorously, much more vigorously than he ever would have dared. Damn it, if that was how it was to be done, he could do it too! But deep down, he knew he couldn't—because the fury with which Sorel stirred was accompanied by an incredible suppleness.

"See that beautiful sheen?" he said. "Like satin! To achieve that, you have to go to the limit. But now you have to watch out. One drop too many of cream, one wrong stir, and everything will be ruined. The chocolate will start to sweat, turn gritty, and taste stale. For didactic purposes it might be useful to let that disaster happen intentionally, but if you taste this, you'll understand right away what a crime that would be."

Still moping, Joop took a lick. He closed his eyes and sighed deeply.

"You see?" said Sorel. "With something this divine, you won't say 'Just right.' Such a calm response is no longer possible. You will either be left speechless, or burst out laughing, or start swearing—because you have just tasted how incredibly delicate the balance is. It is not for nothing that we use the word 'delicatessen.' And the more delicate the balance, the more intense the ecstasy. Not only to create such an impossibly precarious moment of balance, such a moment of hyperharmony, but to hold it captive in a chocolate, even if only briefly—that, my dear boy, is the most beautiful thing you can achieve in our craft."

Greatly moved by his own sermon, Sorel took a towel and wiped the sweat from his forehead, and perhaps even a few tears from the corners of his eyes, although Joop couldn't vouch for that.

"And what happens now?" he asked.

"What did you say? Oh, we leave everything to cool down. This afternoon we'll take dollops of this and cloak them in a tasty but unobtrusive layer of dark chocolate. But it's already past noon. Time for lunch!"

While Frédérique served one last customer, Joop and Sorel left the shop.

What a morning. And what a contrast to his life in Holland. There he would have been cycling home under a gray sky around this time, after an utterly boring lecture on the influence of blah-blah on blah-blah-blah. Here in France, the sun shone, and on his very first day in the chocolate shop, he had already experienced a moment of hyperharmony.

Sorel beamed too. "God, my boy. Are we ever going to have fun together!"

Like the day before, the door had barely opened when Ronnie-Boy Johnjohn charged toward Joop, yapping loudly. This time it took a while before Madame Sorel came after him, almost as if she was granting him a few bites out of Joop's ankles. She grabbed him at the very last moment, though, and pulled him into the kitchen behind her.

Joop followed his master into the dining room. After working all morning in the sweet fumes of chocolate, he felt a bit queasy, so he stilled his strongest hunger pangs with bread from the basket on the table. Sorel poured them both a glass of wine and they drank to a fruitful collaboration.

At that moment, Madame Sorel entered with a tureen of vegetable soup.

"Our little Dutchman is a fast learner," said Monsieur Sorel, tucking a corner of his serviette into his collar.

"Oh, I don't know about that," said Joop with a modest smile.

"He certainly is a fast eater," said Madame Sorel coldly. She removed the empty basket from the table and went to the kitchen to cut more bread.

During the meal, the conversation about hyperharmony continued.

"The more delicate the balance, the more intense the ecstasy" also applied to the ripeness of fruit.

"Take an apple," said Sorel. "If it's ripe, you can easily leave it in the fruit dish for another week. If it's mealy, you can always go to the green grocer and buy a new one. Flavor guaranteed! Just right. Nothing wrong with it at all. As solid and reliable as a German car or a good marriage."

"Oh yes?" said his wife.

"But if a peach is ripe, my dear boy, and I mean truly ripe—that is to say juicy, sweet, and smooth-textured—you have to grab the moment immediately. Because that moment of perfect ripeness is also the very moment the process of decay sets in. In that fleeting moment, ecstasy and melancholy coincide."

Joop was about to mention the apricot he had tasted in Provence once with his family, but then he saw Madame Sorel and, just in time, remembered the earlier incident with apricot jam.

"Yes, in that fleeting moment, ecstasy and melancholy coincide. That is how the sense of taste, more than any of the other senses, lets you experience the impermanence of joy. What's more, you contribute to it. In that respect our sense of taste is unique. You can only appreciate such a peach by destroying it at the same time. After all, you are eating it. By tasting paradisiacal joy, you are also tainting it. With every bite you take, a veritable drama occurs. It's the Fall of Man over and over again."

"Jérôme!" cried Isabelle.

"What's the matter, dear? You think I'm exaggerating again?"

She pointed to his wineglass, which he had absentmindedly filled to the brim for the umpteenth time.

"Damn it, woman, it's Joop's first day! We have something to celebrate!"

"Now if it had been his last day . . ." she muttered.

"What did you say? He understands everything, you know."

"You think so?"

They both looked at Joop, who, mouth still bulging, was already lifting the lid of a dish to serve himself a second portion.

To provoke his wife, Sorel increased the tempo of his wine consumption—and thus that of their guest. And with the coffee, which unlike the brew at breakfast now had a wonderfully rich flavor, he let Joop sample a local liqueur.

Sorel stretched and got up from the table to go and lie down for half an hour.

"Shall I help you with the dishes in the meantime?" Joop asked Madame Sorel.

"Are you crazy?" cried Sorel from the doorway. "You need to rest too. We have a long afternoon ahead of us."

Joop grinned contritely at his hostess, but she was already on her way to the kitchen with the first dirty dishes. There was nothing else for him to do but withdraw to his room.

It had become swelteringly hot and muggy there. He threw open the windows and closed the two creaking shutters. Then he flopped onto his bed, which was as gratifyingly soft as the fluffy interior of a baguette. What a country! What a life!

But Joop had to get used to the enormous quantity of food and alcohol that he put away each day at noon. He found it difficult to get up after the siesta and start working again.

With a bloated belly and a bad headache developing, this time it was he more than his short-winded master who had trouble climbing the hill. Since leaving Holland, he had been troubled by constipation. The white baguette he had been gorging on at every meal worked as a cork, and it was coming under increasing pressure. That whole afternoon nasty cramps pierced his abdomen and made him feel faint.

Sorel too seemed to be in bad shape. While working, he grumbled about a supplier who had cheated him for the umpteenth time, about a customer who wanted to talk to him in person about the smallest trivialities, and about Frédérique, because she hadn't managed to stave off that customer. As long as his master complained about other people, Joop was safe, but inevitably he too would come under attack.

"What kind of shoddy work is that? Throw that junk out! What did I get myself into? What did I get myself into?"

The seething gastric juices and painful fermentations in Joop's bowels only subsided late in the afternoon. Sorel's mood improved too. Perhaps his bad humor was also a matter of indigestion.

A kind of mildness came over his master now. He even became a bit sentimental, saying what an extraordinary boy Joop was, how beautifully concentrated he was when he worked on a chocolate, and that he wished he were a painter so he could capture that moment.

Joop had years of experience in dealing with disdain. He would make himself small and retreat into his own little world. But he had no way at all of dealing with compliments. Now, with Sorel observing him so affectionately and saying such nice things about him, he blushed and looked quickly in the other direction.

Their workday ended at about seven o'clock. While Frédérique came into the kitchen with a mop and soapy bucket, Sorel took Joop to the café, where they drank a pastis with his friends Hubert, the butcher, and Maurice, from the post office.

Hubert was a good-humored fatso who was no threat at all to Joop, but Maurice, a well-groomed dandy who would have been a more normal sight in England, took pleasure in embarrassing him.

"You know what Voltaire said about Holland?" he asked.

Joop shook his head.

"*Canaux, canards, canaille.*"

Of the three friends, it was Maurice who snickered most at the joke, but when he noticed Joop sheepishly laughing along with them, he stopped.

"So you think it's funny? I bet you don't even know what I said."

"Hey, Momo!" protested Hubert. "Leave the boy alone."

When they returned home from the café, madame had prepared another divine meal.

Again wine was the subject of heated discussion between husband and wife. When Jérôme persevered and opened a second bottle, Isabelle took revenge by not looking at him again for the rest of the meal. Again the tension didn't bother Joop, so savory was the food.

"Madame," he said, with an expression of pure bliss on his face. "This is too delicious."

"Oh yes? Don't eat it then, if it's too much for you."

Canaux, canards, canaille: canals, ducks, and—that evening in his room Joop looked up *canaille* in his dictionary—scum.

After a week, the situation at the Sorels' had become unbearable. That her husband wanted to drink himself to death in honor of the lodger was his business, but that Ronnie-Boy Johnjohn hadn't eaten all his food for a few days now because of the tension in the house was unacceptable to Isabelle. The Dutchman would have to leave.

Fortunately, Joop could move into the apartment above the butcher's, which had been unoccupied since Hubert's son had left for Cambodia a few months earlier with the Foreign Legion.

The bare floorboards with bed, table, and chairs reminded Joop of van Gogh's room in Arles, a painting they had discussed in class recently. Except that here, there were no paintings on the walls, only numerous medals, and photographs taken during earlier campaigns of the Foreign Legion. One of them showed a group of soldiers, including presumably Hubert's son, posing proudly next to a dead elephant. Amid this show of arms, there was also a photograph of Brigitte Bardot in her bikini on the beach at St. Tropez.

Joop didn't have to pay rent. Sorel had already arranged everything with Hubert.

"You're here because I invited you, right? But remember, not a word about this to my wife."

Joop still ate the midday meal with the Sorels. Jérôme had managed to convince Isabelle that a master had a duty to supply his apprentice with food during the working day. But now, he spent the evenings alone in his van Gogh apartment. Although he didn't have to pay rent, he still had to be careful with the little amount of money he had brought with him from Holland. His evening meal consisted of a baguette and cheap Camembert or a piece of *pâté de campagne,* and a glass of simple table wine from a bottle that lasted him all week. Sometimes he ate a tomato or a piece of fruit as well. Once a week, he treated himself to meat or fish.

Despite the frugality of his life, he experienced some of his most intense moments of joy in that room. He didn't have to be on good behavior for anyone, he could do just as he pleased. With tears streaming down his face, he would pull the skin off a ripe peach, one of those hyperharmonious peaches that Sorel had talked about. And if he stopped crying right away, it wasn't from shame, but because the lump in his throat had made swallowing the morsels of peach more difficult and thus hampered the intensity of the ecstasy.

He wallowed in the romantic notion of a premature death. He would succumb as a van Gogh of taste, felled by the intensity of his own experiences. His life as a whole had become one fragile moment of hyperharmony. This couldn't last forever; it had to be followed by a premature, unnatural death. He imagined Peter addressing those gathered around his grave. "This young man lived!" his friend would say, voice breaking. "*Lived!*"

At other moments he imagined a brighter future. He had been unfortunate to have grown up in the wrong country among the wrong people. Only now, here in France, as a connoisseur among connoisseurs, had he found his place. Here, intense pleasure was a perfectly normal part of everyday life. He would live happily ever after! Why not?

Thus far he had gone through life as a timid, withdrawn soul so as to bear the derision of his family, so as not to be noticed, so as not to offend anyone. He was worthless—that had been drummed into him for years on end. He was unmusical and stupid and, what's more, unathletic. And he didn't like olives, and chocolates were boring . . .

Canaux, canards, canaille. Just let them cackle, all those Dutch ducks, all that Dutch scum, for he was no longer one of them. He, the ugly duckling of yesteryear, was now a swan.

The Natural Arrogance
of Swans

The chocolatier Jérôme Sorel was utterly convinced of his own superiority. For Joop, who had just realized he was no longer a duck but a swan, the feeling of superiority was anything but self-evident. He had yet to master that air, that natural arrogance. He bobbed along, so to speak, in the wake of his big hero, trying to imitate him in everything.

Most of the chocolates could be kept for three or, at most, four days, some not even for one, so that almost every day some had to be thrown out. For Joop it was an intensely tragic moment when those beautiful works of art, untasted and thus unloved, met their end. But not even then did his master lose his dignity. It was almost elegant the way he let them slide off the tray into the garbage bin, giving some a gentle nudge with his knife to help them along.

"I can hardly eat them all myself," he said when Joop asked about it, "or give them away to passersby after the shop closes. Isabelle may think I'm hopeless in business matters, but I'm not that stupid. Of course there are colleagues who sell their leftovers for half price, but I think that's absolutely pathetic. So, whoosh!"

Once again he gave a reluctant chocolate a push.

"This isn't as dramatic as it seems, you know," he said,

laughing at Joop's look of horror. "When I was your age, it used to really upset me. I experienced every unsold chocolate as a defeat. But one day I realized I could get even more upset about the chocolates I did sell. When I saw another one of those wretches standing in my shop, I was repulsed by the idea that one of my noble chocolates would serve as his fuel, supplying him with just the amount of energy needed to have some dull-witted thought or to give his hairy arse a good scratch. Seen in that light, the garbage bin didn't seem so bad after all.

"In other words, it's better to say good-bye to a chocolate the moment you have finished making it. What happens after that doesn't matter anymore. Remember that, my boy, because it's crucial for your peace of mind as a chocolatier."

Joop frowned. "But what about all the enthusiastic customers then? Like the Parisian the other day, who drove more than a hundred kilometers out of his way just to buy your chocolates? That must give you some satisfaction?"

"Oh, Joop, compliments are easily given. Feed a pig a chocolate and it too, will grunt contentedly. No, my dear boy, all the real stuff happens here in the kitchen. The moment you go out the door, even as you enter the shop, the big void begins, where nonsense reigns supreme."

The customer was a necessary evil, a "wallet with a hunk of flesh attached to it," with whom Sorel wanted as few dealings as possible. That was what Frédérique was for. By the way, that he had put such a beauty in his shop was not to please the customers, as current theories on sales techniques would lead you to believe. Her role was to intimidate them.

"She only has to tilt that little chin of hers, straighten her shoulders, shake those beautiful little breasts ever so slightly and the potential troublemaker is lost. The women feel ugly and the men, inadequate."

Still, there were always customers who were impervious to

her beauty, who thought themselves so important that they needed to speak to the boss personally, usually about something incredibly trivial. That's when all hell broke loose in the chocolate shop.

One afternoon Frédérique knocked on the kitchen door three times. Red alert.

"Come with me, Joop," said Sorel, rolling up his sleeves.

A mother and her little daughter were standing in the shop waiting for them. As if having stepped out of a Renoir painting, they both wore straw hats decorated with a ribbon, long dresses, and gloves. Only the parasols were missing.

Angélique would be celebrating her birthday soon with a few of her girlfriends. If monsieur would kindly assemble a box of chocolates suitable for eight-year-old girls. That is, not too bitter and preferably without liqueur.

"And Frédérique's advice was not quite to your liking, madame?"

"Oh, monsieur, I in no way wish to doubt the expertise of your assistant. I only want the very best for my daughter and would therefore be most grateful for your personal opinion."

"But, of course, madame. One moment."

He came out from behind the counter and walked toward one of the tables, where two old ladies were sitting drinking coffee.

"May I?" he asked them.

He came back with a dish of sugar cubes, which he emptied out onto the scales.

The woman stepped back in horror. "What's the meaning of this?"

"Not too bitter and without liqueur. Just the thing for eight-year-olds, madame. Would you like to try one, dearie?"

"Don't touch, Angélique! Don't touch!" And she took her daughter by the hand and pulled her out of the shop.

"Would you put the cubes back in the dish, Frédérique? Come on, Joop, we've wasted enough time already."

In the kitchen Sorel sat down on a stool. Still shaking from excitement, he grabbed a towel and dabbed the sweat off his forehead.

"I hate children," he said. "That racket, that uncontrolled energy, but especially those disgusting eating habits. They're always seen as being so fragile and so vulnerable. Rubbish! If you watch the way they stuff themselves and with what, they're just blind, greedy caterpillars. It's we adults who are the fragile, discriminating butterflies. A lot of rich people come here thinking their rich little caterpillars deserve expensive little sweets. But this is no damn sweet shop! To appreciate a chocolate, taste buds have to be as developed as for the ripest, smelliest cheese. Till the age of thirteen, fourteen, you might as well feed the little brats sugar cubes."

Joop looked at his master full of admiration: unwilling to make concessions, convinced of his superiority.

Bit by bit, his own charisma was growing too. He practiced on Frédérique. Once, when he had walked into the chocolate shop as a shy student of art history, she had been the last obstacle on his route into the world of Monsieur Sorel. Now, she was the first obstacle on his route back to the outside world, in his new capacity as self-assured apprentice chocolatier. For an inexperienced boy of twenty, it was no mean feat to keep a poker face while walking past that stuck-up little chin and those dangerous female shapes. But he too had a chin he could stick in the air, and he had every reason to do so. He had just left Monsieur Sorel's holy kitchen, which she was only allowed to enter to clean.

Now, as he walked down the street, the hunch in his posture had disappeared. Correspondingly, he was treated with more respect. The fishmonger, who had fobbed off an old, sticky piece of cod on him two weeks ago, now looked for the best possible trout for him—"caught fresh this afternoon, below the waterfall."

That evening, there was no exquisite sauce to drape over the fish, the way he had eaten it not long ago at Madame Sorel's. But simplicity also had its charm. *Hup*, into the frying pan; *hup*, flip it over, and done. There was still a drop of white wine in the bottle—a bit sour, but nice and cold. With a baguette and simple tomato salad, he sat down to eat at his table.

After his first taste of fish, tears sprang to his eyes. Another one of those delicate moments of intense joy. They just kept coming. What a country! What a life!

"And now for love," he said aloud.

He had no idea where that remark came from, but the silence that followed it was unfathomably deep.

Oh yes, love. Now that he was experiencing so many beautiful moments, his need to share them with someone was growing. Yes, of course he shared some of them with Sorel, but that was different.

For want of better, he now added trout to the picnic basket in his imaginary *déjeuner sur l'herbe* (he would worry about how to serve the fish warm later). The painting still dominated his romantic fantasies. While the picnic basket became increasingly filled with well-defined delicacies, the woman in his vision remained vague aside from the fact that she was naked. Since his short-lived infatuation with Corinne, no other candidates had presented themselves.

Suddenly he felt terribly sorry for himself, so totally alone in a strange country, here in his van Gogh room, stared at from the wall by Brigitte Bardot and from his plate by a dead trout. He became increasingly somber as he prodded the last bits of fish off the bones with his fork. That is to say, the last bits from the first side. That was the good thing about a trout like this:

turn it over, and it was as if you had conjured it back and the party could start all over again.

Joop took grateful advantage of this second opportunity. What do you mean, lonely? The true connoisseur didn't mind eating alone. He had learned that recently from Monsieur Sorel.

A Slightly Too Long Weekend

There was a long weekend ahead. After Isabelle Sorel had announced she was going to visit her mother in Angoulême, her husband was in excellent spirits.

"And she's taking her doggy, too, her doggy, too," he sang as he worked. "Oh Joop, it has been so long since I've had the place to myself. I've invited Hubert and Maurice for dinner on Sunday. We'll cook up a feast and shamelessly stuff ourselves, drink and shoot the breeze till all hours. Why don't you come too? Maurice has promised to make one of his exquisite little soups, Hubert is bringing a suckling pig from his shop, and I'm doing my bit, too. I guarantee it, my boy, it's going to be a real bacchanal!"

Joop eagerly accepted the invitation.

". . . doggy, too, she's taking her doggy, too."

That Saturday afternoon, Sorel stopped work earlier than usual to do the last shopping for the Sunday banquet. As soon as Joop was finished with the batch of chocolates he was working on, he could go home too.

Joop beamed, not because of being let off early but because of the confidence his master showed by leaving him alone in his kitchen. And then there was tomorrow's feast to look forward to. His mouth was already watering.

When he came out of the kitchen to go home, he sailed past

Frédérique with a self-satisfied smile. Like a nobleman tossing a coin to a leper, he wished her a pleasant weekend in passing.

"I'd be careful if I were you," she said.

Joop turned around. "Be careful? Why?"

"The strangest things happen sometimes at those parties at monsieur's house," she said with a wicked little laugh.

"What do you mean by that?"

"Oh, it doesn't matter. 'Naïve' is Monsieur's favorite flavor, and I don't want to spoil it for him. Have a good weekend yourself, my little Dutchman."

Heart pounding, Joop walked down the street to his apartment. How "almost" were those almost amorous glances of his master when he worked in the kitchen, how fatherly his affection, how innocent the many endearing forms of address such as "my dear boy" or "my little Dutchman"? Could it be that . . . was Sorel . . . Oh God, no!

Was that why Madame Sorel was so unfriendly to him? Was that why she was frustrated? Was that the reason they had never had children? And those two friends of his, fat Hubert with his greedy eyes and shiny red lips and skinny Maurice with his silk chokers, cigarette holder, and exquisite little soups, might they also . . .

Oh, nonsense. Frédérique just wanted to frighten him. She was jealous of the intimate bond he had developed with her boss in such a short time. It had nothing, nothing at all to do with that other business. Tomorrow was just an innocent wine-and-dine feast, by chance with three older men.

But he kept pacing back and forth in his apartment, until it finally drove him mad and he went to the café next to the butcher's to phone Sorel and cancel. He had just met a few students in the café, he concocted on the spot, to which the commotion in the background added credibility. They had invited him to spend the weekend with them in a summer house on Lac des Settons in the center of the Morvan.

"Oh?" said Sorel. "Too bad you can't come. Well, what fun would it be with a group of old men anyway? Enjoy yourself, then."

So nothing was wrong, thought Joop, after he hung up. That nasty Frédérique with her insinuations. Never in his life had he eaten suckling pig. But still—and now he blushed deeply— there was that one little incident he preferred not to think about, when he hadn't been stirring the chocolate sauce smoothly enough and Sorel had come up behind him and massaged his shoulders. Was it an illusion after the fact or had he really felt something then, a hard bump pushing against his backside?

That night he couldn't sleep. How sincere had Sorel been when they first met and he had spotted a connoisseur in him? How genuine were his motives? He kept thinking of Charlotte's lover, Manfred, that ugly old man who talked naïve conservatory students into his bed by crediting them with exceptional musical talents. Were all old men phonies who were only out for one thing?

Ulterior motive or not, Sorel had too much power over him, that much was clear to him. Outside the kitchen of the chocolate shop he led an isolated existence, apart from the apéritif with Hubert and Maurice and the midday meal at the Sorels'—but Sorel was always present. The excuse he had invented in the café about those students hadn't appeared out of the blue, but had come from a genuine need for the company of people his own age. To meet young people—how in God's name did you do that? He had barely even managed it in Holland.

The next morning, an idea occurred to him when he bought a package of coffee in the little supermarket and noticed a basket with swimming trunks near the checkout. He chose a pair of trunks, went home for a towel, and followed the signs to the municipal outdoor swimming pool, traditionally a meeting place for young people. In the changing room, it turned out the swimming trunks were a few sizes too small, so that his bottom bulged out every time he took a few steps. After spreading out his dingy little towel on a stubbly patch of grass littered with cigarette butts, he looked around furtively, scared to death one of the three men might discover him here, when, by his own account, he was supposed to be in the Morvan with his student friends. Then he tried to read the newspaper. But his attention was caught by two tough guys at the edge of the swimming pool who kept throwing three screaming girls into the water.

"*Patrick, arrête!*"

"*Lucien, non!*"

The girls couldn't get enough of it, and Joop couldn't get enough of them—the way they climbed up out of the swimming pool time and again, slender and graceful in their tight black bathing suits, and with that gorgeous southerly tint to their skin. But nor could he keep his eyes off the muscular bodies of Lucien and Patrick, who stood waiting for the girls. Children of the gods, they were, all five of them. Frowning, Joop stared at his own drooping shoulders and pale, hairy chest. He pinched his side and noticed he had gained weight. Would he ever be able to cultivate a body like that of these two boys? Standing up, he stretched his trunks over his bottom again and walked toward the pool, then climbed down the ladder and diligently began his first lap. He stuck to the breaststroke, because when, during swimming lessons as a child, he swam the wretched crawl—with which Patrick (or was it Lucien?) was now agilely slicing through the water— he had always swallowed half the pool. It was a lost cause. After three laps he gave up and returned to his towel. Back in the burning sun, he tried to read the newspaper again. On the way over here, he had chosen *Le Monde* in the newspaper and tobacco shop because he had wanted to look intelligent. But what a deadly dull, headache-inducing paper it was, with no photographs.

After a few hours he decided to pack it in. His body had failed miserably and was now on its way home, painfully burned by way of punishment. That evening it was his mind's turn to have a go at socializing. He went to the café where he had phoned Sorel to cancel dinner, in the hope of meeting some nice young students after all. But it was almost deserted, and he paid his tab after his first beer.

He was in bed by ten—red from the sun and red from shame—knowing that at that same moment a wonderful feast was taking place at his master's house. That wretched Frédérique! Because of her, he was now missing out on a tender suckling pig. But at the same time a Hieronymus Bosch-like scene imposed itself on him, in which not a suckling pig but a stark-naked, tender young apprentice was on the spit and being fondled by three drooling devils. Despite this frightening vision and amid all his painfully burned body parts, his member now stood firmly erect. That's what you got, of course, from a day of sun and swimming with all those beautiful bodies around you.

After another bad night, Joop only began to feel better halfway through the holiday Monday. Workweek ahead! It wasn't the end of the world that he hadn't managed to meet any young people. It wasn't the end of the world if Sorel had ulterior motives. He was still a brilliant chocolatier from whom there was a lot to learn. To keep a little more distance—that was all he needed to do.

Nathalie

The suckling pig was heavenly, recounted Sorel. And the cottage in the Morvan was idyllic, feigned Joop. After his difficult weekend, it was a relief to be back on the job. And when they walked down to the Sorels' house for the midday meal, Joop was even happy to see madame's sourpuss face and to hear Ronnie-Boy Johnjohn's growling. Everything was back to normal, and as usual the food tasted divine.

Deeply content, Joop walked toward town while his master had his siesta. Usually he would go back to his apartment and also lie down for half an hour, but today he chose to go to the little park built along the top of the city walls, where he sat down on a bench to enjoy the beautiful view of the wooded hills of the Morvan.

He hadn't been sitting there for long when a strikingly young mother approached him pushing a baby carriage. She couldn't be much older than nineteen or twenty. Her refined features and elegant figure reminded Joop of Sorel's remark that children were the fat caterpillars and adults the fragile butterflies. If she had been just any beautiful girl, like the ones he had seen at the swimming pool, he wouldn't have dared to look at her so blatantly. But the baby carriage ruled out any dangerous tensions between them right from the start. The young mother looked at him equally unabashed. Then she smiled, a smile so sad and vulnerable that it cut Joop to the quick.

That afternoon in the chocolate shop, he couldn't get her out of his thoughts. From behind the bars of her premature motherhood, she had smiled at him, the carefree young man on a bench in the park enjoying his half hour off, a freedom she had lost forever, a freedom she had perhaps never even known.

That evening in his apartment, he was still thinking about Nathalie, as he had dubbed her by this time. She had a blond ponytail and possibly even blue eyes, but that was where the similarity to Dutch girls stopped. Grace, that was the essential difference, if he compared Nathalie's feathery tread with, for instance, Daphne's brusque manner. And Daphne had generally been considered the beauty queen of first-year art history. How to explain the difference? Perhaps it was a question of diet, he mused. Anyone who was stuffed with hodgepodge and custard from a young age couldn't help but become ungainly. On the other hand, anyone raised on refined French food automatically became elegant.

And stayed elegant, even in the dire circumstances of premature motherhood. What was the underlying story? Where and by whom had she become pregnant? Was it by the farmhand, in the hayloft during some village celebration? Or in the back of the pickup truck of the fellow from the Peugeot garage? Or else in the backroom of some posh lawyer's office? And was she unhappily married now? Or had the father abandoned her and the child?

Joop would do anything to run into her again. As a noble chocolatier, he would kneel before her: *Voilà, mademoiselle.* A homemade chocolate presented on a red-velvet cushion, a chocolate, followed by a kiss on the hand and a declaration of love. O Nathalie, I have come to rescue you and to love you.

And the baby? Hmm. Like Sorel, Joop wasn't a child

lover. But he was all too willing to be a stepfather for the sake of his unhappy nymph.

The following afternoon he refused a second cup of coffee at the Sorels', so he could rush back up to the park in the hope of seeing Nathalie again. And sure enough, there she was, sitting on "his" bench, in fact. Joop quickly chose a seat a few benches away. She was reading a book, meanwhile rolling the carriage gently back and forth to help her baby fall asleep. From the cover, it looked like a Harlequin Romance. Dreams of a knight in shining armor—while the real knight was sitting only a few benches away . . .

Heart pounding, he stood up, but then, as if his movements were governed by some powerful magnet, he resolutely turned away from her and left the park in a hurry. He had simply chickened out. Dejectedly he walked past the clock tower in the direction of the chocolate shop. Someone like Peter would have approached her without a moment's hesitation and started some corny conversation—about the baby, of course. Oh, what a darling, oh what a sweetie. In broken French, but on target all the same.

The next day she wasn't there. And in the subsequent days Joop understood why the Morvan was famous for its bad weather. The clouds hung as low as they did in Holland, but here it rained more relentlessly. If by chance there was a dry spell just after lunch, he would rush over to have a look in the park. And another look if it was dry after work. And then, just to be sure, he looked in other parks, too. And finally he even looked when it rained. To no avail.

But then, on the following Monday, the lovely summer weather returned, and so did Nathalie. As on their first encounter, he sat on the bench and she came walking toward him with the baby carriage.

He would never forgive himself if he didn't take action now.

But it wasn't even necessary, because she beat him to it. With a beautiful voice (how could it not be beautiful?), and addressing him with the formal *vous*, she asked him what time it was.

Joop looked at his watch, and stammered that it was a quarter past two.

She now studied him with an intensely critical eye.

"By the sounds of it, you come from Holland, too," she said in Dutch.

"Yes," he said, crestfallen. "And so do you."

"Oh, how awful!" She covered her mouth with her hand. "How awful!"

After recognizing the disappointment in each other's looks, they both burst out laughing.

She sat down beside him and couldn't stop laughing about the crazy misunderstanding. Talking about misunderstandings, little Marie-Louise wasn't her baby. She had been here as an au pair for several months with the Bouchard family. You could see their beautiful house over there on the hill to the right, one of those new houses on the outskirts of town. She chattered on merrily. Even though Joop had to revise his clever little theory about grace and diet, and even though his romantic visions of the noble chocolatier and the sad young mother now went up in smoke, she was still a nice girl.

She considered herself rather ordinary. There were so many girls who did this kind of work for a year or two. No big deal. But he, a Dutchman doing an apprenticeship with a French chocolatier, gosh! She looked at him with big eyes. It made him feel shy yet manly at the same time.

"By the way, I have to go back to work," he said. "But why don't you come and eat at my place sometime?"

Yes, she liked that idea, and he noticed she was blushing.

They walked out of the park together. Now, they looked like a very young mother *and* father with baby, judging by the affectionate look of the old woman walking toward them. Meanwhile, Joop was thinking about what he would cook for her. Something simple in any case. He had learned from his earlier attempt to win a girl's heart. Nothing too fancy. He didn't even have the money for that. He would try to surprise her with his nonchalance, with a straightforward tomato salad, for instance, but then made with those dark red, heavily aromatic tomatoes that you could buy here at the Saturday market, with a generous shot of oil and vinegar and some finely chopped basil over the top. And then perhaps a trout like the other day? No, maybe not. Such a sweet, innocent girl might be frightened by a complete fish on her plate. One thing was certain though: a homemade chocolate with the coffee. Although . . . No, no chocolate with the coffee. At least not on the first date.

"By the way, what's your name?" he asked, as they were about to leave in opposite directions.

"Mine? My name's Emma. And yours?"

"Joop," he said, sighing deeply.

She burst out laughing again. "Joop and Emma. How Dutch can you get!"

Simplicity

A hearty omelette and a tomato salad, a baguette and cheap red local wine. That was all.

After dinner, Joop poured coffee with a remarkably steady hand, steadier at least than the trembling hand that held up the cup. Where danger is imminent, only one person can be the most afraid, and Emma had taken that role upon herself.

But the distance between their chairs and the single bed had now become so small and compelling that Joop, inexperienced as he was, didn't know how to deal with it. So he suggested taking an evening stroll along the city walls.

Once they were outside, everything took care of itself.

He put his arm around her. When they stopped at a place with a scenic view, they gave each other a cautious kiss. They sat down in the park where they had first met. There they looked deep into each other's eyes, which sparkled beautifully in the light of the streetlamp near their bench. Then they kissed.

Hours passed. Neither of them wanted to be the killjoy, but, in the end, Joop extricated himself from their embrace. He had to start early the next morning in the chocolate shop. Emma had to get up even earlier to give little Marie-Louise her first bottle. As befitted a gallant young man, he walked her all the way to the Bouchards' house. They had both envisaged a last passionate kiss at the gate, but the neighbors' watchdog made such a fuss they had to abandon the idea.

Dawn was approaching by the time Joop floated through the empty streets back to his apartment. From the bakery on the corner, the delicious smell of fresh bread spread across the square.

Complications

Y ou look terrible!" cried Sorel. "Did you hitchhike to work or something?"

"Sorry, but I overslept and had to rush to get here on time."

"Stubble with chocolate. It's just not acceptable."

"I can go home and shave if you want."

"No, no, it's too late now. I'll look the other way today."

Despite his lack of sleep and Sorel's annoyance, Joop began that day with an inspiration he hadn't felt before. *"Au bain-marie"* suddenly sounded so erotic! And it was no less than titillating to feel the gurgling water reverberate through the handle of the wooden spoon that he was using to press and spread the piece of melting chocolate over the bottom of the inside pan. The chocolate needed to be stirred lovingly, stroked, pampered, teased. It was only now, after the night with Emma, that he really understood what Sorel meant with these words. But there was another reason, too, for his unprecedented virtuosity that morning. It was as if Emma were here in the kitchen watching him, full of admiration, and he was trying to impress her with everything he did. Oh, Emma! She was going to drop by at his place during the siesta. He couldn't wait.

"My God, boy, what's the matter with you today?" said his master, now standing beside him.

Joop looked down and smiled shyly.

"I've met a girl."

"Oh, is that it." Sorel turned the burner off under the pan. "Then go home."

"But . . ."

"That you come in here unwashed and unshaven is bad enough. But that dreamy look in your eyes and that feeble hand you're stirring the pan with, that's enough to make me sick to my stomach. A chocolatier has to be clear-minded and concentrated at all times. Making chocolates is a cold hard science! So get the hell out of here!"

Deeply insulted, Joop undid his apron.

"Not sick, I hope?" asked Frédérique, when he walked through the shop a moment later.

All morning, Joop paced back and forth in his apartment, at first because of the conflict with his master, but as the hours passed, more and more in nervous anticipation of Emma's arrival.

When the doorbell finally rang, he flew down the stairs to open the door for her—but also for the baby carriage and its contents, which he had conveniently eliminated from his image of their romantic rendezvous. Together, they lugged the heavy vehicle upstairs. The little one seemed to be having an off day. Tormented, Joop stood by and watched as Emma took the screaming, red-faced monster in her arms and walked around his room holding her. When she finally put her back in the carriage and sat down on the bed next to Joop, he immediately started to kiss her, wildly and uncontrollably, as if to make up for lost time. Because he had resolved to go further than the night before, he undid the buttons of her blouse with trembling fingers. Unfortunately, he didn't get farther than some clumsy fiddling with her bra straps. Little Marie-Louise started to scream again. And what's more, Emma said she didn't have much time. She still had a hundred and one things to do for the Bouchards that afternoon. And he had to be back in the chocolate shop soon too, didn't he?

"Yes, yes," said Joop, sighing deeply.

The visit had lasted less than fifteen minutes, and they were already lugging the baby carriage downstairs again.

On the street, Joop received one last pat on the cheek.

"The day after tomorrow," she promised. "And then, without the baby."

As he trudged upstairs dejectedly, he thought it might not even be such a bad idea to return to the chocolate shop for the afternoon. If Sorel still wanted him, that is.

Smoothly shaven and right on time, he took up his position in front of the chocolate shop. When his master, returning from his siesta, waved to him from a distance, Joop heaved a sigh of relief.

"Am I ever glad to see you here, my boy. I was afraid I had chased you away forever."

"You were right, though. I wasn't all here this morning."

"What's done is done. Come on. That absurd little incident has taken enough of our time."

Master and apprentice were both shaken by their first real argument and were a good match for each other all afternoon in trying to prove their good intentions.

"I'm happy for you," said Sorel. "I really am. Very glad you've met a girl. Too much longing in that area"—he cleared his throat—"isn't good for an artist. This will calm things down."

Joop, in turn, asked his master all kinds of purely technical questions, to show he could indeed approach his work as a "cold hard science," even if he was head over heels in love.

"Why don't you both come to our place for dinner sometime?" suggested Sorel, again outdoing his apprentice. "I'm sure Isabelle would like to meet her, too."

"She's Dutch," warned Joop.

"Oh dear. Forget the invitation then."

Puzzled, Joop looked at his master. Then they both burst out laughing.

With that, the air was cleared once and for all.

Joop hadn't expected the invitation to really materialize, but a few weeks later he and Emma were invited to the Sorels' for the midday meal on Sunday.

On the way there, he gave his girlfriend a few last tips.

Emma joked that it was like going to visit her parents-in-law.

"But that's what this is," he said in all earnestness.

The hostess turned out to be a hundred percent better than Joop's horror stories. All her wrinkles expressed friendliness, and she showered Emma with compliments. About her beautiful earrings, about her adorable summer dress, about her superb French. What's more, the horrid little monster Ronnie-Boy Johnjohn came running over to Emma, tail wagging, and when she sat down at the table, nestled at her feet, something he normally never did with strangers, according to madame. If anything, it was Joop's holy Jérôme Sorel who gave Emma an uneasy feeling. His greedy look, for example. It was exactly the way Joop looked at her—a touch too intense and penetrating—when she undressed in front of him. And the piqued grimaces monsieur made when groping for the correct word as he expounded, were also familiar to her from a more intimate context. And when madame put a platter of cheese on the table after the main meal and he grumbled approvingly—it was as if she heard Joop after they made love, when she snuggled up against him and stroked his chest.

They were striking resemblances, which she preferred not to think about for too long. But she only had to look at Joop for a moment and she melted. It was so sweet the way he beamed with pride throughout the meal now that his girl-friend had met with such approval.

"You'll take good care of him, won't you," Sorel insisted, as they said good-bye to each other at the door. "He's such a remarkable boy."

Then he gave her a slightly too wet kiss on the hand, so that she kept wanting to wash her hands for the rest of the afternoon.

Le Déjeuner sur l'herbe

One day Joop and Emma went for a picnic in the woods. They followed a path along a creek until they arrived at a sunny meadow. There, a dam of earth had been built right across the creek so that a deep pool had formed.

After they spread the blanket and sat down, Joop looked around contentedly. He told Emma about the painting by Manet, *Le Déjeuner sur l'herbe,* and how this spot reminded him of it.

Emma blushed. She smelled trouble.

At first Joop had no intention whatsoever of living out his fantasy. He knew that after years of daydreaming, reality could only be a disappointment. But when he saw his girlfriend blushing so seductively, he couldn't resist the temptation.

At his request she obediently took off her clothes.

"You're beautiful," he said solemnly, eyeing her from head to foot.

She responded with an insecure little laugh, which didn't quite suit the hallowed atmosphere Joop had in mind.

The peach he peeled for her was a disappointment, too. Now, of all times. For weeks on end he had bought the most succulent peaches at the market, but now, of all times, the skin was too tight and the pulp was stringy and tasted sour and watery.

"I'm going for a swim," she announced after finishing her peach. She didn't feel comfortable and in the water she could hide her nakedness, at least for a while. "Are you coming, too?"

But no, Joop preferred to watch her.

The bottom was swampy, which always made her flesh creep and then gave her the giggles.

Joop frowned. Another wrong laugh that didn't help the atmosphere any.

Emma dove into the water. Elated and noisy, she splashed around, the way people do when they are swimming in water that is too cold. Did he really not want to come in? Oh, come on now! No?

Resigned, she swam to the middle of the pond.

Joop was glad she was finally quiet so he could admire her undisturbed. But all of a sudden she let out a cry and waved her arms frantically in the air. A monster of a trout had brushed against her leg. When she realized what had happened, she burst out laughing. All things considered, though, it was a bit too scary to stay in the water any longer.

Teeth chattering violently, she came out of the water. Because they didn't have a towel with them, Joop took off his shirt and rubbed her dry as best he could.

A little lovemaking then? he thought, as his girlfriend held on to him, shivering.

According to Sorel, if the basic recipe wasn't right, it didn't help to add more ingredients. But still, against his better judgment, Joop now took off the rest of his clothes.

They lay down on the blanket between the picnic stuff. The blazing sun was unrelenting, so that even Emma's perfect skin now showed small irregularities, not to speak of his own body. Because she hadn't been able to dry herself properly, her skin felt tough. And she still had goose bumps, so it was probably the cold rather than arousal that made her nipples so hard.

Joop now felt ill at ease too. Greater than the kick that they were doing it outdoors was his fear that they might be spied on. A rustle in the bushes was enough for him to look up in alarm like a frightened rabbit.

As a result, their lovemaking was more hurried than normal.

He knew it would end in disillusionment; he had known right from the start. And yet, to camouflage his disappointment, he pretended he had never been so excited. To make it even more special, at his initiative they tried all kinds of new positions, in which they seemed to be made more and more of elbows and knees and less and less of soft parts. In one of those impossible knots, Emma began to wiggle her hips so wildly that Joop couldn't hold back anymore and didn't pull out on time.

"Oops."

In no time, Joop extricated himself from their entanglement.

Emma pulled the picnic basket toward her and began looking for a serviette.

"You don't think . . ." he asked her.

"No, probably not. There's only a small chance."

They were both glad to be able to get dressed. Joop uncorked a bottle and poured two cups of lukewarm red wine. Emma had become hungry and tore off a big piece of baguette.

If he was honest with himself, any given love scene in his sweltering van Gogh room could be classified as perfect — when, glistening with perspiration on his narrow bed, they took all the time in the world for each other, a glass of cold white wine within reach and urged on by the screaming swallows out in the courtyard behind the butcher's shop. But as he stared out over the black water of the trout pond, his mind churned at full speed in an attempt to filter out all the bungling from the scene that had just taken place.

Retroactively, Joop declared the picnic in the woods the absolute highlight of his sojourn in France, and therefore the absolute highlight of his whole life. Yes, Emma was at her most beautiful that day as she rose up out of that dark pool in the woods. And he was at his happiest. What more could he wish for, a young chocolatier in the heart of France doing an apprenticeship with the brilliant Jérôme Sorel, and then, on his free Sunday, making love to a seductive wood nymph in an idyllic meadow of flowers. It was one of those impossible moments of hyperharmony, of the kind Sorel had talked about so often, a moment almost too good to be true, one that carried the seed of its own undoing.

Adieu, Nathalie

T hey were sitting in "their" little park, where they had met for the first time, when Emma told him.

"I think it was that one time, by the pond in the woods."

"Are you sure?"

She nodded.

"Strange, eh? Now I'm really going to be that young mother you took me for in the beginning."

Joop smiled sourly, then stood up and walked to the scenic point, where bridal couples often posed to be photographed. A baby. That was the last thing he needed. Some thirty feet below him was the road that led to the Sorels' house, and he imagined himself walking there with his master. Blind, greedy caterpillars they were. He could hear him saying it.

Couldn't something be done about it? Weren't there shady doctors in back rooms, with long needles and ominous little pans, who could take care of this little problem? Or out there in the Morvan, a backward and impoverished region, wasn't there some little old woman who knew her herbs, who could drive out the fetus with a mean brew? But such interventions could go terribly wrong; at school they had read a dismal novel on this theme, featuring a seventeen-year-old working-class girl from Leeds. Couldn't Emma jump off this little wall fifty times to induce a miscarriage?—he meant to the side where he was standing now, of course, not over it and into the depths. His knees became weak at the thought.

"Say something," said Emma.

He looked over his shoulder at the still-graceful girl sitting there on the bench, with her pale face and large frightened eyes. He thought of his sister Rosalinde, as he had seen her at the height of her pregnancy, gasping and puffing, eyes dull from exhaustion. He shuddered at the prospect that Emma would slowly change into such a cumbersome mother animal.

When he finally came and sat down beside her, she began to sob. He put his arms around her and patted her back, dutifully and also a bit impatiently. Letting herself hang limply in his arms she seemed to weigh a ton. Infinitely heavier than the traveling bag he had carried with him as his sole burden when, only two months before, he had ventured out into the world. Longing for that lightness, he gazed at the vast hilly landscape of the Morvan.

"No, Emma," he said with sudden resolve.

He let go of her and shifted away.

She looked at him, frightened. "What do you mean, no?"

Joop sighed. How could he make this clear to her? "Look. You have to understand that a chocolate consists of three layers."

Despite the seriousness of the situation, Emma burst out laughing. "What does that have to do with it?"

"To begin with, there is of course the interior and the exterior," he explained patiently. "Otherwise known as the filling and the coating. The subtle play between these two layers is definitive for the quality of a chocolate. But there's a third layer too, which, according to Sorel, is just as important. He calls that layer the *'entourage.'*"

"The entourage?"

"Yes, that's the environment in which a chocolate comes into being. It's about more than just a well-equipped kitchen, Emma. The right entourage implies a way of life—simple, clear, and orderly, with as little nonsense surrounding it as possible."

Emma's face clouded over. "Nonsense?"

"In the entourage of a true chocolatier, there's no room for a child."

"But you don't have to take the child to work with you." Emma's lower lip began to tremble. "Damn it, Joop, what are you trying to say?"

"That it's better if we don't see each other anymore."

"Don't be silly! This is your responsibility too, you know! You can't walk away from this."

"I'm sorry, Emma, but I can."

As if to prove his point, he stood up from the bench. The midday break was almost over and he was expected back at the chocolate shop.

"Are those stupid chocolates so important that you'll drop me just like that?"

"I've been clear about my priorities right from the start," he said coolly.

"You know what you are? A heartless bastard!"

Without turning around, Joop walked out of the park and headed for the chocolate shop. Poor Emma. Perhaps he had played it a bit too hard, but he only had to think about the baby and he knew why.

Under the circumstances, work went rather well that afternoon. Joop had almost forgotten that anything was the matter when Frédérique knocked on the kitchen door at five-thirty. Telephone. For Joop.

His master frowned. It was against the rules.

First Joop heard only sniffing on the other end of the line, but with stops and starts, it finally came out that Emma had phoned her mother in Holland. She had already quit her job at the Bouchards' and would be going home by train that same evening. Still, she let silences fall at strategic moments, presumably to give him the opportunity to stop her.

"Shall I take you to the train then?" he asked. "Hello?"

She had thrown down the receiver.

"Problems?" asked Frédérique cheerfully.

"Oh, no. Everything's fine."

After work, he went into the cheese shop on his way home to treat himself to the ripe goat's cheese that had been enticing him for the past several days. At home he sat down at his table with a glass of red wine, a piece of baguette, and the cheese. Divine! If only Emma could taste it! But at that moment she was already in the evening train, leaving Avallon, en route to Paris. Only then did he realize what damage he had done that day.

Damn it! If only she hadn't twisted her hips so wildly that day at the trout pond, there wouldn't be any problem now. They could have continued their idyllic little life with a picnic now and again, taking breaks between delicacies to make love . . . The ideal entourage for a young chocolatier. The emphasis had to be on "now and again," because lately he had spent far too much time with Emma and paid far too little attention to the chocolates. That Sorel had been irritated with him lately was absolutely justified. But unfortunately it was too late now for "now and again." The timeless lovemaking with Emma was over forever now that there was a little time bomb ticking away inside her. A child.

Poor Emma. But her mother would take care of her. From all the stories he had heard, it was clear they were very close. And, like so many mother-daughter tandems on earth, they would surely manage, complaining about him in the meantime —that heartless bastard who had left his wife and child in the lurch. But would it really have been so much nobler to have stayed with her against his will? As a tormented chocolatier, a bad husband, and an even worse father? Wasn't his deed a sign of profound self-knowledge? And wasn't it, in the end, more caring to leave her at this early stage when she was still young and attractive? She would have no trouble at all finding another man, even if she had a child. He had seen with his own eyes how well a baby carriage suited her. Really, it was better this way. Later she would be grateful to him.

But no matter how hard he tried to ease his conscience, the image of the departing train cut straight through his soul. To come to a screeching halt in the middle of the night. Joop knew the night train from Paris to Amsterdam all too well: they let it stand for hours on end in a harshly lit train station somewhere in Belgium. That is where his beloved now sat, a prisoner in a no man's land, between yesterday's beautiful dreams and tomorrow's grim reality. Just as he, too, lay awake at this moment, his eyes so accustomed to the dark now that he could distinguish every object in the room . . .

Oh, Emma!

Then, sure enough, the tears came. What did she mean, "heartless bastard"? If only she could see him now, she would understand how difficult his choice had been and that he was anything but proud of himself.

Yet strangely enough, this last thought filled him with a loftier sort of pride. That he was capable of such reprehensible behavior in order to protect his artistry. Heartless bastard? Certainly. But anyone seeking the divine must by definition be a bit inhuman. He had dared to take a stand. His work would be more forceful and compelling as a result. Sorel would greatly appreciate his decision.

But by enjoying his badness, he felt doubly bad, doubly guilty. Which made him feel good again, which in turn made him feel bad again. Thin layers of guilt and pleasure alternated with each other, as wafer-thin as the layers in some of Sorel's chocolates. Life was so . . . subtle.

But meanwhile, somewhere in Belgium, in a harshly lit station, a girl sat in a train staring out the window, a desperate girl, with a broken heart and a baby in her belly. And it was all his doing. Oh, Emma!

Now, it was no longer a question of growing accustomed to the dark that enabled him to see everything in his room clearly, but of dawn shining through the curtains. Although he hadn't slept a wink, he got dressed and made coffee, so that he was ready to rush over to the bakery on the corner of the square as soon as it opened.

Consolation that morning came in the form of a *petit pain au chocolat,* which he usually avoided. He found the pastry too greasy and heavy, and sometimes you were already halfway through it before you found a skimpy little staff of chocolate somewhere in the bottom of the bun. But his craving for cacao was so strong that he couldn't wait for the chocolate shop to open. Fortunately, the baker had been in a generous mood that night. Joop was lucky with the first bite.

It was six-fifteen. By this time the train would be moving again, and before long it would be crossing the Dutch border. *Adieu, Nathalie.* Farewell, Emma. Take care. He had survived the most hellish night of his life. A new day was dawning. On to the chocolate shop!

Man with a Mission

A re you all right?" asked Sorel. "You look a bit pale."
"Oh, I didn't sleep so well. That's all."

After he washed his hands, Joop went straight to work. He had resolved not to bother his master with the ups and downs of his love life. Only after a few days, when he had recovered from the initial shock himself, would he tell him that Emma was no longer part of his entourage.

Blinking with his bloodshot eyes, he tried to focus on the mountain of almonds he had to chop finely.

"You didn't have a fight with your girlfriend, did you?"

Sighing, Joop laid the chopping knife on the board. Now he had to tell the whole story.

"What a shame," said Sorel when he was finished. "You were such a nice couple."

Now that the anticipated support failed to come, the abyss of doubt and remorse that he had tried so hard to close during the night opened up again. Only this time, there would be no dawn to make everything seem brighter.

"But children don't fit into the life of a chocolatier," Joop insisted. "You said so yourself, didn't you?"

"Oh, I say a lot of things. You shouldn't always take an old misanthrope seriously."

"But I totally agree with you! I want to make chocolates,

not start a family. It's only here in the kitchen of your chocolate shop that I'm really happy."

"God, my boy," said Sorel, taken aback. "I think you really
mean it."

"Of course I mean it!"

Joop blushed. The old feeling, the magic between master
and apprentice had returned.

"Then I just don't know what to say to you right now. Or
rather, I know exactly what to say to you. Come, leave those
damn little nuts for now. You and I need to have a serious talk
about the future."

Joop's heart started pounding. He had occasionally fantasized
about eventually taking over the chocolate shop. Of course he
preferred to see his master continue for years on end, but if he
ever did grow too old, Joop would be ready. That he had turned
Emma out onto the street without batting an eye was the ultimate
proof of his loyalty to the chocolate shop. That was why for the
very first time Sorel now dared to discuss the future with him.

They walked to the café, where they usually only went
after work.

Sorel ordered two coffees and asked Joop if he wanted
anything else. He wasn't referring to the croissants in the bell-
jar on the counter, but to the row of liqueur bottles behind the
barkeeper. With a sleepless night behind him and a full day's
work ahead, Joop was wise enough to decline the offer, but
Sorel ordered a *marc de Bourgogne* for himself. The first sip was
enough to trigger a fit of coughing. Swearing, he pulled out a
handkerchief to wipe his mouth.

"As you can hear, my dear boy, my health leaves something
to be desired."

Joop nodded sympathetically.

"I don't like to admit it, but Isabelle is right. I can't do it anymore. My battery is empty, Joop. You must see it too, I think."

"Oh, monsieur, you're not doing too badly, I'd say."

"You're right. I agree. At least, as long as I'm busy with my own work. But if I have to watch out for you, too . . . then I'm totally exhausted by the end of the day. So I think it's better, Joop, if we hereby end your apprenticeship."

"What? My apprenticeship? You can't be serious."

"I have been meaning to talk to you about this for a while, but I didn't have the courage. Now I must. That you let Emma go just like that, while you had such a lovely future together . . . And why? For an old grouch like me? So you can hang around in a hole like Avallon?"

"But I feel perfectly at home here. For the first time in my life! And I still have so much to learn from you."

Sorel pointed to Joop's cup of coffee. "Sure you don't want anything with it? Of course, my boy, of course you do. Jean-Pierre, give this boy a marc too."

Marc de Bourgogne, the same drink they had had when they first met. Joop could no longer suppress his tears.

"Oh God, no, please don't," said Sorel. "I can't stand it!"

He gave his handkerchief to Joop, who, with one last sniff, managed to get a grip on himself.

"Someone is waiting for you, my boy."

"I'm not sure about that, after I treated her so badly."

"Oh, come on! She adores you. The way she looks at you with her big blue eyes; she melts every time you say or do something. It's true. It makes me jealous when I see it."

Joop took a hefty swig.

"And the baby, then?" he asked.

"Well, I have no experience in that department. Apparently they're quite enjoyable when they're your own."

"But what am I supposed to do, back there in Holland?"

"Listen well, my boy. It might even be interesting for you to return to your native country. You've talked often enough about the atrocious eating habits of your fellow countrymen. Is it not a noble task to educate them? To return to the Lowlands as a missionary of haute cuisine? To open your own chocolate shop there, for example?"

Joop couldn't muster more than a doleful little laugh.

Sorel pulled out his wallet. "You have to promise me one thing, Joop. That you won't hitchhike. How much do you need? A hundred francs? Two hundred? Here, take this. And you should go now. Before I break down. And you don't want to be around for that. There's nothing so pitiful as a tearful old man."

Stunned, Joop walked back to his apartment, the wad of francs in his pocket. There, he fell onto the bed and howled like a dog. After he had cried his eyes out, he kept lying there for a while, his face pressed into the wet pillow. Then he pulled his traveling bag out of the cupboard and started packing.

Exactly twenty-four hours after Emma's departure, Joop caught the train from Avallon to Paris. Exhausted from all the emotions, he slept like a log, only to wake up in the Gare de Lyon with the man opposite him tugging at his sleeve. In the metro, on his way to the Gare du Nord, he was once again a young man with a traveling bag. But how different he was from the young man on the journey down, on the quest to find his freedom. Now he was a man with worries, a man with a woman and soon even a child.

The harshly lit station where the train from Paris to Amsterdam stood for hours was in the south of Belgium, just across the border with France. On the platform, customs officers kept walking resolutely toward each other as if they had something extremely important to communicate, as if, for instance, they had just heard that there was a wanted criminal in the train. But, once together, they stood there totally relaxed, chatting and smoking cigarettes. It was as if they deliberately put on this performance to torment the waiting train passengers.

Emma had undergone this same torture the night before. How cruel he had been. A question of inexperience. Like a young recruit who took his task much too seriously, he had guarded his artistry like a military object. The mild view of an older chocolatier had been needed to help him see that there was more than enough room for a woman in his life, and even for a child. If only Emma would take him back now.

Finally, at five o'clock in the morning, the conductor blew his whistle, and with a gentle lurch, the train began to move. As dawn slowly approached, Joop watched the hills gradually collapse and the flat countryside begin. Between Brussels and Antwerp, it clouded over, and just before the Dutch border, the first raindrops fell. The farther north they went, the harder it rained. Dotted diagonal lines stretched across the windows, as if the train itself was crying because it had to travel through such ugly countryside.

Back to Holland, thought Joop bitterly. Back to the Lowest of Low Countries!

You had to have a mission to abandon culinary paradise for this gloom. Otherwise you couldn't survive. Otherwise you would go crazy.

Part 4

SLAVERY

Victory Lap Around
the Duck Pond

The young chocolatier thought he looked strikingly noble, the way he stood at the door in the pouring rain with a red rose in his hand and the traveling bag at his feet.

The woman who opened the door was less impressed. "I don't know if Emma wants to talk to you," she said. "But I'll go and see."

A century later, the woman reappeared in the doorway.

"If you go upstairs, it's the second door on the left," she said, handing him a towel to dry off his hair.

Emma was sitting on the bed in her nightgown.

"Hello, Joop."

He caught a glimpse of a pale face without makeup before she hid herself behind her raised knees. She wrapped her hands around her ankles and started rocking gently back and forth.

Joop sat down beside her.

"Here," he said, offering her the rose.

"Yes, nice. Put it down on that dresser over there."

Because she refused to look at him, Joop addressed his words to her bare feet. He told them how terribly sorry he was. That he had acted in panic, and realized the error of his ways after a sleepless night.

Emma stopped rocking and looked at him incredulously.

"Did you come all the way to Holland to tell me this?"

"Yes, Emma."

He blushed because he was deeply moved by his own story but also because it wasn't quite true.

"And you were allowed to take time off just like that? When are you going back?"

"I'm not going back."

"What?"

Now he had to glue the remaining half of the story to his earlier half-truth.

"My apprenticeship had entered a final stage anyway," he concocted. "And Monsieur Sorel didn't mind ending it a bit earlier."

"So you're here to stay in Holland."

"I'm here to stay. I plan to start my own chocolate shop."

Emma had to think about this for a while.

"I hope you're not going to blame me one day for having left France on my account," she said at last.

"No, of course not, Emma."

"Really?"

"Really."

"Come here . . ."

She took Joop's hand and guided it under her nightgown to touch her bare belly. Then she placed her own hand on top of his. Joop understood that this was meant to be a poignant moment, during which the two of them were to contemplate the little wonder growing inside her. To please her, he smiled amicably.

It was enough to dispel her last suspicions. The gleam in her eyes changed to a glisten, and a tear rolled down her cheek.

"Oh Joop!" she said, throwing her arms around his neck. "Joop, Joop, Joop. What a strange boy you are!"

When she finally let go of him, she in turn began to reassure him. His dream to start his own chocolate shop was her

dream, too. Of course she couldn't help with the actual chocolates, but she could help with the outer layer, the *"entourage."*
The necessary licenses and diplomas, a suitable location, a
loan—she would look into all those things for him. And when
the business finally opened, she would maintain the contacts,
the way Frédérique did for Monsieur Sorel, and do the book-
keeping, and . . . and she would cook for him, really cook, she
meant, the way she had learned during her stay at the
Bouchards', a midday meal too, if necessary, French-style.
Only if he were happy in his kitchen with his chocolates
would she be happy too. All the "nonsense" around it would
be her responsibility, especially taking care of the child. He
wouldn't be bothered by it at all. She could guarantee that.

"Easy now," he said, gently stroking her back, meanwhile
gratefully taking note of her promises.

"I bet the two of you are ready for a cup of tea," said her
mother, when Emma came downstairs with Joop to officially
introduce him.

Hannie turned out to be nicer than she had seemed at the
door. She had predicted that Joop would show up within a
week, but she hadn't wanted to make it too easy for him by
welcoming him with open arms.

Joop and Emma married in private, with Hannie and
Emma's best girlfriend, Ingrid, as witnesses. As long as the
location of the future chocolate shop was still uncertain, the
newlyweds would live with Hannie.

During the first months of her pregnancy, Emma was happier and more in love than ever. As yet, there was no sign at
all of a cumbersome, exhausted mother animal.

When he had walked with her through the streets of
Avallon, Joop had only had eyes for her. The town and its
inhabitants had merely served as a romantic décor. But here

in Holland he enjoyed showing her off. It struck him how many men gaped at her with wide eyes. When they subsequently looked at him, though, their eyes narrowed. He saw them thinking: How can such a measly little bastard land such a beautiful girl? It should be against the law.

Yes, people, this little bastard was in fact a swan! In physical terms perhaps smaller than you, but in the finer world of the palate, in a perfect position to look down on all of you. As befits a swan when it makes its way around a duck pond.

There were plenty of reasons for looking down.

Like hodgepodge, pea soup, and sausage rolls.

Or the disgusting quantities of dairy products with which the Dutch washed down their food.

Or the baguettes and croissants with which modern bakers tried to impress their customers. Monstrosities, every one of which should be considered an insult to a friendly nation.

Not to speak of the restaurants that thought they could pass off their mediocre fare as haute cuisine just by sprinkling French accents over the menu!

And then the people who visited such establishments, the Dutch snobs who ate well or thought they ate well — because it was the thing to do, not because they tasted any of it. The most irritating subspecies were the wine connoisseurs, who could drivel on ad infinitum about good and bad years and who knew exactly which wine suited which meal. But did these people themselves suit the meal? They never asked themselves that!

Emma listened attentively to everything he had to say. She believed in his mission, she loved him. And he looked so sweet when he got worked up about something.

Less charmed were passersby or fellow passengers in the tram, bus, or train who occasionally overheard bits of his tirades.

"Well, well," such an angry duck would quack. "What pretension!"

Like the bald man with the fringe beard sitting opposite them in the train en route to Amsterdam, who was irritated to death for miles on end but only dared to make a comment when he got out at Naarden-Bussum, a few stops before Amsterdam. He threw Joop one more dirty look from the platform.

No sir, thought Joop, *not pretension. "Style" was the word. But they had never heard of that here in Holland.*

He and Emma were en route to Peter and Corinne's.

Joop kept thinking about the notorious picnic in the dunes, when the two of them had treated him to their foreplay, then withdrawn ever so discreetly and, upon returning, had cheered him up with the prospect of a lovely girl in the future. His time would come.

Well, generous friends, here she was.

Their mouths fell open with amazement when they saw her. Joop even had the impression they were a bit upset. It was perhaps easier to wish an unhappy friend all the good things in life than to grant a happy friend his happiness.

Corinne poured some tea and went around with a package of cookies.

"No, no, not for me," said Joop, a bit annoyed.

He was explaining to his friends how infinitely more sensual the French were than the Dutch and hence at the same time more spiritual. It was because all the senses were taken equally seriously, not ranked from high to low as they were here. Why should a delicious chocolate be less noble than a fugue by Bach?

"And yet," said Peter, "if I'm perfectly honest, I'd rather eat an ordinary Verkade chocolate bar than a fancy chocolate. Just straightforward, simple chocolate, no fuss and bother."

"You see, now that's typically Dutch!" cried Joop, triumphantly. "Dead ahead, straight to the horizon, as flat and unmysterious as a polder landscape. Everyone appreciates that, whereas a filled chocolate tends to be considered excessive, even slightly suspect. Yes—because it has a hidden interior, and he who hides something isn't completely honest, is he?"

"Take it easy," said Peter. "Each to his own taste, I would say."

But there was no stopping Joop now. "They just can't do it—make a decent chocolate here in Holland. The play between exterior and interior, the gradual revelation of a secret, the contrasting or else echoing of textures. It's all much too difficult and much too subtle. With Dutch chocolates, it's grit your teeth and then, yuk! A mouthful of misery. No, if I had to choose, I'd prefer the Verkade chocolate bar too."

"My God. This guy is unbelievable."

A tense silence followed.

"Gosh, Jopie," said Corinne at last. "You've sure changed in these few months."

"Gotten fat, you mean," sneered Peter.

"Oh yes," said Joop. With a smile as tender as that of a pregnant woman, he ran his hand over his belly. "That French food, eh?"

Joop's triumphant journey inevitably took him to Swaanendal, too. After having continually postponed the visit, he phoned one Sunday to say that he was back from France and that he wanted to come around to introduce someone to them.

"You won't want to stay for dinner, I hope," was his mother's first reaction. "Rosa's already coming with Wouter and the children, and I might not have enough food in the house."

"Don't worry," said Joop, laughing. "We definitely don't want to stay for dinner."

Like everyone who set foot on the estate for the first time, Emma was impressed by the avenue of beech trees and the stately house it led them to. Halfway down the avenue, they ran into Joop's brother-in-law, Wouter, who was out collecting beech nuts with a baby in a buggy and a child at his side.

"We were sent out to do this," he explained. "Your family wanted to make music undisturbed."

"Rosalinde too?" asked Joop, surprised.

"And how!" he said, with a glum face. "Her appetite for it has come back with a fury lately."

When Joop and Emma set foot in the music room courtesy obliged the quartet to stop making music in order to welcome the newcomer—which didn't endear her to them any.

"We're going on in a moment," Françoise cautioned her, "but first we'd like to get to know you, of course."

Joop knew his family. Emma was too beautiful. That sparked intense aggression in his mother and sisters. His father, too, was out of sorts, judging by the fury with which he rooted around in his pipe before finally lighting it.

Françoise's "getting to know" Emma amounted to cutting her down to size. With a barrage of questions she was quick to discover that Emma was of humble origins, no longer had a father (ah!), and was not at university.

When Emma admitted she knew absolutely nothing about classical music but that she liked Vivaldi's Four Seasons, the battle was over.

Charlotte sniffed derisively, then spun round on her stool to play a triumphant chord on the piano.

Joop glared indignantly at his eldest sister.

"By the way, did anything come of that orchestra in Over-ijssel?" he asked, by way of reprisal.

"Let's change the subject," she muttered.

"Well, then we have some news," said Emma. "Don't we, Joop?"

As they had agreed en route to the estate, he was the one who told his family that Emma was expecting.

"An accident, I presume," said Françoise. "But by the looks of it, you are both happy enough with it, so I won't be making a faux pas if I congratulate you, will I? And will there be a marriage? Already done? Marvelous. Then we owe you a present."

The coolness of his mother's reaction was matched by the exuberance of Rosalinde's.

"Oh, how wonderful! I'm going to be an aunt!"

She headed straight for Emma, bent over awkwardly to kiss her on both cheeks, and promptly sat down beside her on the couch. "Hey, congratulations! How far gone are you?"

Did she have trouble with morning sickness, she wanted to know. And if she needed baby clothes, she had a garbage bag full for her at home in her attic. And she knew a few handy exercises if her back started to bother her. And, oh yes, if she was interested in maternity clothes . . .

"Sorry, sis," Charlotte interrupted her, "but do you really think someone like Emma would wear your shapeless clothes?"

Laurens observed the scene with an amused smile, sucking contentedly on his pipe and remaining silent.

Françoise turned to Joop. "And I guess you'll be looking for a job now, so that you can support your little family. In the catering business, perhaps?"

"I have an appointment tomorrow with the bank. About a loan. I'm going to open my own chocolate shop."

"Well, well," said Charlotte. "There's just no end to it."

"So, that appeals to you, does it?" asked Françoise. "The life of a shopkeeper?"

"Not so much a shopkeeper, mother. More an artist."

The Daalder Quartet burst out laughing.

"What's so funny about that?" asked Joop angrily.

"Oh, oh, oh," said Laurens, as he knocked his pipe against the ashtray to empty it. "Our little Michelangelo is going to have a go at chocolates. How about it, girls, shall we have another go at Schubert?"

Joop stood up. "Come on, Emma. We're leaving."

He might be a swan, but these ducks and their rude cackling were still dangerous to his peace of mind. It was better to have as little to do with them as possible.

No, he received so much more warmth and support from Emma and her mother.

That same evening, Hannie sat for hours behind the sewing machine. For Joop's appointment with the bank, she had taken one of the suits of her deceased husband out of the cupboard. The sleeves and trouser legs were too long and had to be shortened. Because the material was so sturdy, one needle after another broke, but she hadn't complained once.

Later in the evening, Joop stood in front of the mirror. Young man in suit. He would have preferred to be wearing a chef's apron, but he had to be patient for a while longer.

As Hannie plucked a thread off the jacket, Emma kneeled down to shake a trouser leg so it would fall more handsomely over the shoe. Then the two women stepped back to take stock.

In the mirror, Joop saw how the mother nodded approvingly and the daughter beamed.

A Charming Plan

"Let me first emphasize what a charming plan I think it is," said Mr. Ter Horst of the Dutch Retailers' Bank. "Thank you."

"There's no lack of enthusiasm. On the contrary."

Joop nodded happily and felt the knot of his tie press against his Adam's apple.

Years later, he still cringed at how incredibly naïve he was at that moment not to have immediately heard the enormous "but" through the banker's compliments.

What followed was a long enumeration of all the flaws in his draft business plan.

Mr. Daalder hadn't done enough market research. Was there really any need for a new chocolate shop in Holland? The Dutch simply weren't connoisseurs. Yes, there were always exceptions, but they had their favorite addresses already. The less fussy people—which was to say, almost everybody—could satisfy their needs at the better bakeries or sweet shops. Would it not be wiser therefore to offer a wider selection, like in those shops? Because you had to be pretty damned good to venture onto the market with just one product.

And Mr. Daalder's aim—"to awaken the Dutch people's sense of taste"—however commendable, showed little sense of reality. The bank understood "aim" to be something much more trivial: how the aspiring businessman intended to pay back his debt, and within what time frame. Nothing more, but certainly nothing less.

Wasn't Mr. Daalder perhaps a trifle too young, to take on the heavy responsibility of entrepreneurship? Would it not be more advisable to first serve under an established chocolatier—or in a better bakery if need be, or even in the sweets section of a large department store, if need be—so as to learn the tricks of the trade? If Mr. Daalder were to come back in about five years with a more carefully worked out plan (five years? exclaimed Joop. Oh yes, Mr. Daalder, but you're young, so Father Time is still on your side), in about five years, then the bank would certainly be willing to reconsider his plan. But for now, Mr. Ter Horst thought it inappropriate for the bank to provide a loan.

"Well, that's clear then," said Joop. "I'll just go to another bank."

"Of course, you're perfectly entitled to do that," said the banker, amiably, "but I give you little chance of success."

What a coward, thought Joop, when he was back at the bus stop and loosening his tie.

He submitted his plan unchanged to another bank. He received a letter saying a subsequent meeting was not considered opportune.

A third bank was equally uninterested.

In a last desperate attempt to obtain start-up capital, he approached his father. Would he be prepared to advance him his inheritance—that is, one third of the estate—so that he could negotiate a mortgage. He would be able to pay back the lost interest to his father—or else to his sisters—with the profits from the chocolate shop.

Joop had seldom seen his father so angry. To carve up a beautiful estate, with such a rich history, after it had been kept together with such great effort through the centuries, and that, for the sake of a glorified sweets shop! How dare he!

He should have known. It was taboo within the family to talk of the estate in terms of money or inheritance. This had to do with Uncle Albert, who still resented Laurens for having bought him out for a song when their parents' inheritance had been divided. Joop foresaw that history would repeat itself in his generation. One of his sisters — he guessed Charlotte — would take on the noble task of conserving the estate, and he and Rosalinde would naturally be prepared to renounce their inheritances. After all, as an aristocrat with a sense of history, one was supposed to stand above vulgar money matters. So he couldn't rely on building his chocolate shop on an inheritance — either now or in the future.

Joop came to the depressing realization that he had already been back in Holland for longer than his apprenticeship in France had lasted. Apart from the course material for obtaining his tradesman's diploma and an information package about the necessary licenses that he had recently received in the mail, he hadn't come one step closer to setting up his own chocolate shop. Emma didn't complain aloud yet, but her belly was like a silent reproach, and growing bigger by the day. *Hey, breadwinner, let's get moving.*

One evening she came and sat beside him on the couch. After first putting an arm around him, she broached the painful subject ever so carefully, afraid as she was of hurting him.

Perhaps (pat) — it was only an idea (pat, pat) — perhaps it wasn't such a bad idea after all to follow the banker's advice and to work first for an established chocolatier (pat). To learn more about the business side of the métier, to which, at Monsieur Sorel's — absolutely rightly, of course! — no attention had been paid. The aim, naturally, was still to start his own chocolate shop as soon as possible (pat, pat). He mustn't forget that his dream was also her dream. And she was sure those banker's "five years" could be shortened a bit, there was no doubt about it! (Now, he was even given a kiss.)

"Joop?"

She had long convinced him, but he didn't want to admit to it. He stood up, mumbling something about taking a shower, and walked out of the room.

The Job Interview

I n his search for work, Joop's choice fell automatically on Otto Vermeulen and Son, "the famous chocolatiers from Baarn," because they were generally considered to be the absolute summit of chocolate making in Holland. Not that he was terribly impressed. By the same token, the Vaalserberg, near Maastricht, with all of its three hundred meters, was the absolute summit of geographical Holland.

Joop had become acquainted with the firm's work long ago, in the form of Rosalinde's extra-bitter chocolate *R*. And, it had to be said, despite the little scented violets and the profusion of whole hazelnuts, he owed his first positive experience with chocolate to the craftsmanship of this Otto Vermeulen.

Joop ignored Emma's advice to first check if they needed an extra hand. It might sound arrogant, but they would be stupid not to hire someone of his caliber right away. And no polite telephone call, formal letter, or introductory meeting could ever compare to the persuasive powers of a homemade chocolate. Through Monsieur Sorel, he ordered a large slab of chocolate, vanilla pods, a bottle of almond liqueur, and various other ingredients. It cost a pretty penny, but fortunately Emma was willing to dip into her savings for it ("Your dream is my dream").

He toiled away in the kitchen till all hours of the night, complaining about the inferior equipment, about the bottoms of

the saucepans being too thin, and about his own cooking ther-
mometer that he had brought with him from France but that
seemed to react more slowly here. Was it because of a different
air pressure at sea level, or did it just seem slower because of
his impatience? And for whom was he sweating away in the
kitchen anyway? For a bunch of Dutch chocolate boors who
probably weren't even worth it! According to Sorel, it was
better to say good-bye to your chocolates the moment you had
finished making them, but that was precisely the problem now.
He still had to apply for a job with them. God how he hated
being dependent on someone else's opinion.

In the end, he managed to produce three acceptable chocolates, of which two were intended for the Vermeulens and one
disappeared into his mouth as a sample. Although he could
taste all the imperfections of Hannie's kitchen as well as all his
own doubts and frustrations, he noticed at the same time that
he hadn't forgotten his craft yet.

By now it was three o'clock in the morning. After working
for so long and with such deep concentration, Joop had withdrawn totally into himself, so that Emma scared the wits out of
him when she appeared in the doorway. She had a surprise for
him, which she now pulled out from behind her back. It was a
fancy little box of shiny gold cardboard, designed especially
for his interview chocolates. All those hours that he was in the
kitchen, she had been working on it in the dining room. She
proudly showed him the ingenious lid, which she had thought
up all by herself. Just a gentle pinch of the box and it jumped
open. And you only had to prod the lid gently with two fingers
and it shut again. Nice, eh? She let the box jump open again,
this time to show him the red velvet-lined interior, the edges of
which she had trimmed with gold thread. And? Did he think it
was pretty enough?

Pretty enough? Joop exploded. What kind of nonsense

was that? Surely she knew how he detested ribbons, bows, and frills. All they did was to distract. Good chocolates spoke for themselves.

Emma turned pale, dropped the little box, and ran upstairs to her room.

After his adrenaline level had fallen and he had caught his breath, Joop regretted his fit of anger. Sighing deeply, he went upstairs to reconcile.

Emma was lying on the bed, her face pushed deeply into the pillow.

"Sorry I was so sharp," he said. "But this is a matter of principle. It's a beautiful little box, but . . . Emma, where are you going?"

She had stood up abruptly and was walking past him out of the room.

He followed her downstairs, where she sat down at the dining-room table again. Lips pursed, she folded a new box in no time, this time from gray cardboard and with no decorations.

"Satisfied?"

The box bounced over the table toward him.

"Yes," he said timidly. "Really. That does much more justice to my chocolates. Thanks a lot."

He walked around the table to give her a kiss, but she shielded her face with her arms.

The next day, Joop took the train to Baarn to present his chocolates to the Vermeulens. When he saw the shop window, he had doubts about the whole undertaking. The gaudy little candy violets on the chocolate letter from years ago had been no accident, and Emma's fancy little box would have been perfect among all the crystal and tinsel. On a slowly turning tray, the same pretentious chocolates kept passing by ad nauseam. Milk chocolate and white chocolate were present in abysmal abundance, and any bitter chocolate was adorned with bilious green or pale pink icing, which had been piped over the top in thin little stripes or sumptuous curls. Joop also spotted the cherry-brandy chocolates he hated so much.

The shop window also served as a trophy cabinet. On a large tray lay the many Gold, Silver, and Bronze Chocolates the Vermeulens had won over the years at the national chocolatemakers' convention held in the hotel-restaurant The Seventh Dune at Egmond aan Zee, as the certificate next to it announced. There was a framed photograph of Otto Vermeulen standing as proud as a peacock next to a laughing Cary Grant. But the pièce de résistance lay on a little pillar draped in purple velvet: the only medal ever won by a Dutch chocolatier at the prestigious *Wiener Pralinenwoche*, the Viennese Chocolate Week. It was only a Bronze and already eight years old, but still.

This was a temporary solution, Joop reminded himself, to quell his urge to flee. He took a few deep breaths, then went inside. Sniffing around, he smelled not only the usual cream fillings and liqueurs through the chocolate, but also the perfume of the many posh ladies who were sitting in the tearoom enjoying their Vermeulen chocolates.

"Sir!" resounded a female voice, sternly. "Can I help you with something?"

"I'm here to see Mr. Vermeulen," replied Joop coolly. Anyone who could take on Frédérique could take on any unfriendly chocolate saleswoman.

"Father or son?"

"Oh, the father will do. But both are okay, too."

"Oh, so you don't have an appointment. May I ask what it's about?"

"I'm a chocolatier, and I've come to offer my services to the Vermeulens."

"Then you'll have to write them a letter first."

Joop put the box of chocolates down on the counter. "Just give them this. They'll want to speak to me."

Father and son, Otto and Erik Vermeulen, were sitting together in the office when there was a knock at the door.

"Enter!" they cried in unison.

It was Anja, coming to tell them there was a young man in the shop who wanted to work for them. And he had brought something with him too. Homemade, she mustn't forget to add.

The old Vermeulen picked up the box and carefully lifted the lid.

"Hmm," he said. "The presentation is dismal, but at least he's used good chocolate. Let him come in for a moment."

"Are you sure about that, Pa?"

"Who knows, it might save us an advertisement."

A moment later, Joop was shown in by Anja.

"I see you haven't tasted my chocolates yet," he said, shaking their hands.

"Very astute of you, my friend," sniggered Erik.

He looked like a frat boy, with his straight blond hair and reddish face. His father, sitting slumped back in his chair, resembled an old patriarch of the walrus kind, who demonstrated his power primarily by being fat and sluggish. How different from Jérôme Sorel!

"So," said the old Vermeulen. "Start by telling us about your training."

Enthusiastically, Joop began to talk about the apprenticeship he had done in France, but he was immediately interrupted by the father.

"Sorel? Never heard of him."

"And that's a bad sign," added his son, lighting a thin cigar in the meantime. "It's a small world. The people who really count always run into each other at the international festivals and competitions."

"It's against Monsieur Sorel's principles to compete."

"That's a good one!" cried Erik, sucking on his cigar and blowing a series of little circles.

Joop looked at him disapprovingly. "Taste first, then judge, I would say."

"And he's cheeky, too. Did you hear that, Pa?"

The father gestured to his son to keep quiet. Then he turned to Joop.

"What we think of your chocolates doesn't really matter."

"I don't quite understand."

"What matters is what the customer thinks of them."

"The customer?" said Joop, horrified. "Are you serious?"

"Oh, I get it," said Erik. "First the competitions are beneath monsieur, and now the customers are no good, either."

"Just smoke your cigar, boy. And you, Joop, come with me for a moment."

The old Vermeulen picked up the box of chocolates and walked to the tearoom with Joop. Nodding to the left and right, he greeted various ladies before stopping in front of a table where a woman sat with her daughter of about twelve, who was dressed in riding attire. They were drinking tea and lemon, and between them was a little plate with crescent-shaped chocolates, which they nibbled on nonstop.

"And a good morning to you, ladies!" said Otto Vermeulen cheerfully. "I'd like to introduce you to Joop Daalder. He wants to come and work for us, and to prove his skills, has made two chocolates. Would you dare to sample them for me?"

"Oh, what fun!"

The woman took the little box and carefully lifted the lid. "There's no poison in them, I hope? Ha ha ha!"

She rooted out the first chocolate then passed the box to her daughter.

"Hmm," she said, after the first bite. "Yes, yes." She put the rest of the chocolate into her mouth, looking obliquely upward to concentrate better on the taste. "Not bad at all," was her final assessment, after she had swallowed the last morsel and wiped her mouth with a serviette. "I miss the usual Vermeulen touch, but there is hope yet, I'd say. Anne-Marie, what do you think?"

Her daughter made a face as she put her half-eaten chocolate back into the box. "Just give me a *cédille au Grand Marnier*," she said, grabbing the last one off the plate.

"Ah, come on, dear, now you're not being nice. The poor boy has worked very hard at this! You will hire him, won't you?"

"If you can wait five more minutes, madame, I'll come and tell you."

"Oh, oh, Mr. Vermeulen! You're making it all very exciting, you know."

He snapped his fingers to indicate that Joop should follow him back to the office.

"A score of one out of two," reported Otto to his son.

"Ouch," said Erik. "Not so good, eh, fellow?"

"Oh, such remarks don't mean a thing to me. I know perfectly well when my chocolates are good or bad."

"Then I'm afraid the point of our visit to the tearoom has completely escaped you. My patience is starting to run out, young man."

"It's about time, Pa."

"Be quiet for a moment, Erik. What I totally miss in you, Joop, is respect. Respect for me and my son, but especially respect for the customer—because a Vermeulen chocolate is nothing other than a congealed moment in a dialogue. Oh yes, a dialogue, one that has been going on for generations between our family and our customers. We offer, the customer comments; we modify, the customer comments again. And it's been that way for more than a hundred and fifty years. I want you to let that sink in, boy. A dialogue that has lasted more than a hundred and fifty years! And then you brazenly walk in here thinking you can interrupt us just like that with your home-made little statement? Where on earth did you get the nerve?"

Joop folded his arms and said nothing.

"The idea, I would say, is that you apologize now," said Erik.

"Oh really? Well, sorry then."

Shaking his head, the old Vermeulen made a note in his diary. "I'll expect you here on Monday morning at eight o'clock."

"What?" said Erik, who was as surprised as Joop.

"And there's a three-month probation period."

"But Pa—"

"Those chocolates of yours didn't look bad at all, we happen to be short of personnel, and you'll save us the trouble of interviewing. But that attitude of yours sure needs to be worked on. Respect, eh, boy. That's what it's all about."

"Yes, Mr. Vermeulen."

"But Pa—"

"End of discussion. I suggest you give him a tour of the kitchen. I'm going to the tearoom to inform that lady and her daughter of my decision."

"A word of warning, Daalder," said Erik, as he walked to the kitchen with Joop. "My father is nicer than I am."

For the hundred-thousandth time that day, Emma looked out the window. And, yes, there he was at last! But, oh dear! Judging by his gloomy expression the interview had not gone well. She walked to the front door ready to comfort him, and so was totally surprised to hear he had been hired.

"Oh Joop! I'm so proud of you!"

As she threw her arms around him, Joop stared sullenly in front of him. Of course he had been hired. If this was enough to make her proud, what was her pride worth?

Requiem for a Pear

T hey moved to Baarn, where they rented an apartment above a florist's shop that was within walking distance of the Vermeulens' chocolate shop. Emma brought in a few girlfriends to help paint and decorate the baby's room. That way Joop could concentrate fully on his work.

He had little to do with Otto Vermeulen. Now and again, the old boss came into the kitchen to show an important customer around or to consult with his son, but most of the time he spent in his office phoning or in the tearoom delighting the ladies with charming little compliments.

"Oh, Mr. Vermeulen!" they would moan with their mouths full of chocolate, quickly grabbing a serviette to prevent brown drool from dribbling down their chins.

It was Erik who managed the kitchen on a daily basis. In addition to Joop, there were two trainees from the confectioners' school, Flip and Rogier, who were usually deployed for the rougher stirring, beating, and chopping work.

From day one, it was clear how differently they worked here. According to Sorel, it was essential when making chocolates to take the time for everything. But there was no time here at Vermeulens'. Not only did the busy shop require a constant supply of fresh chocolates, but orders from outside also came pouring in all day. Suddenly a few *grands plateaux* would have to be prepared for a wedding, or a thousand cream-filled chocolate truffles churned out for a surgeons' conference in Amsterdam.

Joop was forever at odds with his boss. Erik thought he worked too slowly, but for Joop, working faster was synonymous with skimping. He quoted Sorel, who had taught him that you had to caress chocolate lovingly, to slowly get it in the mood, and never to force it.

"Hey, you dirty rascal, how about saving that sort of stuff for your wife," said Erik, to the great amusement of the two trainees. "Here, it's just upsa-daisy!" And he turned the heat up under the pan.

When Joop mentioned Sorel again the next time he was given an instruction, Erik exploded.

"Your yakking on about that French master is starting to bore me. And don't think you're original either. All those young chefs and patissiers who've done a month's training somewhere in France come back with the same blah-blah. They've all done an apprenticeship under some culinary god. They all act as if French cooking is their personal discovery. And then all that griping about how terrible it is here in Holland. And that laughing about what country bumpkins we are. Okay, fellows, I say in turn. If you know everything so well, prove it. Open your own restaurant or patisserie or chocolate shop, and make it run at a profit. Then we'll talk again."

From that moment on, Joop wisely restrained himself. But it still hurt him to see how lovelessly the chocolates were treated, and to have no choice but to be an accessory to it. One day he even discovered that they fiddled with the ingredients. Those *cédilles au Grand Marnier,* for instance, the crescents of orange peel coated with a thin layer of chocolate that that snobby little Amazon had been so crazy about—not a single drop of Grand Marnier went into them. For a number of years now, the Vermeulens had been using a much cheaper Spanish orange liqueur.

"But that's downright deception of the public, isn't it?"

"We've never had a single complaint," said Erik.

Smiling sardonically, he watched as his employee dejectedly dragged the pieces of orange peel through the bath of fake Grand Marnier.

"You should see entrepreneurship as an Olympic hurdles race," he explained in the meantime to Flip and Rogier. "The trick is to only just get over the hurdle, to only just keep the customer happy. Our holy Joop here sees this differently, of course. He wants to jump over the hurdles as high and beautifully as possible, preferably with a triple backward somersault. That might be fine and dandy if you work in a little medieval village somewhere in France, where time has almost stood still and customers will show up no matter what, but as a modern business we can't allow ourselves to work like that. If we did, the competition would overtake us in no time."

Joop came home utterly depressed that evening.

"Your time will come," said Emma with a sigh. By now she was in her ninth month and no longer had the energy to cheer him up. Supporting her back with her hand, she grimaced with pain as she slowly lowered herself onto the couch. "Go ahead and call Monsieur Sorel if you like."

Lately they had mountain-high telephone bills. As an antidote for the humiliations he had to undergo every day in the Vermeulens' kitchen, Joop had a long conversation with his master almost every evening.

"Oh oh, my boy," said Sorel, after he heard the story about the Grand Marnier and the hurdles race. "Now that is the intensely cynical ideal of the capitalist: 'Just good enough.' In my dictionary, it's called: 'As bad as possible.' It makes me so sad, Joop, so sad. And it's getting worse all the time, now that the Americans call the shots everywhere.

"I'll tell you a tragic story about a pear from my childhood, the Duchesse de Quimper. A fruit so delicate it didn't even melt on your tongue but instead seemed to evaporate. And with a taste, boy, a taste . . . It was only available for one week a year, two at most, or sometimes not at all, for it was not uncommon for the whole harvest to fail. The tree was prone to fire blight and other diseases, and had to be disbudded at exactly the right moment using an extremely specific technique. The blossom was sensitive to frost, rain, and wind. And if pears finally did hang from the branches—sometimes more, sometimes less—you could only pick them if they were absolutely ripe, because if they were taken from the tree too soon they would remain bitter and sour. They were too delicate to be piled up, and were highly perishable, so they could never be transported very far and had to be sold as quickly as possible. In short, a fussy, fickle pear. But also a pear to love.

"Then the dwarf fruit trees came on the scene, which were picked so easily and yielded twice as much fruit per tree, and therefore twice as much money. Orchard after orchard of the finicky Duchesse de Quimper has been chopped down over the years to make way for these indestructible dwarf trees, which grow rock-hard pears that can be picked rock-hard and that land in the shop rock-hard. Whoever has the patience can forever turn them over on the fruit dish at home. With a bit of luck, after a week or two, they will be more or less ripe on one side. And for whoever doesn't have the patience? Oh well, he'll still have a pear-shaped piece of fruit in his hand that tastes like an apple. Pretty good, wouldn't you say? They're available everywhere and at all times of the year, these just-good-enough pears, and they're not expensive. In economic terms, a huge success story.

"And the Duchesse? Nowadays, you occasionally see a lone tree near a farmhouse, completely gone wild, with under-sized, worm-ridden fruit that rots away before it ripens — because the farmer is too old to climb the ladder and trim the tree properly, and his children have no time for it anymore. They prefer to sit in the cinema and look at the latest Holly-wood junk. Before long, there won't be anyone left who knows how to do it. Exit Duchesse de Quimper! Forever!"

It fell silent on the other end of the line, and Joop thought he heard a sob.

"Monsieur Sorel?"

"And then those bastards still have the gall to claim that the free market guarantees quality! But please, let's change the subject, dear boy. This is too depressing. How is your charming wife doing?"

"Fine," said Joop, looking over his shoulder at the cum-bersome mother animal snoring on the couch. "Just fine."

Marcel's Birth

The most beautiful moment of his life? Without a doubt, the birth of his son.

That is what Wouter said to Joop by way of preparing him for the overwhelming experience that lay ahead of him. And although his brother-in-law was known as a sober-minded scientist, Joop actually saw him wipe away a tear.

"And the birth of my daughter was also very beautiful," he added quickly. "But then I had experienced everything once already."

During the week that Emma was due, there was a constant coming and going of all kinds of women in their apartment. In addition to Emma's mother and her best friend Ingrid, there were the professional caregivers: the obstetrician, the midwife, the district nurse, the maternity assistant—Joop constantly confused their jobs and their faces, and didn't even know exactly how many people were involved.

"You must be the wet nurse," he said, opening the door to one of them.

"Well, I hope not." With a condescending snort of laughter, the woman walked past him to the kitchen.

One Saturday afternoon, after the contractions had reached a peak and Joop had worked through the telephone list, the different ladies arrived in quick succession, then convened secretively in the bedroom. Joop was left alone in the living room. Witnessing such a delivery was nothing for him, Emma had said, and he had agreed wholeheartedly. As he sat on the couch staring blankly into space, he heard her groaning softly and the others prompting her loudly. Hours passed, during which the bedroom door occasionally opened and one of the women slipped out to fetch something from the kitchen or bedroom. Taps were turned on and off, buckets were filled and emptied, the toilet was constantly being flushed. Ingrid came to ask him where she could find clean washcloths ("Never mind; I'll find them"), and whispered consultations were held in the hallway. He was about to stretch out on the couch when Elske (the midwife? the attendant physician?) came and sat down beside him, slurping on a cup of instant bouillon.

"So, young man. Are you ready for it?"

After the obligatory chat, he must have dozed off, because the next moment his arm was being tugged and Hannie was leaning over him.

She was crying.

"What's the matter?" he asked, startled.

"What's the matter? You have a son!"

Sure enough, he now heard a baby crying.

Amid a circle of women, Emma was sitting straight up in bed, deathly pale and soaked with perspiration but radiant, with a bundle in her arms of white toweling concealing something deep pink. All the women looked in Joop's direction, happily anticipating his reaction.

"Come on, girls," whispered Elske, "make room for the proud father."

"Well," he said, sitting down on the edge of the bed and looking more closely at the crinkled little face with its sticky black hairs. "So that's him."

When the fatherly emotions they were hoping for failed to materialize, the women decided Joop was so overwhelmed by emotions that he simply couldn't express them. This conclusion enabled them to be deeply moved even when he accepted the little bundle from Emma without visible enthusiasm.

Joop would have liked to call him Jérôme, a suggestion that was resolutely dismissed by Emma. Startled by her own adamancy, she had gone out of her way to explain that her negative reaction had to do only with the name, not the person. But Joop wasn't angry and didn't insist. After all, the deal was: the baby was for her and the chocolates were for him. So it was better for him not to get too involved in the name giving. Besides, there was the danger that Sorel, who was anything but a child lover, might be insulted by a little namesake.

In the end, Emma chose the name Marcel Anton Daalder—Anton after her deceased father, of course, and Marcel . . . ? Well, there was a good story behind that, as she would tell everyone who came to admire the baby, each time anew. It went like this: When she had worked in Avallon as an au-pair, she had often taken little Marie-Louise Bouchard to the park. There, she sometimes saw a nice young Frenchman sitting on a bench, a shy, sensitive type. She had imagined he was a poet, who came to the park for inspiration. She had even thought up a name for him: Marcel. When, one day, she finally gathered up the courage to start a conversation with him, he turned out not to be a French poet at all but a Dutch apprentice chocolatier, and . . . Exactly! It was Joop! And the funny thing was that Joop had also thought up a story around her and had given her a name too: Nathalie.

"So if it had been a girl, would you have called her Nathalie?" asked one clever visitor.

Emma looked at Joop questioningly, her radiant smile now somewhat hesitant.

"Who knows," he said diplomatically.

But everyone sensed what the real answer was.

After that, Emma left the Nathalie part out of the story—which she sometimes had to tell three times a day during the first weeks after the delivery. Her friends and family lined up to admire the little wonder, including the uncles and aunts on her father's side.

Joop's contribution to the family visits stood in stark contrast to this.

On the third day, Peter and Corinne came to visit.

"Who would have ever imagined it!" chuckled his friend. "Papa Joop!"

When Corinne saw the little one lying in the crib, she cooed with emotion. "Oh, what a little mite, oh, what a little darling. Oh, Pete, shall we, too?"

"Well, dear. I would say let's have a cup of tea first."

Rosalinde and Wouter also came to visit during the first week. While their two children obediently started to play on the floor, the dreaded garbage bag full of baby clothes that Rosalinde had been going on and on about was emptied out over the maternity bed. The pieces of clothing were held up one by one and praised at length, before being neatly folded and landing on one of the countless piles that were forming on the bed.

"Oh, what a darling little shirt! Look, Joop."

Meanwhile, Wouter bent over the crib.

"A newborn has got to be the most beautiful thing there is," he whispered. Again, Joop saw his eyes glisten.

The most beautiful thing there was? A ripe apricot perhaps, or Madame Sorel's roast leg of lamb with garlic and rosemary, or perhaps Emma swimming naked like a forest nymph in a trout pond. But a baby like this?

Joop's lack of enthusiasm was becoming conspicuous, but

when one of Emma's girlfriends said something to her about it, she immediately became defensive. Joop wasn't happy at his work, which was why he was so preoccupied lately. And he just happened to be a special sort of person, a refined chocolatier, an artist. And artists just happened to react differently than other people to the normal things in life.

As mild as she was about Joop, she was incensed about the fact that his parents and Charlotte only came to see little Marcel after three whole weeks. The gift Charlotte had brought for her nephew was a trinket from a Chinese shop worth no more than a guilder, a poorly finished wooden cart with the sharp heads of little nails protruding on all sides. Joop's parents' gift was a larger model of the same cart, and already fell apart while it was being unwrapped.

Now that his parents had been plucked out of their natural environment, it struck Joop more than ever how much they had aged. Every time Laurens lifted the traditional celebratory rusk with aniseed sprinkles toward his mouth with a trembling hand, dozens of the sprinkles bounced over the floor. And because of the top dentures that had recently been put in his mouth, he had great difficulty getting the rusk down.

"Just leave it, silly."

His mouth full, he wasn't able to respond to his wife, but his eyes shot fire.

"So, shall I hold the baby for a moment?" asked Françoise. "Then I think it's about time for us to leave."

To Emma's great delight, Joop finally seemed to become enthusiastic about fatherhood the next day, when an enormous package arrived from France. Together on the bed, they studied the impressive array of stamps glued all over it. On that alone, the Sorels had spent more than Joop's parents on their whole gift!

Laughing, Emma pushed the package into his hands. He should open this one.

"Look how beautiful!" he called.

Triumphantly, he held up a giant teddy bear. How charmingly it grumbled when tilted, just like a Frenchman who was contented with his meal. And then those little overalls that Madame Sorel had dressed it in just for fun, which were really meant for the baby. What quality! And such a handsome design! No, you wouldn't readily find something like that here in Holland.

But the excitement about the gift was short-lived.

To Joop's disgruntlement, within a few weeks Marcel had already outgrown the overalls, evidently designed for the delicately built French baby, not for a Dutch milk guzzler.

And the more time passed, the more somber he became.

Since the delivery Emma only halfheartedly listened to his stories about the problems at his work, while she listened twice as hard to every little peep from the baby room. To make matters worse, lately her cooking wasn't up to par. Everything tasted bland, as if she empathized so strongly with the baby's world that she too would have preferred to eat baby food. When he complained about this one day, she explained that the family doctor had told her to use fewer herbs and no onions and garlic because of breastfeeding. Otherwise Marcel would have even more problems with colic.

So that was it. That damn milk!

That horrible white liquid that had made Emma's beautiful breasts swell so badly that they hurt and had become off bounds for him. That liquid, which sometimes dripped out of her nipples or even shot out in little jets in all directions, long before the baby had started to suckle. And now that same milk was dictating their menu!

A chronic shortage of sleep didn't make his mood any

better. At least three or four times a night, he would hear Emma get up with a tired sigh and shuffle off to the baby room in her slippers. *Click, clack, click, clack.* And there he was, wide awake again. The grace that had once allowed him to imagine her as French had completely disappeared.

No, he had fallen into the trap.

Like a mythical Lorelei, Emma had risen up out of the dark water in the Morvan to lure him to his fate. He only just managed not to say it aloud. He had promised Emma never to blame her for having left France on her account. But perhaps he didn't have to blame her for anything anymore. He had Marcel for that now.

Yes, it was all his fault. Marcel had driven them out of paradise. Marcel had changed the graceful wood nymph into a cumbersome mother animal, and condemned his father to hard labor in the infernal kitchen of Erik Vermeulen.

Time passed. Joop wasted away; the little one thrived. He sat up straight, got his first teeth, and began to crawl. He stood up, took his first steps, and started to babble. But that was about all, thought Joop, who had noticed painfully few signs of sensitivity or intelligence in the year and a half that he had been observing his son.

The child had hopelessly clumsy coordination. He simply knocked things (or other children) over or pushed them out of the way with his little arms, without it ever occurring to him that he might walk around them instead. Straight ahead! That seemed to be the only instruction his brain was able to pass on to his limbs. And if the obstacle was too big, a temper tantrum ensured that Mummy dear came running. That was all he needed to get a handle on the world.

It was sometimes said there is nothing like a shared meal to bring people together. For thousands of years, kings, merchants, and peacemakers had gratefully made use of this fact.

But from his earliest childhood, Joop had also experienced the opposite. Nothing creates greater distance than the sight of a fellow human being feasting on something you can barely get down your throat. The Daalder Quartet, for instance, with their mugs of fresh cow's milk. And now, his son, with his vegetable mashes and banana mushes. To make things worse, he ate according to the principle: for every three spoonfuls that went into his mouth, two came back out again. It was such a repulsive sight that in a perverse sort of way, Joop enjoyed it, the way some people watch horror films for pleasure. But it didn't make him any happier.

One rainy evening in September, he came home after a particularly rough day at work. Two new trainees from the confectioners' school had started that morning, so that Erik had worked harder than usual at making a fool of him all day. Emma was standing in the kitchen preparing a sickly mush for Marcel. Sighing, Joop walked through to the living room. There he encountered a gruesome battlefield.

The floor was littered with little pieces of foam rubber originating from the four ripped-off and dissected limbs of Jérôme, as they had named the beautiful teddy bear Marcel had received from the Sorels. The decimated head and torso had been tossed into a corner. Amid the remains of his victim, without the slightest sign of remorse, the culprit was now cheerfully playing with a toy car.

"Goddamn it! You bastard!"

Joop swept his son up off the floor and lifted him high into the air. But he was not violent by nature and came no further than gently shaking him.

Marcel hesitated. He loved flying through the air, but the quivering, crimson face just beneath him didn't look good. Adding up the contradictory sensations, he didn't know whether to rate the total experience with a plus or a minus.

Until his mother came storming in.

"Joop, control yourself!"

So it was a minus.

Marcel started screaming.

"Have you gone completely mad? And all that for a stupid bear!"

Joop carefully put the crying child back on the floor and walked out of the room.

As Emma picked up her little child to comfort him, the front door slammed shut.

The Golden Chocolate

There were men who abandoned their wife and child from one moment to the next ("Just buying cigarettes"). Near the station, he was tempted. But where should he go? Back to Avallon? No, Monsieur Sorel wasn't up to taking him under his wing again. Besides, Joop realized he had left his wallet at home.

Before he knew what he was doing, he had walked all the way back to the detested chocolate shop. By this time, the cleaners had already closed the shop and gone home, but the tray with decorated chocolates was still turning gaily in the shop window. Two spotlights were also still burning, one aimed at the medal from Vienna (now ten years old!), the other at the plate with the celebrated chocolates from Egmond.

Joop suddenly had an idea.

He would compete for that year's Golden Chocolate. Why not? As far as he knew, it was an open competition, the only condition for participation being that you had to be employed in a chocolate shop, patisserie, or restaurant. That he hadn't participated before was because of Sorel's principled objections to such competitions. The greatest triumph already took place in one's own kitchen, and there was nothing that a prize could really add to that. But it was easy for Sorel to talk. Joop didn't have his own kitchen in which to celebrate triumphs.

For more than two years now, he had been following someone else's stupid orders. Taunted every day by Erik Vermeulen, he longed for recognition.

When he came home, little Marcel was lying in his crib snoring like a prince. Emma had swept up and thrown out what was left of the bear, and was sitting on the couch reading the newspaper. Kissing her on the forehead, Joop apologized for his fit of anger. With surprise—and gratitude—his apologies were accepted.

Then he presented his plan to her.

Emma warned him not to expect too much from it.

"You and I know how good you are, but as you always say yourself, there's no room for new talent in the conservative world of chocolatiers."

She was right of course. The jury in Egmond not only served the established order, it was composed of it. Otto Vermeulen had sat in it often enough and Erik only the year before. Was it not a lost cause from the very outset?

The Golden Chocolate probably was. Joop was realistic enough to acknowledge that. But if this year's jury had any guts, then surely the Silver Chocolate was a serious possibility. God, would that ever surprise the Vermeulens! And with a Silver in his pocket (a Bronze was okay, too, or even an honorable mention, if need be), he would stand stronger when applying to the bank again for a loan. Banks loved achievements. All the more now that he was no longer an unemployed young idealist but a breadwinner, indeed, a father. Banks loved fathers.

After he had registered for the competition and paid a substantial registration fee, he received a fat envelope containing a confirmation of his participation, additional details, and a piece of cardboard with all kinds of flaps and dotted lines and the logo of the hotel-restaurant The Seventh Dune printed on the outside. He was to make twelve identical samples of the same chocolate, with a maximum weight of twenty-five grams each, and they had to be packaged in the enclosed official competition box.

Just as when he had made the interview chocolates for the Vermeulens, he ordered his chocolate and all the other ingredients from Monsieur Sorel, without daring to confess to him the despicable purpose for which they were intended. When he had received everything, he shoved all the hateful little milk pans and bottles and nipples into a corner of the counter and set to work. Already he felt better than he had for a long time, despite all the deficiencies of an ordinary kitchen. Better to be one's own boss in a deficient kitchen than someone else's slave in a well-equipped kitchen.

To attract attention amid the storm of chocolates at Egmond, Joop opted for simplicity. He conceived a specimen made of bitter chocolate and filled likewise with bitter chocolate, but of a slightly coarser texture, and with just a drop of *marc de Bourgogne* as the only added flavor. Sorel would be proud of him. But when he tasted the filling, he hesitated. Would a Dutch jury not be inclined to label such a simple chocolate as "superficial" or "predictable"? He decided to add more liqueur than he himself cared for, as a concession to Dutch taste, which found the combination of alcohol and chocolate "mature" and "distinguished." On the one hand, Joop was deeply ashamed. Bowing to potential criticism was a cardinal sin in Sorel's eyes. On the other hand, he had sold his soul to the devil anyway by participating in this competition, so he might as well do his utmost to win.

In the week before "Egmond," the old Vermeulen for once rolled up his sleeves and came to work in the kitchen again. Nowadays, he only dirtied his hands when there was a prize to be won. To build his little masterpieces, he naturally claimed the best place in the kitchen, along with the best equipment and everyone's attention. With the most horrid clichés, and sometimes with absolute nonsense, he played the wise old man, a perverse caricature of Jérôme Sorel. In previous years, Joop would have fumed, but now that he was taking part in Egmond himself, he almost pitied this inflated toad, who took himself so utterly seriously. As could be expected, he designed a chocolate as pompous as a Wagnerian opera, crammed with flavors and dramatic effects, with, at its center — the man just couldn't help himself — a whole hazelnut. "Dead wood," as Sorel would call it.

On the day of the competition — traditionally the third Sunday of October — Joop traveled by public transport to Egmond aan Zee with his box of twelve chocolates. From the bus stop he had to walk half a mile through the dunes along the private road of the hotel. His heart started beating faster when he recognized Erik's canary-yellow Porsche in the parking lot. The gray Volvo of the old Vermeulen was parked beside it. Joop felt just like Cinderella, showing up at the ball unexpectedly. In which case the two Vermeulens could play the roles of his jealous older sisters.

He joined the line of people standing at the hotel entrance. His fellow chocolatiers had dressed neatly in suits, and their wives had put on their fanciest dresses and covered themselves in jewels. Joop was almost sorry he hadn't let Emma come along. She would have outshone them all. To start with, she was fifteen years younger than most of the ladies standing here, but, more important, with her less flashy clothes she would have had that much more impact. Which was also what he hoped to achieve with his simple chocolates.

At the entrance, a lady in a pink suit handed him a list of participants. After every name was the number of the table to which the chocolates were to be taken.

This was the beginning of what he would later call "the Egmond nightmare": his name was not on the list.

Going against the flow of people, he tried to return to the woman at the entrance. He caught her attention by holding his box of chocolates up in the air and pointing to it wildly. She gestured to him to keep walking. He had no choice but to follow along behind a few other chocolatiers into the room with the numbered tables. Here, he accosted a woman in a yellow suit with a clipboard under her arm, who was walking back and forth between the various tables. Itching with impatience, she listened to his story, looking over her shoulder all the while to call visitors who had lost their way to attention.

"Hello, sir, madam, you have to go that way! I repeat: Will all those taking part in the competition hand their boxes in here. Will all the other guests be so kind as to proceed to the auditorium!" To Joop she said that if he wasn't on the list, he wasn't a competitor. "So you too, sir, to the auditorium, please!"

The lady in the pink suit, who in the mean time had moved from the front door to the entrance of the auditorium, couldn't make any sense of Joop's confused story.

"Please go in, sir. We're about to start."

The doors were closed behind him. There was nothing else for Joop to do but look for a place to sit. He found one, in the very back row. The bleached-blond woman seated next to him looked at the box of chocolates he was holding on his lap with surprise.

"They made a mistake," he whispered.

"I see," she said, nodding as if everything were clear now.

The opening words were spoken by the owner of the hotel-restaurant The Seventh Dune. He thanked the various sponsors, without whose generous contributions this twenty-fourth edition of the Golden Chocolate could never have taken place, along with the many volunteers who had been busy day and night to make this year's event another resounding success. It became a painfully long story, partly because the audience was so foolish as to clap at every opportunity.

In accordance with tradition, while the jury members were out tasting, one of the participating chocolatiers gave a lecture about a specific aspect of the métier. This year, Pepijn Verbeek, from the chocolate shop De Bonbonnière, in Groningen, had the honor. The lights in the auditorium were turned off for the slide show of his trip to Venezuela, where he had visited a few cacao plantations. Very fascinating. Beautiful country. Beautiful people, too. But very poor. On seeing the slide of the Indian girl with the shy laugh standing barefoot in front of her hut, a sigh of emotion rippled through the auditorium. Although Joop sighed about quite different things at that moment, squirmed restlessly in his chair, and didn't follow a word of the story, the Indian girl was still engraved in his memory years later. Whenever he imagined her, he felt the same knot in his stomach as he had felt then.

After the slide show, it was time. The floor was given to the jury chairman.

This year, too, the chocolates were of an exceptionally high quality, he announced, which certainly hadn't made the work of the jury members any easier (applause). Nonetheless, after much deliberation—oh, and tasting, of course (ha ha ha!)—they had come to a decision.

First, there was a long series of honorable mentions. Each time, a chocolatier came onstage—the one smiling radiantly, the other fighting disappointment. Each received a handshake from the jury chairman, a medal, a bunch of chrysanthemums, and a round of applause from the audience that sounded more bored each time.

After that, the Bronze Chocolate was awarded with a slightly longer story and a slightly larger bunch of flowers.

The same applied for the Silver, the color Joop had awarded himself in better times.

"And now, the moment I'm sure everyone has been waiting for. The winner of this twenty-fourth edition of the Golden Chocolate, for many years a prominent and inimitable chocolatier, and with his present entry—the *grande merveille de noisette*—as brilliant as ever, you've probably already guessed it: Otto Vermeulen!"

Joop had allowed for this possibility beforehand. Otto Vermeulen, as brilliant as ever. But under the present circumstances, to have to watch as his daily tormentor was fêted made his nightmare complete. The man received a standing ovation. Joop had no choice but to stand up too, but thank goodness he couldn't clap—because of the box of chocolates he was still holding in his hands.

When the ceremony was over, there were snacks and drinks in the foyer for the guests. Joop walked around in a complete daze. An expression of despair was carved in his features like a mask. When he saw the jury chairman standing alone for a moment, Joop accosted him. The man didn't know what he was talking about, and pointed out that it was improper to complain to a jury member right after the prize giving. The only person who had the patience to hear him out was the bleached-blond woman who had sat next to him in the auditorium, the wife of one of the chocolatiers who had received an honorable mention. She really found it very, very sad for him. Not that it would change anything for him, but if he liked, she would be happy to taste one of his chocolates. No? No, of course not, of course she understood.

The answer he was seeking came in the form of a hand landing firmly on his shoulder.

Erik Vermeulen.

"So, kid," he said. "You should read your contract more carefully. Ever heard of the competition clause?"

Erik had his coat on and was already walking toward the door. Joop ran after him to ask him for an explanation.

"Thank goodness a jury member-friend tipped us off," he said, as they walked across the parking lot together. "He thought it was strange that one of our employees had entered under his own name, but the organizing committee assumed you would have asked for our permission. No such luck. My father was furious. 'If you don't expel that upstart from the competition immediately, I'll withdraw my contribution.' Well, naturally, the choice was quickly made. But what a dirty rat you are, Daalder. We teach you the tricks of the trade and you go behind our backs to take part in Egmond. Not that your garbage would ever have won a prize, but you just don't get away with something like that!"

They were now standing beside Erik's Porsche and he was already inserting the key into the lock of the door.

"So you two knew all along," said Joop. "Why didn't you say anything?"

"Now wait a minute, mister! Who should have said what to whom here? If I had had my way, you would have been fired on the spot. But Pa is much too nice. Pa wanted to give you one last chance, but to teach you a lesson at the same time. 'We won't say anything,' he said. 'We won't spoil his fun. Let him come to Egmond with his homemade chocolates. He has to feel that he's done something wrong.' Now here's where I do agree with Pa. I want you to feel it, too."

Erik Vermeulen had opened the door of his car. He was about to step in when suddenly he made an unexpected turn.

The next moment, Joop was lying on the asphalt groaning with pain.

Erik had belted him in the stomach.

From close by, Joop heard an engine start up, followed by the sound of a cardboard box being crushed under a tire.

"And?" asked Emma.

Strangely hunched over, Joop stumbled into the living room, collapsed on the couch beside her, and burst into tears.

That night they made love for the first time in a long time. Joop took grateful advantage of the opportunity, though for Emma it was clearly more out of pity than because she really felt like it. But the pain in his stomach rivaled his excitement, and Emma seemed a bit too relaxed, the way she just lay there smiling at him encouragingly. It made him feel lonelier than ever.

Suddenly the body underneath him tensed.

Cries from the baby room.

Joop had barely rolled off her when Emma was already standing beside the bed with her nightgown on again.

For the sake of form, he shouted, "Damn it!" but actually he was relieved.

"Sorry, darling. To be continued later?"

She kissed him on the forehead and walked *clickety-clack* to the baby room.

Space

The period of despair came to an unexpected end. It began with a telephone call from Rosalinde at an ominously early hour of the day. Their father had died in his sleep that night, probably from a brain hemorrhage.

"Oh, Joop," said Emma, who had followed the conversation from a distance. She went to put her arms around him.

He didn't need to be comforted, but, so as not to hurt her feelings, he waited a few moments before extricating himself from her embrace.

When he had dressed and phoned to say he wasn't coming to work, he sat down to a large breakfast. It was nice not to have to hurry for a change. After a second cup of coffee, he left at his leisure in the direction of Swaanendal.

Following the initial numbness, the atmosphere there had now turned feverish with all the funeral arrangements. Charlotte and Rosalinde were busy discussing the text for the obituary. Evidently the few friends who had been informed had spread the news, for the telephone didn't stop ringing. The sisters took turns answering.

"Yes, thank you. Yes, completely unexpected. Yes . . . No, not at all, it's very nice of you to phone."

Françoise sat petrified in her chair. Without her eternal book, she looked strangely naked. The star of the show—as she called Laurens—had already been taken to the funeral home. She didn't go in for vigils and that kind of nonsense. Dead was dead and the sooner you got used to it, the better.

"Arranging the snacks. Isn't that something for you, Joop?" said Charlotte, with a cynical snicker.

"Come on," said Françoise, with the same snicker. "Let's keep it affordable!"

Joop was assigned another "dumb job"—filling out envelopes. To avoid duplication, he first had to make sense of his father's illegible handwriting and the many deletions in his three tattered address books.

When he arrived home late that evening, it turned out Emma had stayed up to comfort him after everything he had been through. She was amazed at his calmness. Perhaps the grief was very deep and still had to come out? She had adored her own father and had had to do without him from a young age, a loss that had shaped her life. It was not only difficult to imagine but it hurt her, too, to see Joop so unmoved. Did it really not affect him at all?

In the end, she felt angry, not at Joop but at the deceased. She had met Laurens a few times and had heard the stories about how it used to be at home. Joop's apathy was the ultimate proof of the lovelessness with which his father had raised him.

The day before the funeral, Joop struggled until late in the evening with the text for his speech. Emma was moved to tears as she watched him suffering at the dining-room table. He wasn't wearing shorts and knee stockings and he was drinking wine instead of lemonade, but aside from that, he looked just like a schoolboy driven to desperation by a difficult homework assignment.

He would be the third speaker, after his two sisters. If their Saint Nicholas verses were already worthy of inclusion in an anthology of contemporary Dutch poetry, what would that make their speeches tomorrow? Eloquent, sensitive, heartrending, you name it. And he had to add something to that, when his father's death barely affected him?

"As long as you say something, even if it is awkward," said Emma.

Dissatisfied with the weak, hypocritical story he had on paper, but too tipsy from the wine to keep working on it, Joop went to bed at one-thirty. For hours, he was haunted by bits and pieces of his speech, until it dawned upon him why he wasn't getting anywhere. Father duck was dead, whereas he was a swan. After this illuminating thought, he knew what he had to do the next day and fell into a deep sleep.

As he sat with his family in the black limousine that drove behind the hearse, and his sisters ran through the scenario once more, Joop announced that he had decided not to give a speech.

"Sure, take the easy way out!" cried Charlotte. "What an incredible coward you are!"

"You'll regret this for the rest of your life," added Rosalinde, more as a curse than a warning.

"Oh, don't mind him," said his mother, in a voice so cold and full of loathing that it sent shivers down Joop's spine.

But he braved the wrath of his family and stuck to his decision.

The weather was glorious. He couldn't have chosen a more beautiful day, remarked a few of the guests rather naughtily. A strangely festive atmosphere prevailed in the auditorium. The Daalders stood for beautiful music, so that despite their grief, a lot of people looked forward to what was coming. And so it became deathly still the moment Charlotte — thinner and paler than usual, as if she herself had just returned from the underworld — sat down behind her harpsichord, which had been brought to the funeral home for the occasion. After adjusting the stool to the right height, she turned and faced the public.

"According to the famous harpsichordist Manfred Scholl, there is no more comforting music than Prelude Number eighteen in G-sharp minor from the second part of *The Well-Tempered Clavier*, by Johann Sebastian Bach. This is what I am going to play for you now."

With the very first notes, handkerchiefs already appeared. And that was only the beginning. The music became only more beautiful. That Manfred Scholl was right! People reminded themselves to ask her exactly which prelude this was. There was nothing wrong with that, was there? So beautiful, so beautiful. And the fact that now and then a run wasn't perfect, well, on a day like this, it simply emphasized human failings. The playing of the mourning daughter was all the more moving because of it.

The final chord had barely died out when Charlotte took a few sheets of paper from behind her music books and walked with them to the lectern. What she had managed with the harpsichord, she now did all over again with words. The sentences were absolutely exquisite, one more beautiful than the next, like a series of sprightly Romanian girl gymnasts who, after the most daredevil of stunts, land perfectly on their feet and even manage a radiant smile as they do so. And it all seemed so effortless—the accuracy with which Charlotte portrayed her father. With the right dose of humor too. That she managed this, despite her grief, was nothing less than a miracle.

People felt sorry for Rosalinde, who now took her place behind the lectern. What on earth could this younger, less remarkable sister, who had always been overshadowed by her talented older sister, possibly add to this? That became clear soon enough. Her words were perhaps less poetic, less polished, but they came straight from the heart. While Charlotte had cast her light on the deceased so that everyone remembered him as clear as day, Rosalinde brought him back to life with her warmth. But why compare speeches or sisters anyway, when they complemented each other so beautifully? Laurens Daalder would have been proud of his two daughters. What a talented family, and what a beautiful funeral so far.

After Rosalinde sat down, the lectern remained unmanned for just a bit too long, causing some consternation in the auditorium. People looked at each other questioningly, their eyes as round as the two O's in Joop's name. It was Joop's turn now, wasn't it?

But, in the end, it was an older man who walked to the lectern. Oh dear, wasn't that Laurens's younger brother, who had gone into business and behaved so objectionably when Laurens had assumed responsibility for the estate? People braced themselves for what was to come.

After the soft, refined voices of the Daalder daughters, Albert's awkward bellowing came as quite a shock: "Farewell, Doctor Daalder, your dumb little brother salutes you!"

Oh, oh, oh, there was no hiding hard feelings here. And, by the way, it should have been "Professor Daalder." But once people became accustomed to the sound of his voice, it turned out there was nothing sinister behind his words. The admiration for his brother was totally sincere. People looked at each other pleasantly surprised. Where emotions were concerned, there was a lot to be learned from such uncomplicated souls as this. They could be so spontaneous! Those who had thought ill of him now felt ashamed of their overly hasty judgment, and subsequently lost themselves in pondering the profusion of mental twists that they were burdened with as intellectuals, and for which they paid a nasty price on occasions like this.

Whereas the daughters had not lost their self-control for a moment, when he evoked childhood memories Albert was so overwhelmed by emotions that he had to shorten his speech and leave the stage in a hurry.

Joop? Joop now perhaps?

But no, now it was the turn of a long series of little old men and the occasional little old woman — friends and ex-colleagues. Many of them came with a quotation from world literature, but not before they had first described their quest for it in the minutest detail. The quotations, often in a foreign language and occasionally in ancient Greek, were undoubtedly very appropriate, but they dragged on and were not always equally audible. To be perfectly honest, after a flying start, the ceremony was beginning to falter.

There was a great sense of relief when Charlotte took her place behind the harpsichord. Bach again. Perhaps a bit less overwhelming than the first piece, but beautiful all the same.

Now Joop? No, now the doors behind the coffin slowly opened. Sunlight and birdsong flooded the auditorium, and four dark figures loomed up in the bright backlight. They were the pallbearers, who would carry the deceased to his final resting place.

A long procession followed them through the graveyard — headed by the widow, supported on either side by her two daughters. Behind them came son-in-law Wouter and the two grandchildren (my, hadn't they grown!), followed by Joop (fat!), and what's-her-name-again (beautiful girl, by the way).

Would Joop say something at the graveside then?

When everyone had gathered around the grave, glimpses of recognition flashed back and forth — but briefly and discreetly. People didn't want to bother each other during this final moment of farewell. After a few people had laid bouquets, the coffin slowly sank into the ground. Whoever wanted to could scatter some earth over the coffin with a little shovel, but when one of the guests offered it to Françoise, she turned away brusquely.

Above the crackling gravel, on the way back to the reception hall, tongues started to wag for the first time.

"Strange, though, that Joop didn't speak."

"Well, he always was the odd man out, of course."

Joop had to be present in the reception hall together with his sisters and mother to receive the condolences. It helped that he was the last one in the row because by the time the people reached him, most of them had already used up all their ammunition.

Next to him, his sisters were showered with compliments.

"Beautifully played, beautifully spoken."

"Chapeau!"

"I don't know if I could do that."

But there was also one shaky old lady who, holding her handkerchief in front of her mouth, came especially to Joop, grabbed him by the forearm, and looked deeply into his eyes.

"I completely understand that you didn't speak, Joop. Don't blame yourself for anything!" But she gave him such a nasty pinch when she said "anything" that she probably meant just the opposite.

A sheer endless line of seemingly perfect strangers filed past, all of whom turned out to know him very well. Joop had several déjà vus, as if the person shaking his hand had already done so five minutes earlier.

When the frayed end of the line finally came into sight, it included a figure who was behaving rather badly. His loud voice and raucous laughter were inappropriate enough, but he had committed a deadly sin by already fetching a bun and coffee for himself while the others stood neatly in line even though they were faint with hunger. It was Joop's cousin

Nico, the rascal who had left for Canada after high school to pick tobacco and who had been there ever since.

To those interested enough to listen—their number was rapidly dwindling—he talked about the wonders of the New World. After ten years in Canada he spoke Dutch with a thick North American accent. There was space in Canada, he was saying, space such as Dutch people could hardly imagine. The city of Toronto was as big as the province of Utrecht, and situated on a lake—Lake Ontario—with a surface area as large as the Benelux. And that was only the smallest of the Great Lakes! And then there was the harsh climate there. Minus thirty was perfectly normal. He held his bun five feet above the floor to show how deep the snow had been that winter.

His listeners kept lowering their voices to provide him with a good example.

"What did you say?" he blared at them. "What?"

By the time it was Nico's turn to offer his condolences to his family, Joop had already learned that he had lingered in the tobacco business for a few years, but had now started his own business with a Canadian friend called Stuart. They sold and installed a new kind of filter system in swimming pools and hot tubs. It was hard work but good money. It so happened that he was in Holland visiting his parents when Uncle Laurens died. By the way, that was a fantastic speech his father had given, didn't they think?

Now that the line had disintegrated, the two cousins kept talking to each other.

Nico wanted to know how Joop was doing.

Hmm.

Joop told him about his apprenticeship in France and about his exciting plans for his own chocolate shop, but for now, he was forced to work for a boss, after a frustrating trek past every possible bank to obtain start-up capital.

"Now that's typically Dutch!" bellowed his cousin. "Whether it's a chocolate shop or a vacation park, or some other neat initiative, a Dutchman always pulls a long face. 'Well . . .' he says, and names ten reasons why it won't work. You know what I mean? Go to a Canadian with the same idea and he says, 'Wow!,' gives you ten handy tips, and, what's more, offers to help. That's the essential difference between here and there: the difference between 'Well . . .' and 'Wow!'"

Then Nico came up with had a brilliant idea. Why didn't Joop open a chocolate shop in Toronto? The banks were much easier with loans there. And you didn't have to worry about tradesman's certificates or business plans, public enquiry procedures, Nuisance Acts, and all that bureaucratic crap, just *hup!*—and you had your own business. He could raise the idea with Jerry Somerville, his financial adviser.

"If I managed, why shouldn't you? Come on, man. Come on over to Canada. I'm not kidding."

Canada and chocolate. The combination reminded Joop of long ago when the war had just ended and the Canadian soldier had kneeled in front of him to give him an inedible bar, his very first encounter with chocolate. "Here you go, sonny." Was it only now that the noble gesture gained significance? Did the real liberation only come twenty-four years later? Then again, Canada and chocolate; it was also an awkward combination.

"Well," he said at last. "I don't know. Do you think there would be a market there for high-quality chocolate?"

"You should hear yourself!" laughed Nico. "Now you're doing it too! 'Well . . .' Don't be so Dutch, man. Try to say 'Wow!' for a change."

While Nico began talking louder and louder, the indignant whispering around them became more and more vehement. Typically American, two old ladies agreed—to charge through the proverbial china shop with such clamor.

Nico really wasn't aware of a thing, but several times Joop had seen Emma gesture frantically that he should put an end to the conversation.

Charlotte took one last sip of coffee before putting her cup down on the saucer with a loud bang. Then she cut through the crowd, heading straight for the two offenders.

"Hey, Charlie girl!" cried Nico. "How's life?" Thanks to her withering look, something finally seemed to dawn on him. "I mean, given the tragic circumstances, of course."

"May I speak to you for a moment?" she said to Joop.

She led him off to a quiet corner.

"We're used to Nico misbehaving, but that you encourage him at the funeral of your very own father is a disgrace. You should be ashamed of yourself!"

Rosalinde now joined them. She had a message for Joop. "Mama would prefer you don't come back to the house afterwards. It's a gathering for the inner circle, and you . . . You're not part of it anymore!" She took to her heels in tears.

Joop understood they were aiming for a definitive break, but the strange thing was that it made him feel elated, as did all the angry faces around him. He almost wanted to do a little dance or jump for joy. Grinning broadly, he walked back to his cousin. That crazy character suited his mood perfectly.

"I can see it right in front of me," Nico continued. "Daalder's Chocolates. Come on, man. Why not?"

It was just like the old days, when his tough cousin jumped over a ditch and then stood on the other side urging him to do the same—only this time, the ditch was the Atlantic Ocean.

Part 5

SELF-EMPLOYED

A New Start

Dazed from the long flight, the first in their life, Joop and Emma trailed along behind Nico through the arrivals hall.

When they left the terminal through the automatic doors, it was as if an oven door had opened.

"Ninety-one degrees!" cried their host proudly. "For you, that's . . . minus thirty-two . . . that's sixty-nine—oh no, fifty-nine, divided by nine is . . . oh well, who cares, you can feel it."

Soon after, they were sitting in the backseat of his Chevrolet in the busy stream of traffic on the 401, a twelve-lane freeway that undulated across the city like a wide ribbon. The urban sprawl went on in every direction as far as the eye could see, ostensibly without a nucleus, as if a giant Marcel had scattered handfuls of houses all around him and then randomly placed small clumps of high-rise apartments among them. Occasionally, it became frighteningly dark inside the car, when a huge truck lumbered past them. It could happen on either side, because you were allowed to pass on the right here, bragged Nico. And when they left the freeway, he turned right on red at the first traffic lights. Apparently that was allowed here too.

But Nico showed them the most exotic traffic rule when they left the busy arterial road after a tiring forty-five-minute drive, and were driving through the shady streets of his neighborhood. It was the four-way stop, an intersection where traffic from all directions had to halt and the car that had stopped first was the first one allowed to drive on again. This rule required a degree of civility that only Canadians could manage. In a country like Holland, everyone would promptly crash right into each other.

In Nico's backyard, they were served a glass of Coca-Cola; that is, a glass filled with ice cubes with some brown liquid squashed up against the sides. Meanwhile, Nico started the barbecue and, above the roar of the neighbor's lawn mower, informed his guests about the many advantages of Canada over Holland.

After dinner, Emma phoned her mother to say they had arrived safely and ask how little Marcel was doing. They were dead-tired from the flight and the six-hour time difference but they had trouble falling asleep because of the sticky heat. With an almost sadistic chuckle, Nico had warned them that it barely cooled off here at night.

The next morning he gave them a lift to St. Clair Avenue, where they were to view some business premises. Emma was shocked by the shabby appearance of the street, by the grubby little shops, by the numerous parking lots where garish billboards called attention to pizza, donuts, and car wash. Everything became even uglier because of the telephone and electricity wires, which cut through every image like scratches on a roll of film. She hoped Nico would keep driving. It had to get better farther along. But he stopped just beyond an unused lot, in front of three gloomy shops of dark-brown brick, the middle one of which was vacant.

Ouch.

Joop had to swallow hard, too. But then he remembered that an artist feels at home anywhere as long as he can practice his art. Sorel had said that not long ago in response to hearing about their plans to emigrate.

As arranged, the owner, Dario Graziano, was waiting for them in the adjacent shop, the ice-cream parlor of his nephew, Tony. He hugged Joop like an old friend and greeted Emma with a kiss on the hand and words of flattery. After he had treated them to a cup of weak coffee that was passed off as espresso, they walked with him to the shop next door.

It was cool inside. Air conditioning was no luxury in this climate, certainly not where making chocolates was concerned. When Emma heard the metal boxes whirring away so eagerly, though, she wondered how many chocolates Joop would have to sell every hour in order to pay the energy bill. Joop was more worried about the musty smell that was circulated together with the coolness. But apart from that, the space appealed to him.

At a ten-minute walking distance from the shop, they went to look at a possible house to rent, in a quiet street, dark green from the maple trees. Emma recognized the shape of the leaves from the Canadian flag. Children were playing in the middle of the street with hockey sticks and a tennis ball. Playmates for Marcel?

The owner, waiting for them at the door, assured them that this was a good, safe area where only decent, hard-working people lived. Like Nico's house, this one was dark and stuffy. The windows were small and, moreover, fitted with screens that veiled the outside light with a gray haze. Proudly, the owner pointed out the five faithful servants that would be at madam's service night and day. He was referring to the household appliances. In addition to a disproportionately large refrigerator, a washing machine, and an oven, for the first time in her life Emma became acquainted with a dishwasher and a clothes dryer. But it was only when he opened the kitchen door and showed them the backyard that she really became enthusiastic. Not because of the patch of barren ground on which a few moth-eaten bushes stood, but because of the black squirrel that fled along the top of the wooden fence in elegant little arcs. Marcel would just love that!

When Emma asked Joop what he thought after the tour, he shrugged his shoulders. The house was of minor importance to him. It was for her to decide. She would have preferred that he come with her to look at another house, but he thought it was a waste of time. Instead, he took the subway downtown to conduct a little exploratory market research in preparation for their meeting at the bank later that day.

On the advice of his cousin, he visited Eaton's department store, a palace of bad taste at least ten times the size of Amsterdam's Bijenkorf. He took the escalator down to the food department in the basement. The atmosphere there was distinctly English. He passed an extensive assortment of marmalades and preserves and little tins decorated with charming scenes from Beatrix Potter and filled with blackberry- and quince-flavored candy. There were cakes with pale pink, mint-green, or lilac whipping cream piped on top, hues he would have associated more with soap than with food. The chocolate department was enough to make you cry. Or laugh your head off. In Dutch chocolate shops, at least it still smelled of chocolate. Here, the dominant scent was peppermint. Chocolates filled with toothpaste . . . You had to be of English descent to come up with that idea. Joop had seen and smelled more than enough. He left Eaton's and crossed the street to Simpson's, the big competitor and an equally big palace of bad taste. Here too the food department was hidden in the basement, as if they were a bit ashamed of all the garbage they were selling. Finally, he walked to a branch of Laura Secord, a chain of shops specialized in chocolates and sweets. He came, he smelled, he did an about-face. He walked back to the subway entrance in a giggly mood.

A Dutch banker like Mr. Ter Horst would have pursed his lips: if this kind of shop dominated the most economically attractive locations in the city, then apparently there was no market for better-quality chocolates in Toronto.

But fortunately Mr. Somerville of the Bank of Commerce, with whom Emma and Joop had an appointment that afternoon, had a completely different attitude.

"Just-call-me-Jerry" was a cheery little fellow with the same build as Joop. And, who knows, perhaps the fact that they could look straight in each other's eyes had a positive effect on the conversation.

They sat down in the freezing cold of his office. Nowhere in Toronto did the air conditioning work so furiously as in the banks, as if, with financial transactions, heads had to be kept as cool as possible. Emma, who for the occasion had put on her beautiful red summer dress, even got goose bumps.

Fresh from downtown, Joop was able to express his amazement directly to Jerry that in a city of two million inhabitants—with immigrants from every corner of the globe (he had been fascinated by all those different faces in the subway just now), who brought with them a wealth of culinary traditions—that in such a cosmopolitan city decent chocolates were nowhere to be found, was nothing less than a downright disgrace! Jerry empathized with his client. He thought a European-style chocolate shop was a brilliant idea. Toronto was more than ripe for it. And when Emma presented the financial side of their plans, he was deeply impressed by her business sense. Together they would form a fantastic team. As far as he was concerned, they could have a loan right away. He gave them papers to take home with them so that they could read everything through at their leisure.

Emma and Joop looked at each other. Was it that easy here? Wasn't there a catch somewhere?

That evening, Nico had to laugh at their misgivings. It was not for nothing that so many farmers and adventurers had emigrated here from the fifties onward. Unlike in overpopulated and overregulated countries like Holland, where you had to fill out three forms before you were even allowed to break wind, there was enough room here for everyone to do what he liked. New ideas were welcomed — by the banks, too.

And sure enough — within a week, Joop had arranged what he hadn't been able to achieve in Holland in four years: a loan, a suitable location for his chocolate shop, and all the necessary licenses. After the contracts were signed, Emma flew back to Holland to pack everything and to fetch Marcel from her mother's. Their emigration was a fact.

After a flying start, it was inevitable Joop would meet with a few minor setbacks: a summer flu, probably caught because of the constant shifting between the sticky heat outside and the dry coldness inside; Canadian customs, who charged absurdly high import duties for European products and equipment; the almonds, which he therefore ordered from California instead of Provence, which were incredibly large and flawless but — how could it be otherwise with an American product! — had absolutely no taste. He was also confronted with the outlandishly strict regulations regarding the sale of chocolates containing alcohol. They had to be clearly labeled and kept apart from the other chocolates, and they couldn't be sold to minors. Joop burst out laughing. That one little drop of alcohol? Oh yes, said the inspector of the Liquor Control Board of Ontario, because many little drops put together did indeed represent a danger. Apparently there were teenagers here with such an urge to get drunk that they would even eat a whole box of chocolates to achieve their goal.

The renovations, however, went smoothly. People could work very hard here, Nico had already told them, and unlike workers in Holland, they didn't have to be filled to the brim with coffee to get into action. If there was any cause for delay, it wasn't the carpenters but the marital disagreement about the design of the shop interior. Joop had only one goal in mind: after the frustrating years at Otto and Erik Vermeulens', he wanted to get started as quickly as possible. Emma wanted it to look nice.

"The eye also likes to be pleased."

"The eye is always demanding the lion's share," shouted Joop. "In my chocolate shop, the palate will be doing the talking for a change."

"But surely a lick of paint can't hurt?"

"Oh yes it can. We would have to air the place for a week, otherwise the chocolates might absorb the smell of the paint."

Emma sighed. No dressed-up shop window, no advertisements in the local newspapers, no festive opening. Wasn't he going a bit overboard? Monsieur Sorel lived in France, where refined eating was the norm. Here in Toronto, surely you had to let the people get used to the idea? But Joop wouldn't budge an inch. The name of the shop on the window was sufficient. True quality drew attention of its own accord.

A few days before the planned opening, the adhesive letters — DAALDER'S CHOCOLATES — arrived, in the color of chocolate with a cacao content of at least seventy percent. It took Emma half the morning to draw just the right arc on the windowpane, where the letters were to be placed. Despite her precautions, the first *D* ended up tilting backward slightly because Marcel insisted on helping and had stuck it on the pane before she could stop him. The sticky layer turned out to be so adhesive that she was unable to adjust the slanted letter. But the chocolates spoke for themselves, she reminded Joop, before he could get angry at his son.

On the first day the chocolate shop was open, only three people came to have a look, one of whom was so startled by the vexed look on Joop's face as he emerged from the kitchen that he apologized and left the shop in a hurry. The next day only Dario dropped by with a hideous flower arrangement to congratulate his new tenants on the opening of their shop.

"Don't worry," said Emma to Joop that evening.

"What do you mean?"

He had just had a wonderful day at work. Chocolate clearly responded very differently to the artificial, dry cold of the air conditioning, but he was gradually getting the hang of it. And he had discovered that if you roasted the Californian almonds long enough, they eventually acquired a taste. And the customers? Oh, they weren't important. He was only too happy not to have been disturbed all day.

The heat wave continued. Naked under a damp sheet, Emma lay awake at night worrying, while Joop lay awake thinking of making chocolates. Because it was easier to have sex than to fall sleep in this heat, that was how they sought relaxation. Their languid, sweaty lovemaking reminded Joop of the long siestas in his sultry van Gogh room in Avallon. Holland had been fatal to their love life, that was clear to him now. They had met each other abroad. Perhaps that was why they could only make love abroad.

After yet another tropically warm day, toward the end of the afternoon a greenish-brown thundery sky appeared. It began to rain, harder than they had ever seen it rain before, and just as they were thinking that, it began to pour even harder. Smiling, Joop realized how easily Nico's boastful immigrant's tone slipped into one's thoughts, and he could already imagine the irritated reaction of the stay-at-homes, like Peter and Corinne: "Well, it can rain hard here, too, you know!"

After the thunderstorm, all the dust was rinsed out of the air and the street smelled deliciously green. The next day, the sky was full of friendly little cumulus clouds, which, unlike those in Holland, barely moved an inch. A period of ideal summer weather began, with the temperature hovering around eighty degrees Fahrenheit. A real summer, in other words, not that half-baked business like back home. This was just like France!

"That makes sense," said Nico, who had come to have a look at the chocolate shop. "Toronto is at the same latitude as Bordeaux."

As the weather improved, the stream of customers gradually increased. It occurred to Joop that although cacao was a tropical product, chocolate was perhaps the last thing people wanted to eat when temperatures were tropical. Now that the house was more or less in order, Emma could man the shop more often, so that the customers didn't continually interrupt his concentration. But with her arrival, another kind of nuisance presented itself: Marcel. Because kindergarten only began in September, for the time being he would just have to entertain himself in a corner of the shop. But he didn't entertain himself, nor did he limit himself to that one corner. The racket and the whining drove Joop crazy. Fortunately, Emma found a teenage girl down the street who was willing to babysit.

September came, October came. It gradually became cooler, but the sun kept shining and the customers kept coming. And, more important, they came back. Not that business was booming, but Jerry at the bank was not displeased. At any rate the dreaded dip after three months didn't happen, and Christmas was on its way.

In November, a cold front of polar air settled over the province of Ontario. The first snowflakes fluttered down, the harbinger of a long, severe winter. Time for some old-fashioned Dutch ambiance, thought Emma. She phoned Nico to invite him to celebrate Saint Nicholas's Eve with them, but no one answered. After a few more vain attempts, she finally got his business partner on the line.

Didn't they know yet? Nico had returned to Holland, probably for good. He wanted to start a holiday park there, or something like that. Oh no, they hadn't argued. No, the poor guy had just been homesick for years.

Joop should have known. The moment Nico had persuaded you to take part in his pranks, he himself took off with the wind. But with or without Nico, they were staying in Toronto. Having a family member nearby only created a false sense of security. A true pioneer had to stand on his own two feet. It made the adventure that much more exciting.

Still, there were moments—especially on mornings when he walked to the chocolate shop in the biting cold—that Joop cursed his cousin from the bottom of his heart.

Chocolates and Barbarians

When Joop worked for Sorel, he left it to his master and his able assistant, Frédérique, to defend the chocolates against the barbarians. When he worked for the Vermeulens, he couldn't care less if some dimwit took off with a box of chocolates. Just right, he even thought. Now, for the first time, he had to part with his own children. That wasn't always easy, even if he did take Sorel's warnings to heart that it was better to say good-bye to your creations in the kitchen than in the shop, and that you should never look at your customers' mouths for too long, or at their buttocks when they took off with the loot.

Among his customers were fatsoes of unlikely proportions. Like the man with the triple chin and the enormous flabby breasts who parked his car right in front of the door every morning. He would park double if necessary, so as to walk as short a distance as possible. But even then, he came into the shop panting from the effort it had taken him to hoist himself up out of his car. The box was opened immediately after purchase, and—*plop plop plop*—the first three chocolates disappeared into his mouth like peanuts.

Even worse were the anorectic girls who misused his chocolates to quell their pangs of hunger. As skittish as men who come to buy porn magazines, they would sidle up to the display case, and, lightning-fast, would point out a sizable number of chocolates with their translucent skeleton hands. Often they would say it was a gift. Like the fatsoes, they too would put away the chocolates as if their life depended on it, but they waited until they got home to do it, where they could immediately confess their sin to the toilet bowl.

And between the extremes of the sickly fat and the sickly thin, there were the so-called "chocoholics." These were mostly women whose behavior was irreproachable in their everyday lives, but who writhed unashamedly with pleasure in the presence of chocolate. Chocoholics preferred to operate in groups of two, three, or four, so that they could loudly ridicule each other's addiction and incite each other that much more. The one who indulged most was the heroine of the day. But their enthusiasm was too bestial to count as a compliment. All they cared about was the chocolate, not the craftsmanship that went into it.

Sooner or later, every chocolatier was bound to encounter such extremes of human behavior. It was better to view them as a force of nature and undergo them stoically. But according to Sorel, forceful action did have to be taken at all times against customers who saw fit to interfere with your work. They should know their place. It was take it or leave it.

Now and again, Joop opened the kitchen door ever so slightly to check if his wife was being firm enough with the customers. She was a good pupil, who could dutifully reel off all the stories about the interior, the exterior, and the entourage, about combinations of taste and contrasts of texture. And she had an arsenal of appropriate quotations at the ready—his, and thus indirectly, also Sorel's. Milk chocolate was only meant to give the tongue a moment's rest. White chocolate didn't even deserve its name. Talking with your mouth full wasn't impolite to your listeners but to your taste buds. It was touching to see how her tone became sharper as soon as she noticed he was listening. But Emma was no Frédérique.

And he was no Sorel. There were plenty of reasons for exploding. Did he also sell chocolate cakes? Could he make the same chocolate but then with milk chocolate? Did he ever make low-calorie or sugar-free chocolates? Before long, they would be asking if he could make chocolate-free chocolates! And, sure enough, that very same week a woman sporting a tent dress and a long gray braid came into the shop and told him she had bought chocolates made from carob in a health-food shop in San Francisco. And the nice thing was that for once she didn't get a migraine. An idea for Daalder's Chocolates perhaps? With a question like that, you would have had to scrape Sorel off the ceiling, but even at this, Joop failed to become truly angry. The customers were also to blame for the lack of fireworks. If Sorel accused a fellow countryman of bad taste, war broke out. But a Canadian immediately bowed his head in submission. Sometimes the capitulation was already encoded in the question. "Of course, I don't know much about it, but . . ." or "This may sound stupid, but . . ."

In the early days, Joop was all too happy to kick these passes into the goal.

"Yes, madam, it is indeed rather stupid."

The poor things were visibly shocked by his blunt tone but too polite to end the conversation—so that Joop was able to go on kicking for a while.

"That's very interesting, what you're saying," they would say, slowly edging their way out of the shop. "Thank you very much."

Once they reached the door, they would make a hasty exit.

"Say, darling," said Emma, as she watched the disheartened customer walk past the shop window, "was that really necessary?"

After a series of such incidents, he realized she was right. Canadians didn't have to be put in their place. They were already standing there. They frankly admitted how unsophisticated they were, or that they had difficulty with the strong flavor of bitter chocolate. Their modesty was genuine, their faith in his authority unlimited. No cynicism could withstand such childlike candor. Slowly but surely something special was beginning to develop between Joop Daalder and the natives.

Emma's Grief

Emma took Marcel to school. Emma manned the shop. Emma did the shopping. Emma cooked hot midday meals, French-style. Emma did the laundry. Emma did the bookkeeping. In the summer she knew exactly how many chocolates were consumed by the air conditioning, in the winter she knew exactly how many chocolates were burned by the radiators. Sometimes she used her own savings to pay a bill. There wasn't much room for unforeseen circumstances — the bottom of her reserves was in sight. But she didn't say anything to Joop, because she didn't want him to feel bad. Emma took Marcel to bed and read to him. Emma did the dishes. Like a true pioneer's wife in a log cabin in the middle of the forest, she baked bread in the evenings for the next day, because Joop loathed the bread from the shops.

Meanwhile, for more than a year now she had been walking around with a question she didn't dare to ask Joop, for fear of disturbing his peace of mind. When she finally thought the time was right, she chose her moment carefully. Joop had had a good day. His new experiment with textures had exceeded all expectations. She had fed Marcel early and already put him to bed. She had cooked just a bit fancier than normal, but not too noticeably, otherwise it would look so calculating. During dessert — a homemade raspberry sherbet —

she broached the touchy subject. A second child. It would be so good for Marcel to have a little brother or sister. She had missed that in her own childhood. And she just loved the idea of holding a little one in her arms again.

For Joop it was not open to discussion. They had finally entered calmer waters, they were finally sleeping well again (indeed, Emma thought, nowadays Joop fell into a deep sleep right away. They never made love anymore). Why should they upset the precarious balance? Weren't their hands full enough already with their two children, that is, with Marcel and the chocolate shop?

Emma's fear that Joop would be put out by her question was unfounded. Within half a minute, he considered the subject closed. He sucked the sherbet off his spoon and remarked that the ice crystals gave it a nice texture.

Emma silently mourned the second child that would never be born, and went about her daily chores with grim fervor.

A new customer had started frequenting the shop around that time, a handsome Canadian with an athletic build who looked like a Kennedy. He came to the shop often enough and gave her enough knowing looks—letting other customers go first—for her to figure out that he was coming for her, not for the chocolates. Once when they were alone, he approached the counter. In a soft voice, he said she was the most beautiful woman he had ever seen and that he thought of her night and day. Wouldn't she like to have dinner with him some time. She shook her head vehemently, pointing to her wedding ring and then to the door behind her.

"But I can see you're not happy," he said.

She wanted to deny it, but her voice refused to cooperate.

"The invitation stands. I'll hear your answer next time."

Then she became frightened, knowing that if she responded

to his advances, she would be risking everything. She felt guilty already.

On his next visit, which she had longed for with an aching heart—as a good seducer, he was smart enough not to barge in every day—she asked him not to come anymore.

"Are you sure about that?"

"Yes," she said, sighing deeply.

He saw she meant it and, like a real gentleman, didn't insist. Just like in the movies, he bought an enormous box of chocolates, let Emma wrap it as a present, and then gave it back to her.

It was the last time she saw him.

When she was kneading the bread dough that night, she grieved, not only for the second child she would never have, but also for the Canadian Kennedy she would never be able to love. Oh well. At least Joop was happy, and that was worth something to her too. And the business was doing all right—not brilliantly, of course, but all right. That was no mean feat, something she could be proud of, too. They still had to watch the money, that was true. And there were a few other things she kept postponing. The walls at home could use some paint, and the carpet was becoming matted and even beginning to smell bad. She dreamed of making something beautiful out of the garden, the way all her Dutch girlfriends were doing nowadays (they had reached the age when gardening was considered exciting enough to devote half a letter to). Oh well. She modeled herself after Joop, who wasn't interested in that sort of thing. She modeled herself after the Canadian mothers she sometimes spoke to in the school yard, who never complained about anything.

When her mother came over from Holland for a few weeks, Emma was particularly keen to show her how well everything was going. She had thought up all kinds of nice day trips. Niagara Falls, for instance.

"It's really not necessary, darling," Hannie said, finding her daughter rather tense. "It's you I've come to see, not the tourist attractions."

But she really mustn't miss those waterfalls, insisted her daughter.

One Sunday, Emma drove the sixty miles to the falls with her mother and Marcel.

They walked along the boulevard to the point where you could see the water cascading down right under your nose. Marcel pulled at her trouser leg the whole time because he wanted a cotton candy, but Emma just kept staring at the water, endlessly falling over the edge of the precipice in a furious rush and yet as if in slow motion. She felt her legs grow weak and started crying. And couldn't stop.

Hannie took control. She treated her daughter and grandson to lunch in the revolving restaurant at the top of the observation tower, where you could admire the waterfalls and the upper reaches of the river for ten minutes, before sliding past the flat hinterland for another fifty. She managed to pacify Marcel with a children's menu full of nice surprises, so that she could focus all her attention on her utterly miserable daughter.

While her mother gently stroked her hand and talked, Emma still couldn't stop crying. She didn't care if people were looking. Disappointment in love, they would probably think. Abandoned by her husband. And in a certain sense it was true. Fortunately, Canadians were always extremely discreet. Even the cheerful waitress with the name tag Cindy acted as if nothing was wrong.

"Hi! How are you today?" she had asked her tearful customer.

One revolution of the restaurant was exactly enough to come up with one practical solution. Joop should hire a saleswoman. And if Emma was afraid of the cost, Hannie was prepared to make a contribution. Because it couldn't go on like this.

"What happened?" asked Joop, when the party came home and he saw Emma's swollen eyes and blotchy face.

His mother-in-law was the spokeswoman. For a moment he looked at her reproachfully, as if she were a troublemaker. But he knew her. Before she commented on anything, something really had to be wrong.

A certain Doreen Davis was the first of a long series of fresh, young, dime-a-dozen salesgirls. As long as Emma trained them and instructed them to disturb "Mister Daalder" as little as possible, it was perfectly all right with Joop.

For Emma, it was a great relief no longer to have to man the shop. At last some of the pressure was off, at last she could devote more time to Marcel, who was doing very poorly at school.

Mark's Birth

Marcel was being bullied by a few boys from his class. They called him a sissy and sang, "Marcel, *ma belle*, these are words that go together well."

When the teacher said something about it, the boys appeared to stop right away. But in the school yard, they followed closely on his tail while softly humming the melody. One day Marcel had had enough of it. He turned around and treated the worst offender to a professional right hook. The bullying was literally over in one blow.

Marcel had acquired a taste. From that day on, whoever came too close to him could expect a punch. The result, though, was that he was avoided like the plague and became more isolated than ever.

He observed his fellow classmates with a dark glimmer in his eyes. At a young age, he had already developed a fine nose for hierarchies. He understood, for instance, that the three bullies themselves were rather pathetic, and that they were desperately trying to get into the good books of the most popular boy in the class, a certain Dave Wilson, who clearly ran the show. Among the girls, everything revolved around Shirley Fraser. He discovered even more. Although they had reached an age when it was cool for boys to think that girls were stupid, King Dave and Queen Shirley did socialize with each other outside of school, and so did their parents. Together with a few other classmates and their families, they formed a secret society. From time to time, he overheard something about "Dakoddish," an idyllic place somewhere in the forests north of Toronto where they organized get-togethers in the weekends and during vacations. It was always great fun there. In the summer you could swim and water ski, in the winter you could charge through the snow on snowmobiles, at night you could hear the wolves howl. That was where the real alliances were forged between the leaders of the class, so that as an outsider you were always one step behind. Very occasionally, a boyfriend or girlfriend from the class was allowed to go on one of those weekends. Never him, of course. He wasn't even invited to birthday parties.

When his English improved, he learned that Dakoddish was "the cottage," and that it wasn't one single place but various summer homes of the wealthier families in the vast region of lakes that began some hundred miles north of Toronto. But even in fragmented form, "the cottage" remained Marcel's ultimate goal. To be invited to one of them or, better still, to have one of his own. Only then did you belong. Only then were you truly Canadian.

The children had two full months off during the summer. While the richer classmates took off to the cottage, the less affluent stayed behind in the muggy city. Every summer Emma tried to convince Joop to close the chocolate shop for a few weeks so they could go on holiday together. There was so much to discover in Canada, with all of its impressive natural beauty. But nature didn't mean a thing to Joop, and besides, he preferred to carry on with his work. To keep Marcel busy, she registered him in all kinds of handicraft courses and day camps, where he often misbehaved so badly that he was sent home halfway through the first day.

She took him to the swimming pool, the zoo, Centre Island.

He got bored very quickly and never made friends. When they went to the playground with the wading pool in their neighborhood, she sometimes took a book with her, but she never managed to read more than a line at a time because Marcel would already be bashing someone. Sometimes she tried to talk to him. It saddened her that a child could be so deeply dissatisfied at such a young age.

Why didn't they have a cottage, he wanted to know, like all the other children in his class?

"Not all the children," said Emma.

"The important ones."

When Marcel was eleven, she took him to Holland for the summer. They stayed with her mother and visited lots of old friends. They hadn't had any contact with Swaanendal for years now, but they did visit Peter and Corinne, who had recently left Amsterdam and were now living in a renovated farmhouse. They didn't have any children of their own and weren't accustomed to those of others. Their house was filled with beautiful artifacts — from the bazaar in Istanbul, from an antique shop in Arles, from a glass factory north of Trieste. The host and hostess just managed to contain themselves, but Emma could see that Marcel was driving them crazy every time he careened past one of their treasures. When the sun broke through the clouds, they took their second cup of coffee out into the garden (inspired by Monet's in Giverny), but there, too, they were on tenterhooks, frightened to death the little monster would damage their floral splendor.

Marcel was more dissatisfied than ever. Holland was a stupid country with a horrible climate, where people did nothing else all day but sit around on their rear ends drinking coffee. To cheer him up, Hannie treated them to a few days in a vacation park in the Hoge Veluwe, a nature reserve in the central part of the Netherlands, where he could have fun playing outside with children his own age.

"Look, Marcel," said Emma cheerfully, when they had found bungalow 47 with the help of the little map. "Now we have a cottage too!"

But Marcel wasn't fooled. A cottage didn't have a number. This was a stupid little house in a childish forest, with all those dorky pine trees standing in rows. There were no bears here ("But there are wild boars!" cried his grandmother), no crystal-clear lakes with high rocks along the shores, from which Dave Wilson and his friends would be diving all day long. He was separated from that magical center of power by a greater distance than ever, and was losing precious time frittering away the hours here in Holland. Perhaps it was already too late ever to make up for the time he had lost.

He bragged constantly about Canada to the other children in the vacation park. It was more than five hundred times the size of Holland. In the winter, the temperature could drop to seventy below zero. At night, you could hear the wolves howl.

"So what," said the children.

When a few boys laughed at him because he didn't even know what Ajax was (he thought it was a cleaning product), he shrugged his shoulders and said soccer was a boring sport anyway. Ice hockey was a hundred times more exciting. The Toronto Maple Leafs, now they were heroes. In Canada . . .

"If you say Canada one more time, I'll punch you in the face," said Robert-Jan, the toughest and most popular boy in the vacation park.

"Canada," said Marcel. "Canadacanadacanada."

The boys fought it out on playing field B. All the children rooted for Robert-Jan, but it was Marcel who won and Robert-Jan who ran home crying to bungalow 34 with a nosebleed. His irate father marched over to bungalow 47 to set things right with the mother of the nasty bully.

"I know how punch-drunk you all are over there in America, but that's not the way we do things here in Holland."

After the fight, none of the other children wanted anything to do with Marcel. He spent the remaining days in the pine forest, where he had discovered an ant's nest and entertained himself by cutting the ants into head, thorax, and abdomen with the little scissors on his Swiss Army knife.

Emma was happy once they were back in Canada and the school year had begun again.

But the fights Marcel was involved in became more and more serious. After he had pushed a boy from a lower grade onto the ground for no reason and kicked him in the head a few times, Emma was invited for a talk with the school psychologist.

"Wouldn't ice hockey be something for him?" asked the psychologist. "He'd be able to get rid of his energy in a positive way. And a team sport does wonders for the self-esteem."

She consulted the parents of Dave Wilson, who played ice hockey, and registered Marcel for the next upcoming open day that the club was organizing to select new young players. The youth trainer had the aspiring players do a few skating exercises, then play a match against each other. When it was over, he told Emma he found Marcel very aggressive. She began to apologize for her son until she realized, from the surprised expression on the trainer's face, that "very aggressive" had a positive connotation in English, certainly in relation to ice hockey. He would have to learn to skate better, but the club was eager to have him.

Marcel made such progress that after a few months, he was allowed to play on a higher team, of which Dave Wilson was also a member. The practices and the games took place at a ridiculously early time of day and in a remote part of town. Now that the boys were on the same team, the Wilsons offered to pick up Marcel and take him with them to practice. All winter long, several times a week at the crack of dawn Emma waved good-bye to her son as he slithered down the slippery sidewalk with his sports bag and hockey stick, to the Wilsons' waiting car.

Sometimes Emma was conscience-stricken. Did they really not mind taking the boys every single time? Shouldn't she, once in a while —

"Not at all," said Dave's father, Donald. "No problem."

In the team, the two boys complemented each other well with their different styles of playing. Dave was quick and skated nimbly past his opponents, while Marcel preferred to skate right through them or flatten them at full speed and with his full weight against the sideboards, so that he could take the puck from them and pass it on to the unchecked Dave. Sometimes he had only been on the ice for five seconds and had already meted out the first unauthorized thump, and he'd be sent off to spend two or even five minutes in the penalty box. There in the dock, he felt supertough, and enjoyed the reproachful glances that the coach and the parents of the rival team threw in his direction.

That year their team won by miles. As top scorer, Dave Wilson was declared the most valuable player of the league, but Marcel Daalder derived almost as much status from the impressive number of penalty minutes he had amassed, and became known by friend and foe alike as the terror of the league. Correction: *Mark* Daalder was known as the terror of the league — because from now on he wanted to go through life with that tougher name, not only on the ice rink but also at school and at home.

"Mark?" cried Joop. "What kind of nonsense is that?"

He stubbornly persisted in saying Marcel, but his son became more obstinate by the minute and acted as if he didn't hear a thing.

For Joop, ice hockey was the umpteenth proof that his son was a lout. With the same mixture of disgust and fascination

as when he had observed him as a baby, he watched now as —
under the influence of sport and pubescence — his son's shoulders became increasingly square and the foolish child's face
was pushed up higher and higher by a fleshy bull neck.

He shivered when his son stuffed himself with a stack of
peanut-butter and jelly sandwiches and washed them down
with a mug of milk. The downy mustache and countless over-
ripe pimples didn't make him any more appealing.

He didn't care what he ate, as long as it was a lot. If he
wasn't gorging himself on sandwiches, he was just as happy to
fill his plate for a second time with *boeuf bourguignon.*

"Goddamn it, boy. Do you have any idea how special that
is, what your mother has cooked?"

"Yeah, well? I'm taking a second helping, aren't I?"

Mark looked at his father with total indifference, more as
an obstacle than as a person, the way he sometimes intimi-
dated his opponents on the ice.

He felt invincible, for it had finally happened: he had been
invited up to the Wilsons' cottage for the weekend.

Calm Waters

Joop made chocolates, Emma managed the house and the administration, Marcel threw himself into ice hockey. Things were going well. After the troublesome early years, it appeared as if the Daalders had finally landed in calmer waters.

But one day, Joop was standing in the silence of his kitchen calmly stirring in a saucepan (he no longer heard the rattling of the air conditioning nor the tinkling of the front-door bell), when he noticed that he was in a terrible mood. He stopped stirring and tried to identify where the problem was coming from. An unpleasant memory was the culprit, the unjust remark that his fellow-student Daphne had made to him once at a sidewalk café in Assisi: "Oh, don't you like olives?"

Shaking his head, he continued stirring. The cackle of ducks from a distant past—it shouldn't bother him in the slightest. Work took so little effort these days that he was left with too much time to think. That was all.

But during the rest of the day, he managed to dig up more and more unpleasant remarks out of his memory.

"So that appeals to you, does it, the life of a shopkeeper?"

"Isn't that boring, making chocolates all day?"

"Why Canada, of all places?"

Always in the form of a question. That was the wrapping paper in which the Dutch presented their judgments.

Damn it! The knife had slipped and he had a nasty cut on his finger.

Where did this cackling suddenly come from? Surely he shouldn't be bothered by it anymore! Everything was going well now, wasn't it? He had built up a faithful clientele who thought the world of him. In fact, why should anything at all bother him now? As a true chocolatier, you were supposed to stand above everything, weren't you?

He took his bad mood home with him.

They had a wonderful meal, and later that evening, the house was filled with the delicious smell of fresh bread. But Joop still sat in his armchair frowning deeply. Emma, who was sitting at the dining-room table scribbling like mad, was driving him utterly crazy. She was writing a long letter to Peter and Corinne.

"Shall I leave some space for you?" she asked.

"Please don't!"

He could understand that she wrote to her mother and her girlfriends, but Peter and Corinne were *his* friends. Because of her conscientiousness, he was deprived of the opportunity to let the friendship die a natural death.

Everything was going well here in Toronto, she wrote. The customers thought the world of Joop. Marcel's hockey team had just become champion for the third year in a row, and he had gone north for a weekend with a friend (let's hope they don't run into any black bears!). And, how lovely, Corinne, that the monkshood was doing so well this year. As for herself, she still intended to do something with the garden one day, but there just wasn't any time and she dreaded the amount of work. The soil was poor here.

A few weeks later they received a long letter back from Corinne. Joop read through it quickly. It was the usual chit-chat, about Peter's work at the university and her work at the museum.

They had just been to Paris for a weekend, where they had visited a gorgeous new exhibition at the Louvre. And the phloxes in their garden were in full bloom now.

Peter had scribbled something in the margin too: "Nice for you, Joop, that your chocolates are so popular over there in Toronto! The Canadians probably aren't used to much in that area! Greetings, P."

They probably aren't used to much . . . Joop could have said it himself. But now that Peter had written it, the words acquired a nasty aftertaste. It was as if he meant that the Canadians were easily satisfied.

And then those exclamation marks . . . a variation on the question marks in which judgments were usually packaged.

Joop grew angrier by the minute.

So Peter thought it was easy to play the big chocolatier "over there in Toronto"? Yes, yes . . . It certainly was a lot more difficult to reach the top in Holland. Not because the top was so incredibly high, but because it was so fiercely guarded by a clique of aging arrivistes and their gushing followers. They had staked out their territory with barbed wire and posted signs everywhere saying NO TRESPASSING, PRIVATE PROPERTY, or OTTO VERMEULEN, AS BRILLIANT AS EVER, which amounted to the same thing.

"You're imagining things," said Emma. "He's happy for you."

"Don't you know Peter yet? Sideswipes are his specialty."

"Well, so what, even if they are?"

Even if they are, even if they are . . . She was right. But that old feeling from when they lived in Baarn, that feeling of being a caged animal, had returned full-force. The frightening thing now was that there was no one to blame. He was self-employed, happily married, and had a faithful clientele who thought the world of him.

The next morning he had to force himself to go to the chocolate shop, where he had to contain himself so as not to blow up at the new salesgirl, who asked him just a few too many questions while looking at him with enormous, fluttering eyes. She had a sugar-sweet girl's voice that contrasted sharply with her voluptuous figure, as if it had become stuck somewhere in puberty.

She asked him what exactly a *grand cru* was.

"That's something you don't have to worry about."

"But I'm interested to know."

"But I'm not interested to tell you. Okay?"

"Yes, Mr. Daalder," she said, blushing. "I'm sorry."

"Yes, yes. It's all right."

But it wasn't all right at all! How could Emma have hired such an obnoxious Barbie Doll when he had insisted so emphatically that the girls should leave him alone? On the way home, he decided to ask Emma to fire her on the spot, even if that meant giving her two months' salary. He couldn't stand that doll's voice for one more day, nor those sweet candy colors she always wore, like that fluffy pink sweater she had on today, which hurt not only his eyes but also his teeth.

When he came home, however, he found Emma in tears. A telephone call had come from Holland. Her mother had died. An accident. She had just done her groceries and was cycling home when she was hit by a truck at the roundabout (you know, the one near the new apartment building).

"You two really don't need to come with me," said Emma. "It's an expensive trip, and a funeral is just a funeral."

Father and son exchanged a rare glance of mutual understanding.

"Well, if it's okay with you . . ." began Marcel. It was the summer vacation, and Dave had invited him to come and spend a whole week at the cottage.

Joop preferred to stay at home, too. He had reached a dead end with the chocolates and wanted to force a breakthrough.

Dame Blanche

The obnoxious salesgirl was called Julie Shaw, and she was hopelessly in love with her boss. He was such a sophisticated man, so mysterious and impenetrable. But then, Mr. Daalder was married, and not just to anyone, but to a European woman, stylish the way only European women can be. There was Sophia Loren, there was Catherine Deneuve, and there was Emma Daalder. What could a man like him possibly want with the puppy love of a dumb Canadian bird like her? Forget it, girl, she warned herself, as she dove into her cupboard to search madly for something her boss would think pretty enough to make him finally notice her.

Meanwhile, her boyfriend, Jeremy, sat on the couch playing "Blowin' in the Wind" on his guitar. He was a perfectly good guy, but so decent, so . . . Canadian. He was just like an affectionate puppy, with his oversized hands and his oversized feet and his stupid baby face (and his enthusiastic puffing and panting in bed).

Julie and Jeremy came from Orillia, a small town about seventy miles north of Toronto. They had known each other since high school, and both dreamed of a different, more exciting world. They had gone to the big city, where, to their parents' distress, they were now shacked up together as an unmarried couple. That would only lead to trouble, they were told. Jeremy wanted to become a musician and in the meantime worked as a waiter. Julie wanted to become a journalist and had been working for a short time now in the chocolate shop, where she had promptly fallen in love with Joop Daalder.

When Julie arrived at work that morning, she found Emma Daalder there, dressed in black and wearing dark sunglasses.

"Oh, I'm so sorry, Mrs. Daalder," she said, when she heard what had happened.

It was all she could do not to burst into tears. Mrs. Daalder's grief looked so heartrendingly real. She had probably had a very complex relationship with her mother, like in those artistic European films that were sometimes shown in the alternative film houses, with their long, serious dialogues and uncompromising close-ups of both actresses, alternating with incomprehensible but disturbing flashbacks. And if Julie had to suppress a yawn during such scenes, it was because of lack of concentration on her part, and certainly not because of the film.

She sympathized with her boss's wife, but at the same time her heart began to pound more fiercely. She felt horribly wicked for taking advantage of such a sad occasion, but she knew this was her chance.

"And please," said Emma to her at that same moment, "don't bother Mr. Daalder with too many questions." Despite all the consternation around Hannie's death, Joop had still found an opportunity to vent his dissatisfaction about Julie.

"No, Mrs. Daalder."

A taxi drove up that would take Mrs. Daalder to the airport. When Joop went outside to say good-bye to his wife at the curb, Julie discreetly looked the other way. But when he came back into the shop a few moments later, walked past her, and shut himself up in the kitchen, she thought: and now he's mine.

Lovesick, she diagnosed herself. But that didn't help. Like the hysterical women in the reports of nineteenth-century psychiatrists or the fainting teenage girls at rock concerts, she could hardly breathe when her boss came out of the kitchen with a portion of fresh chocolates. That sullen look of his, above such a tray of delights! But most of all she was in love with his hands. Strikingly small, they were almost like a child's, with soft, short fingers. She could see they would feel warm and a bit clammy and that they would caress a woman's body very tenderly. When she came home that evening, she tried to write a poem about it. "If only I were made of chocolate, then I could melt in your hands! If only I were a chocolate, then . . ." No, it was worthless junk. She tore the sheet out of her diary, also because she suspected Jeremy sometimes read it. He was quite suspicious.

When the enthusiastic puppy wanted to mount her that night, she turned away from him. As long as she couldn't get the man of her dreams, she didn't want anyone else.

"Is something wrong?" asked Jeremy anxiously.

"No, no, I'm just tired," she said, but she stayed awake for the rest of the night.

The next morning she put on her tightest sweater and her shortest skirt. Not without consequences. The female customers showed their disapproval with raised eyebrows, the male customers grinned like idiots and made all kinds of slimy comments. Only Mr. Daalder looked at her as he always had, that is, hardly at all.

He even exploded at her that afternoon. She had just finished with a customer when the kitchen door flew open.

"Could you pronounce the *s* a bit less sharply? I can hear you right through the door: *sss* . . . *sss* . . . *sss!* Perhaps you think it sounds charming, but it reminds me of drops of fat falling on a barbecue. I really can't concentrate this way."

Julie swallowed. Red blotches appeared on her neck that clashed horribly with the light-yellow sweater she was wearing.

"I'm sssorry," she said. Then, laughing sadly, "I mean: I'm sorry."

She was completely at a loss. The rest of the day she could only speak to the customers in stammers and stutters. Now that Mr. Daalder had made her aware of her *sss*, her self-esteem went hissing out of her as if she were a punctured tire. By the time she went home that evening, she was feeling like a limp piece of rubber.

At home, she stood in front of the mirror.

"Ssso sssilly," she said.

She took off her fluffy sweater and her doll-like skirt. In her panties and bra she already looked a lot more mature, she thought. Now for her voice.

Like Professor Higgins teaching Eliza Doolittle how to say "The rain in Spain falls mainly on the plain" in a refined way, Mr. Daalder had conveyed something very valuable to her.

"A penny for your thoughts," said Jeremy, suddenly coming up from behind and putting his arms around her.

With a slightly too hard jab of the elbow, she made it clear she wasn't interested in his pawing.

"Ow!" cried Jeremy surprised. "Jesus, Julie, what's the matter with you lately?"

Joop couldn't sleep because of the muggy warmth, and because of the empty space beside him in the bed. He missed Emma. But at the same time he wondered whether he missed her as a person or only as a reassuring presence, as a stopgap for avoiding his fears. Like with that little note Peter wrote: "Oh no, darling, you're imagining things." That "darling" she threw in everywhere, when had she started doing that? Did this always happen in marriages — that a wife admired her husband less and less and mothered him more and more? And that a man behaved less and less like a prince and more and more like a child? "If you say so, darling!"

❧   ❧   ❧

Julie also lay awake, for the umpteenth night in a row. She lay as far away as possible from her snoring boyfriend to help her think more clearly (and because his body odor had begun to bother her recently). "Jesus, Julie, what's the matter with you lately?" he had asked. And rightly so. She hadn't been honest with him. She was at odds with herself and going through a difficult time. But she was finding her way again now. It wouldn't hurt Jeremy either to take a good look at himself. He should become more self-reliant, stand more on his own two feet, be less dependent on her. Perhaps that way their relationship could still be salvaged.

And Mr. Daalder? She had decided to quit the next day. She would be frank and simply tell him she was too infatuated with him to be able to function properly. She would say good-bye to him with dignity, not as a dumb little doll with an affected way of speaking but as a young woman.

"S . . . s . . . s," she practiced in the dark. "Silly . . . super . . . sex . . ."

The next morning, Julie put on a simple pair of jeans and a nondescript dark brown blouse. All morning she practiced her new pronunciation on the customers. It improved by the minute. Then, during the noon break, she took three deep breaths. Contrary to all the rules, and even without knocking, she entered her boss's sacred kitchen.

He was busy scraping hardened bits of chocolate off the marble slab.

"What are you doing here?" he asked angrily.

"I came to thank you," she said, approaching him.

"What are you talking about?"

"Didn't you notice it this morning? The *sss* is gone. You helped me get rid of it. And all by itself my voice has gone down almost an octave. I feel like a new person."

"That's nice for you. Now go and have your lunch."

But she came closer, and closer still, and without knowing exactly what she was doing anymore, she finally put her arms around his neck.

With that voluptuous young body pressing itself firmly against him, and that mouth fastening itself onto his, it was as if a time machine started working. The frustrations of recent days vanished one by one and he felt himself becoming younger and younger, until he imagined himself in the prime of his life . . .

The transition from adulterous to loving husband went with surprising ease—as easy as it was for Julie to get dressed and go out front to open the shop, and for him to call the operator and request a line to Holland. Today was the day of the funeral. For Emma, it was already nine o'clock in the evening. She was staying at her friend Ingrid's and would be sitting there now with a glass of red wine in her hand recovering from the emotional day. Good timing, this telephone call.

"Was it very difficult?" he asked her. "And how are you doing now, darling?"

Because of the uncharacteristic intensity with which he sympathized with her, because of his lighthearted, almost enthusiastic tone, Emma knew right away that something was wrong. When she asked if Julie Shaw was behaving herself now, she was treated to a succession of half-answers and further explanations—oh yes, for sure, well, that is to say . . . Individually, each answer sounded perfectly innocent, but when heaped on top of each other they formed a towering, unstable thundercloud. And she had seen how Julie looked at her husband. She recognized that lovesick look from earlier salesgirls—and from customers. Like an orchestra conductor or a ski instructor, a chocolatier simply exerted an irresistible attraction on many women. Not that Emma ever felt threatened. The

infatuations ended quickly because Joop never noticed them
and therefore never responded to them. But lately he had been
vulnerable, like when he was put off by that one little comment
by Peter. Those with evil intent might take advantage. It would
be pretty damned opportunistic of that Julie, though, to abuse
the present situation. But perhaps nothing was the matter, perhaps she was just imagining things.

"You don't have to pick me up at the airport on Friday," she
said to Joop. "I can take a taxi."

"Yes? Are you very sure?"

Emma sighed. He wasn't that sympathetic after all.

After the telephone call, Joop went back to work. What
had just happened during the lunch break was a once-only
slipup, a tasty faux pas. Surely Julie would see it that way
too. Now, they must return to the order of the day and act as
if nothing had happened, and, especially, not let Emma notice
anything so as not to hurt her even more. And that wonderful
vitality he felt now? He could use that to work on his chocolates with new élan.

"Bye, Julie," he said, at the end of the workday.

"Bye, Mr. Daalder," said Julie.

Joop slept like a log that night.

When he woke up the next morning, he heard the birds
singing. Thinking of Julie, he stretched contentedly. He had
been naughty, very, very naughty, and that on the day his
mother-in-law was buried.

Joop jumped out of bed. He felt more energetic than he had
in a long time. As he stood under the shower, he even burst into
song, something he had never done before. At breakfast, he ate
twice as much as normal. Without feeling hurried, he was at
the shop in eight minutes instead of the usual ten.

He set to work with new élan.

But when he heard Julie come in half an hour later, a pink

haze blurred his vision and his hands began to shake so badly that he had to put down the knife with which he was carving a wavy pattern in a chocolate.

Don't greet her. He normally never would.

But half a minute later, he stuck his head around the corner.

"Good morning, Julie."

"Good morning, Mr. Daalder."

"Do you feel like having lunch together later on?"

At twelve o'clock, Julie locked the front door and turned over the sign from OPEN to SORRY, WE'RE CLOSED. Then she knocked on the kitchen door. The door opened and Joop pulled her in.

After all the emotions she had been through, more than anything Emma was in the mood for some passionate lovemaking. She put her suitcase down in the hallway and let Joop embrace her, but he didn't seem to understand her patently obvious body language and limited himself to tender little pecks and encouraging pats on the back. Abruptly, she let go of him. She smelled a perfume she couldn't place.

Through the kitchen window, Joop saw how she stood in the middle of the garden with her arms folded. Evidently she needed to be alone, to figure things out for herself. That was understandable after such a heavy loss.

The next morning, Emma drove to a garden center. She filled the trunk with flowering plants, bags of fertilizer, and garden tools, and began working like a dog the moment she got home.

The truth came out. Julie was in love with someone else and wanted to break up.

But why, for God's sake, Jeremy wanted to know.

Julie sighed. He was a sweet guy, but so . . . boring, so . . . Canadian. Sorry.

"You're Canadian, too, aren't you?"

"Less and less," she replied, as she admired herself in the mirror.

Jeremy began to cry.

She felt sorry for him and knew she was being very hard on him, but she couldn't stand it when a guy showed his weaknesses so shamelessly. It confirmed her idea that she had outgrown him.

Jeremy grabbed his guitar.

"Oh Julie, Julie, Julie!" he began singing. "Why Julie, Julie, Julie . . ."

"Oh shut up, for God's sake!"

Jeremy went and packed his things. A few hours later, he was sitting in a bus heading for Orillia. His parents received him with open arms. The big city wasn't the right thing for their kind of people.

The double life suited Joop fine. It was, after all, *très Français* to have a mistress on the side. Or a lover. Emma could have someone too, if she felt the need.

But he preferred not to look in the mirror too often. Although he felt younger than he had in years, strangely enough that roguish smile he had acquired of late made him look older. It reminded him just a little too much of Charlotte's harpsichord teacher, Manfred Scholl.

Poor Emma still suspected nothing. Since her return, she devoted all her time to gardening, having turned completely inward because of her mother's death. Her grief was so heavy, so all-consuming that he didn't know how to deal with it. As a human being, he was too limited, too banal. The best he could do was to show consideration for her feelings through small gestures, for example, by not complaining if a meal wasn't quite up to his standard.

Meanwhile, he had to think up something so he could be with Julie. He could hardly miss the midday meal, which he had elevated to the most important of the day in keeping with the French tradition, and for which Emma always did her best. Instead, he used the age-old excuse of working late. He was brooding on a new chocolate.

"And?" Emma asked him occasionally. "How is that new chocolate coming along?"

"Don't ask," said Joop, sighing.

She looked at him intently, but he didn't flinch.

In the chocolate shop, things were getting pretty wild. Between customers, Julie would slip into the kitchen, where she and Joop made a sport of seeing how far they could go before the next customer announced himself with the ring of the front doorbell. Hair was quickly tidied, blouses and shirts buttoned, flies zipped. Julie ran out front, Joop washed his hands, took a sip of water, and set to work. But a moment later, she was back. And the chocolates? Oh well, the chocolates. Joop worked on automatic pilot.

One evening, after closing time, they thought up something new. Julie lay down naked on the marble counter. Her skin was whiter than white, and Joop thought it would look wonderful if he made a living *dame blanche* out of her by pouring a dark chocolate sauce over her breasts.

Long ago, Emma had spoiled the sacred atmosphere of *Le Déjeuner sur l'herbe* by constantly bursting out in laughter at the wrong moment. Here, exactly the opposite happened. Julie took everything much too seriously. The deadly earnestness with which she looked at him as he walked toward her with the saucepan, her heavy breathing, and the way she closed her eyes now, and would no doubt sigh from pure pleasure the moment she felt the warm chocolate sauce stream over her . . . It was all a bit too theatrical for him.

The magic was gone, and so was his lust. What was this naked girl doing here in the middle of his sanctuary? Sorel would be revolted by the scene! It was far too long since Joop had spoken to him, had dared to speak to him. That was always a bad sign.

"No, this won't work," he said.

He walked back to the stove with the saucepan in his hand.

"What's the matter, Joop?"

Julie sat up, crossed her arms over her breasts, and rubbed herself warm. The cold marble had given her goose bumps.

To talk himself out of the awkward situation, Joop pretended he was being tormented by guilt feelings. That his inability to help his wife in her grief had driven him into infidelity. But that it had to stop now.

"And you didn't think of that before?"

"I'll ask Emma to advance you two months' salary."

"Fuck your money!"

She got dressed and left the chocolate shop in tears.

Joop arrived home late that evening, but earlier than he had during the past few months. When he and Emma were sitting in the living room after dinner, he told her that Julie had quit so that she could spend more time on her studies. Might it not be an idea to hire a slightly older woman this time? These young girls were really so unpredictable.

"Gosh, I'm surprised," said Emma, without looking up from her knitting. "You were happy with Julie, weren't you?"

"Well, happy . . ."

This time she did look at him.

But again he missed a golden opportunity to confess his infidelity.

The next saleswoman was Martha Simmons, an honest, decent woman in her midforties who—after twenty years of faithful service—would witness the demise of the chocolate shop from close up.

After a week of crying fits and helpful conversations with close friends, Julie was over Joop Daalder. He was a callous bastard who had dumped her in the cruellest possible way, but she did owe it to him that in one blow she was rid of her bungling Jeremy and her affected voice. She resumed her studies with unprecedented energy and, armed with a wildly enthusiastic letter of recommendation from her professor, was accepted at a prestigious school of journalism in Vermont. She thus became a classic example of the Canadian dream, which consisted of leaving Canada to pursue a career in the United States.

Joop emerged less favorably from the affair. The rejuvenation cure had only worked temporarily, had taken its toll on his body and soul, and had ultimately hastened the aging process. He now felt every bit as old as the reflection in the mirror that he had avoided so fearfully of late. The mistress hadn't been a muse, had been at most a lovely distraction, but the combination of remorse and fierce longing for her youthful body was even less inspiring. The chocolates remained the same. Work was threatening to become a grind.

The only possibility Joop saw for breaking the deadlock was to confess everything to Emma.

It turned out she had known about it all along. From the very beginning.

"Why didn't you say anything then?" he asked angrily.

"Isn't that the question I should be asking you?"

"Your mother had just died. You were already having such a hard time."

"Very considerate of you, Joop."

In the future, she would prefer to hear about this sort of thing right away. But she was glad that in the end he had decided to tell her. For the rest, she didn't want to waste another word on it.

No scolding, no sanctions. Nothing. Surely she couldn't forgive him just like that? Was he imagining it, was it because of his own guilty conscience, or did her compliments sound slightly less sincere from that day on? And didn't the word "darling" pop up more often than ever? It was as if she spread her revenge out very thinly over the long years of marriage that would follow his little misdemeanor.

Head-on Collision

The soldier at the gate saluted as Graham Kelso drove off the military grounds in his jeep. Task accomplished: that is, the inspection of a number of military graveyards near Verdun. Conclusion: They were in reasonably good condition.

But Graham Kelso was feeling downcast.

Verdun had left its mark on him. The madness and futility of trench warfare were still palpable more than half a century later, as an endless heaviness pulling all hope for a better world down into the ground. A visit to Verdun should be compulsory for every young soldier, thought Graham, so he wouldn't take his task too lightly.

From Verdun his thoughts shifted to Vietnam, from which his country's army had withdrawn recently. Another of those futile exercises that had led to the death of tens of thousands. The weapons were more modern, the mud was warm instead of cold, but apart from that, the same misery.

Graham Kelso grew more somber by the moment.

To make matters worse, he hadn't been able to think up a gift for his wife, Doris, who would be turning fifty in two days' time. An annually recurring drama for him, whereas she always knew exactly what to give. In the end, they would go out together a month or two after her birthday and buy something for her—perfume, earrings, a blouse. "It doesn't matter, silly, I know you love me." They always made a fun day of it. But he still experienced these little outings as a defeat. He so much wanted to surprise her for once.

He had a whole day before having to return to his army base in West Germany. Instead of crossing the border right away and racing at top speed over the *Autobahn,* he decided to drive through France for a bit, in the hope that the winding roads through the picturesque landscape would cheer him up. But it wasn't his lucky day. In no time he ended up on a busy *route nationale* that ran relentlessly and as straight as an arrow through nondescript countryside, with the occasional run-over animal as the only object of interest. It looked like Iowa, it was so boring. After a while, he found himself driving behind a big, rumbling truck. Just his luck. Not that he was in a hurry, not at all, but the cars behind him certainly were. One crazy lunatic after another loomed up in his rearview mirror to hug his bumper and then pass him at the most dangerous moment possible. When they pulled up beside him, the drivers and any passengers with them eyed him contemptuously or held up their middle finger. That was because of the little American flags on his jeep, of course. In this country, he and his colleagues certainly didn't need to count on gratitude. No, the Germans, of all people, were a lot friendlier. Perhaps it would be wise if he were to pass the truck as well; that way there would be a lot less trouble. But by now it had become a question of prestige. Graham refused to let the ill-mannered French goad him.

But then—just below the top of a long, slowly ascending hill, when he was the only remaining vehicle still driving behind the smoking colossus and they were crawling along ever so slowly— the truck driver rolled down his window and made a churning motion with his tattooed arm to indicate that the coast was clear.

Now that, at least, was nice.

He turned on his indicator, and started to pass.

Jesus!

A black Citroën DS was approaching at breakneck speed, flashing its headlights. With a tug of the wheel, Graham just managed to avoid the loudly honking oncoming vehicle and return to his half of the road right in front of the truck.

God Almighty, what a close shave!

His foot shook on the gas pedal for miles to come. How strange, though. Had he perhaps misinterpreted the truck driver's signal? Then another possibility presented itself. A horrible one. The man had intentionally let him pass at the wrong moment. Boy-oh-boy! Anti-Americanism in the French could be grim at times, but that a truck driver like that was even prepared to sacrifice a fellow countryman to send an American to his death, that went a bit far.

Just imagine: Surviving a long career in the army without a scratch and then, just before your retirement, meeting your end in a banal car accident! And poor Doris, who was always so terrified something would happen to him but who put on a brave face because it had been her own choice to marry a military man.

It had become quieter on the road now. The French were all eating. Well, *bon appétit,* fellows. Good riddance! Boy oh boy.

After the next village, the road began to wind and the landscape became gentler. Okay, this was more like it! Take that pasture, for instance, with a few white cows grazing in it and a little village on a hilltop in the distance: that in itself was already gorgeous, wasn't it? He glanced at the Michelin map on the seat beside him. Gosh, this scenic stretch of road hadn't even been accorded a green stripe, imagine that! But perhaps all roads looked scenic if you had just escaped death.

It was in fact enchantingly beautiful here. He passed a sign indicating that in one kilometer, there was a turnoff to Fontenay, a twelfth-century abbey. God, what a shame Doris wasn't with him now. She loved culture.

Suddenly he had an idea for a birthday present, a truly brilliant idea. That stupid truck driver had been a godsend! He would offer Doris a second honeymoon right through this area. He turned left into the side road, and a few miles later, the abbey came into view. Bingo! He parked the jeep at the side of the road so he could draw a circle around Fontenay on the map, then followed the route southward with the tip of his pencil in search of other places of interest. Vézelay, that sounded promising. There he would look for a romantic little hotel.

And so Operation Doris gradually took shape. Goal: To win his wife's heart. That was the key to the good marriage with which he had been blessed. The drive to conquer still persisted. Indeed, the landscape of their love was only becoming more magnificent with age, and so the drive was becoming greater too. Perhaps such a landscape was the only remedy for the infinite grief of Verdun or Vietnam.

His eyes twinkled in anticipation. Would Doris ever be surprised! She could be so enthusiastic. She was just like a little girl then. Wonderful to see her like that. As a precaution against an oncoming car, Graham almost steered his jeep off the road. Easy does it, fellow, he said to himself, for God's sake easy does it. If you kill yourself in a crash now, I'll declare you the Biggest Blockhead in the Universe.

He continued on his way without further incident. He wasn't far from Vézelay anymore, when he came past Avallon. He vaguely remembered something from the history books about the "knights of Avallon." Perhaps nice to have a quick look. He followed the CENTRE VILLE signs, and then . . . no, but how was it possible? The finishing touch: a chocolate shop! Now absolutely everything fell into place. Doris was crazy about chocolate.

⁂

The next day Joop received a telegram from France. Sorel was dead.

He immediately phoned Sorel's friend, the butcher Hubert, to ask what had happened.

He didn't know all the details either, but what he had understood from Frédérique was that an American army officer had come into the shop the afternoon before, who had wanted to surprise his wife on her birthday with her favorite dessert, that is, with chocolate fondue, you know, the dish where you dip pieces of fresh fruit—banana, strawberries, pineapple, it didn't matter what—into a warm chocolate sauce. Would monsieur maybe be willing to come to their hotel room with the fondue?

That the customer was an American and a military man to boot, and, moreover, that he had asked in abominably bad French for something as disgusting as chocolate fondue—it had been too much for poor Jérôme. Gasping for breath at the beginning of what was meant to become a flaming tirade, he had succumbed to a heart attack.

Filled with eternal remorse that he hadn't spoken to his master lately, Joop flew to France to attend the funeral.

In Paris it was already raining. In Avallon it was pouring.

A taxi took him to a little church about six miles outside of town, which, with its walled cemetery, was surrounded by wheat fields. It wasn't the most intimate location for a final resting place, whereas there was so much lovely countryside near Avallon. Moreover, the peace was disturbed by the traffic from the *Autoroute du Soleil,* the new highway that lay just a few hundred yards away from the church.

There was only a handful of people in the church. Hubert,

who in the intervening years had grown even fatter; Maurice, who had grown thinner and was accompanied by a young man Joop had never seen before. Frédérique, who was still beautiful, now as a middle-aged woman. And Isabelle Sorel of course, sitting in the front row, as close as possible to the coffin. The same little bun but now gray. Only Ronnie-Boy Johnjohn, who lay in the aisle at her feet, was remarkably well conserved, until Joop realized this must be a successor.

He went over to Madame Sorel to hug her warmly, antici-pating her emotional reaction. Oh, that he had come all the way from Canada!

But she stayed as stiff as a rod when he embraced her and didn't return his kiss.

"He started drinking again because of you," she muttered, a remark so shocking to Joop that he immediately erased it from his memory.

A side door opened and a priest appeared wearing a long robe. Joop quickly looked for a place in a pew a few rows back.

Since he had first partaken of The First Supper as a boy, at his Belgian friend Pascal Vandenbroucke's, Joop had had a soft spot for the Catholic church. Its God seemed to allow for more joie de vivre than the colorless, scentless, and tasteless atheism of his parents. But this priest was anything but the jovial, red-cheeked fatty he knew from the lids of Camembert boxes. Perhaps it was because of his square-rimmed glasses, perhaps it was because of the routine way he swung the pot of incense through the air and rattled off his Latin texts, but more than anything he resembled a civil servant mechanically performing his daily duties.

"He may not have attended Mass very often," he addressed the gathering, gesturing to the casket with his hand, "but in his own way Jérôme was a devout man. Oh yes, dear friends, a devout man. For what is a chocolate other than a solidified piece of virtue? The word says it already: bon-bon. That means 'good,' twice over. Nothing but good, twice over, dear friends, that's what our Jérôme aspired to. The first good he aspired to was to draw the very best out of the cacao beans and out of the many other priceless ingredients that the Good Lord has bestowed upon us humans. The second good he aspired to was to make his fellow men happy, to inspire them to do good in turn."

Joop shifted back and forth restlessly on the hard church bench. Had the priest actually known the deceased? Even with the commonplaces that might apply to any chocolatier and with which he thought he couldn't go wrong, he was already way off the mark. How in God's name could Sorel, the misanthrope, who viewed the customer as no more than a wallet with a lump of flesh growing on it, be portrayed as a humane Christian? When the priest started talking about Sorel's special bond with children, Joop knew for sure. The man was simply talking nonsense.

After the Mass, the coffin was carried down the aisle and out of the church by half a dozen boys in ecclesiastical attire. As the small procession proceeded across the graveyard in the pouring rain, Hubert offered Joop a place under his umbrella.

At the graveside, the priest murmured a few more Latin texts as he swung the smoking pot of incense in the air. Then he let a silence fall to allow for individual prayer.

The dog started growling.

"*Sst, sst,*" spat Isabelle Sorel, pulling on his leash.

Then it became supposedly quiet, but the raindrops pelted painfully loudly on the umbrellas, and in the distance freight trucks whistled over the wet surface of the *Autoroute du Soleil.*

The priest crossed himself one last time and prepared to walk back to the church.

Is that all? Joop wondered. Why didn't Hubert say something, or Maurice? Surely their good friend couldn't be carried to the grave with just holier-than-thou nonsense and Latin hocus-pocus?

Because no one else did anything, Joop came out from under Hubert's umbrella to say something at the graveside.

"Dear Monsieur Sorel," he said. "All your wisdom, all your anger, I carry within me. Armed with chocolates, I will continue your struggle against the advance of bad taste. Thank you, Monsieur Sorel. Thank you, Papa."

There was little or no response to his words.

Maurice and his young friend glanced at him with crooked smiles. Frédérique was already walking toward the cars with madame. The priest was walking back to the church with the altar boys.

Only Hubert nodded to him encouragingly, without it being clear whether he meant "Good for you" or "It doesn't matter."

The taxi driver, who had waited for him in his car during the service, drove Joop back to Avallon.

There he walked back one last time to the chocolate shop, where he had experienced so many happy moments with his master. An old Renault with Dutch license plates stood half-parked on the sidewalk and Joop had to squeeze alongside it to reach the door.

An *À VENDRE* notice hung on the door, with the telephone number of the real estate agent. Madame Sorel hadn't wasted a moment.

The door was open and the bell still worked. But the shop had been emptied.

With the same haste with which Sorel used to storm out of the kitchen when something was wrong in the shop, an extremely tall man and an extremely tall woman, unmistakably Dutch, now appeared, and told him in impeccable French that it was *malheureusement trop tard pour vous,* but the shop had been sold to them that morning. To avoid further misunderstandings, the woman walked to the door and ripped off the notice.

After Joop had explained who he was, they became a lot friendlier.

Fons and Margot were their names, and they were from Leiden.

"Just by chance we were walking down this street yesterday," recounted Margot, "and we saw this for sale. We've been looking for something like this for years, haven't we, Fons? And you can easily drive down here in a day, that's so nice."

Naturally, it was very sad about the chocolatier. Yes, indeed.

"See that joint there?" said Fons to Joop in the meantime, as he pointed to one of the beams. "It's characteristic of this area."

"Fons is an architect," his wife explained. "He sees that kind of thing right away. Whereas I instantly fell in love with the scent here. Divine, that chocolate! I wouldn't mind if it went on smelling this way for years and years."

That very evening, Joop was sitting in the airplane on his way back to Toronto.

Looking back on his life of the past few years, he felt angry at himself. While he had lost himself in little personal problems and wasted his time on lecherous fantasies about Julie Shaw as a *dame blanche,* his master had been waging a noble battle. A battle that, in the end, had cost him his life.

It was happening worldwide, the advance of bad taste and the demise of refinement, under the banner of the Americans, with their more-more-more, faster-faster-faster, and their stupid army officers like Graham Kelso. You could tell by the Duchesse de Quimper having to make way for the just-good-enough pears, you could tell by the winding country roads becoming *autoroutes,* by the Marcels starting to call themselves

Mark. You could tell by the abandoned state of the French countryside and the smaller provincial towns, where all those thousands of Fonses and Margots so eagerly settled.

"Living the life of a king," that's how they saw it, but they were just maggots devouring a corpse from the inside.

If anything good had come out of this sad journey, it was the promise he had made Sorel at his graveside to continue the battle against the barbarians. Joop had been reminded why he made chocolates.

Emma came and picked him up at the airport. After the chilly reception in Avallon, it was lovely to finally recognize a familiar face in the anonymous sea of people, to finally see someone who loved him. Perhaps she was the only one in the world who still loved him.

They hugged each other warmly.

But as they drove home on the 401, he became somber again.

Cars, cars, nothing but cars. What ugliness, what madness, such a modern city.

"Then I have good news for you," said Emma. "The Wilsons have invited us to come and spend Thanksgiving with them at their cottage."

"You didn't say yes, I hope."

"Oh, come on, darling. I've never seen Marcel so radiant."

Thanksgiving
with the Wilsons

They drove northward, with Emma at the wheel. She had finally persuaded Joop to come too. To help him get over the death of Sorel, it would do him good to get away from everything for a while.

"Don't you think it looks a bit like the Morvan here?" she asked.

"Oh yes?" said Joop. "So I guess we'll see the cathedral of Vézelay around the next corner then, and we can go to that farm over there for fresh goat's cheese."

Morvan, my foot, thought Marcel, in the backseat. Canada is Canada, and it resembles nothing else. He was en route with his family to the Ultimate Canadian Experience: eating turkey in a cottage on Thanksgiving. The moment had finally come when the split in his immigrant's existence would be mended. The worlds of his great ice hockey friend Dave Wilson and his Dutch parents would now fit together like two large portions of a complicated jigsaw puzzle. That was always a major breakthrough. The remaining pieces of the puzzle would then fall into place almost automatically.

Emma was happy, too. She was thrilled to be driving through this unknown territory. It was too absurd for words that they had lived here for this long and never gone anywhere, apart from Niagara Falls.

The farther north they drove, the brighter the fall colors became. It gave her the shivers. Overwhelming, breathtaking; words did not suffice. She wrote a jubilant letter in her mind to all her Dutch girlfriends. *Think of a huge deciduous tree, dear people, and color the leaves the reddest red you can imagine. Put a tree next to it, and make this one bright orange. Add a third tree, and make it yellow. Then repeat all these steps until you have a gigantic forest, all aflame. And it goes on and on, my dear friends, it goes on and on, uninterrupted, all the way to the horizon! And if all this is too much for you, give your eyes a rest with the dark green of an occasional pine tree, and if that still isn't beautiful enough for you, then leave an open space here and there for a lake with a perfectly tranquil surface, in which the whole forest is reflected.*

At last she had found an appropriate response to "the Michaelmas daisies are blossoming like never before this year."

Joop thought the colors were garish to the point of vulgar. "They're much softer and more subtle in the Morvan."

Emma burst out laughing. "Sorry, darling, but now you're going too far. However you look at it, this is simply gorgeous."

He crossed his arms and said nothing more.

They had to leave the main highway at McCrawley Road, a gravel road that ended after ten bumpy miles in a parking lot at the edge of a lake.

Weekend bags in hand, they walked over a dock at which a few luxurious motorboats were moored. They were in perfect time. Within five minutes Donald came sailing up in his boat. Before they went on board, they all had to put on life jackets. Joop's was too tight, which didn't help his mood any.

Once they had chugged out of the little harbor, Donald accelerated. With the motor roaring louder and louder, they shot out onto the lake. The bow rose high up out of the water and pounded unpleasantly hard against the waves left behind by other boats. Left and right people waved exuberantly to each other. Only Joop didn't participate. This obligatory joviality on the water had always irritated him.

Now and again the boat sank back into the water, when Donald slowed down to proudly point out the cottage ("I would call it a villa!") of this or that Hollywood star. He told them that a lot of Americans were crazy about Muskoka, as this region of lakes was called. And that the cottage over there, with the two totem poles, was the Frasers', you remember Shirley, who used to be in Dave and Mark's class, and that one over there, with the mint-green boathouse, was the Marshalls' little retreat. He had been on the board of directors of Eaton's but was retired now.

Donald steered close to the shoreline so that he could show his guests a heap of metal overgrown with weeds. It turned out to be an interesting piece of Canadian heritage. It was where the railway of a forest company had once begun, where the logs that had first been transported over water were loaded onto railroad cars.

The next cottage they passed had been for sale for more than a year now. You know, the recession. But now was really an ideal time to buy. Prices were very low and it was only a question of time before the economy picked up again.

Marcel got excited about the idea. The Frasers, the Wilsons, the Marshalls all had cottages. Why not the Daalders? He looked at his father's miserable face, which lay on the overly tight life jacket like the head of John the Baptist. That was why. With those idiotic chocolates of his, they didn't even earn enough to buy a boathouse.

When they arrived at the Wilsons' cottage after a forty-five-minute ride, Margaret was standing on the dock to welcome them.

"Hi!" she called out. "How are you?"

Marcel went with Dave, his brother Greg, his sister Deborah, and her girlfriend Lindsay for another spin around the lake in the smaller outboard motorboat.

The adults walked up some wooden steps to the cottage, which had been built on the rocks, hidden among the pine trees. Inside, it smelled of turkey, even more so when Margaret opened the oven door and slid out the tray to baste the creature again in its own bubbling juices.

On the table stood four glasses of eggnog, a thick, sweet drink made from egg yolks and milk, which Canadians also drank at Christmas.

"With or without rum?" Margaret asked her guests.

"How about without eggnog?" asked Joop. "And you can leave the rum out too." Emma eyed him sternly. He had promised to behave.

Why didn't the boys go for a paddle in the canoe, suggested Margaret, after the other three had finished their glasses. That way the girls could catch up on the latest gossip.

Joop felt no affinity at all with Donald, but because the turkey was claiming all the oxygen in the cottage, he was glad to be able to get outside.

Again, he had to put on that awful life jacket. What were those Canadians so afraid of? A sudden tidal wave? The Loch Ness monster? When he settled in the bow of the wobbly canoe, he wasn't even allowed to sit on the little thatched seat, but only to lean against it with his backside while kneeling on the hard floorboards. Apparently it was better for the balance.

Silently, they paddled along close to shore. In the distance, the motorboat with the teenagers zigzagged over the water like a bothersome bluebottle, but when Donald and Joop sailed around a promontory, they found themselves in a quiet, tranquil bay where all they heard were their own paddles occasionally thumping against the sides of the canoe and the sucking sound of the little eddies left in their wake.

Although Joop had resolved to stay in a bad mood for the whole visit, despite himself he was impressed. So this was where the calmness of the Canadians came from. It was an almost mystical calmness.

But then something exciting happened after all.

"Look!" whispered Donald, pointing to the shore with his paddle. "A blue heron!"

Its wings flapping sluggishly, a perfectly ordinary blue heron flew up out of the reeds.

Joop burst out laughing.

"You see those everywhere in Holland."

"Really?" asked Donald, awestruck.

At Sorel's graveside Joop had vowed to wage the battle against bad taste. He kept his word, and the Wilsons became his first victims.

After they sat down at the table and the man of the house tackled the creature with a large carving knife and a carving fork, Joop fired away.

What was a turkey, he philosophized aloud, other than an oversized chicken, the way everything on this continent was oversized. The cars were turkeys on wheels. All those grossly overweight people were turkeys on shoes. Canada itself was a kind of bloated turkey. What in heaven's name was the point of all that useless land?

"We wonder that ourselves sometimes," acknowledged Donald, offering his guest a plate of meat.

Joop took a first bite. Very dry. As if the bird wasn't already big enough as it was, the meat seemed to expand in his mouth rather than shrink. It was as if he was chewing on a piece of rope.

The cranberry sauce was passed around.

"Meat with jam?" said Joop. "Interesting concept, but I'll pass."

"Would anyone like wine?" asked Donald, in the meantime.

It was a domestic wine called Northern Delight, with a horrid purple label on which a few Canada geese were waddling around.

"Wine?" asked Joop. "Where? I don't see wine anywhere."

Emma died a thousand deaths that evening. The Wilsons were the most good-natured, hospitable people you could imagine. For years they had taken Marcel to all those hockey practices without a murmur. Countless times he had been allowed to join them at their cottage. And by way of thanks, Joop gave them the full blast.

Now it was the vegetables that were no good. Squash, sweet potatoes, corn. It was like baby food, so sickly sweet. And by the way, did they know that in France corn was only fed to the pigs?

Marcel hid behind his piece of turkey wing. Like a hyena he tore off big pieces and gulped them down. He hated his father.

But despite all the insults, the Wilsons remained friendly. They were all too aware that a traditional Canadian Thanksgiving dinner was seriously deficient to the taste of a true European connoisseur like Joop.

"I hardly dare to ask," said Margaret, smiling dejectedly. "But would anyone like more?"

Emma certainly would. Gladly.

Joop looked at her with contempt. Emma, who normally never took a second helping, but who now wanted to undo the damage he had done. Typically Emma. Noble Emma.

Donald took a second portion as well, so as not to embarrass the guest.

Meanwhile, the children were allowed to leave the table until dessert was served.

Dessert was the umpteenth slap in the face for Joop: pumpkin pie. A cold, diarrhea-colored paste with a floury consistency, in itself an unusual experience. And whoever wanted to could spray a thick layer of fake whipping cream over the top.

When Joop was helping Donald move a bed after dinner, Emma took advantage of the opportunity to offer Margaret her humble apologies for her husband's misbehavior.

"He's having a very difficult time right now," she explained. "As you know, his teacher has just died, and now he's angry at everything and everybody."

"No problem," said her hostess. "He's just very direct. It's refreshing for a change. We Canadians can be so unhealthily polite. And besides, he's entirely right. I am a useless cook."

"That's not true at all!" Emma protested.

"Fibber!" said Margaret, laughing. "Now you're starting to sound Canadian."

Mark Daalder
Gets Ahead

After the disastrous Thanksgiving weekend, the dark glimmer returned to Marcel's eyes.

While most of his classmates worried about the disappearance of the rainforest, poverty in the Third World, and the power of multinationals, he and a few other classmates formed a club nicknamed the Rednecks. They had their hair cropped, and were militantly pro-American, avid supporters of the death penalty, and against premarital sex, although not all the members lived up to this. Like naughty boys pelting passersby with chestnuts from a tree house, so the Rednecks tried to shock their sensitive peers with their hard views.

The friendship with Dave Wilson, who didn't want anything to do with the Rednecks, came under pressure. Dave was still incredibly popular and was elected school captain by his fellow students in their last year. Because of the many activities this position brought with it and the pressure of schoolwork in the senior year, he decided to quit ice hockey.

The big dream of many seniors was to be accepted at one of the prestigious universities in the United States. Dave, for example, aimed for Harvard. Marcel, who was not very bright and didn't have a rich father to pay the high tuition, hoped to land a sports scholarship by excelling in ice hockey.

More fanatically than ever, he scared the life out of his opponents, but Dave's artistry was sorely missed and the team fell back to the anonymous middle of the league standings. When Marcel twisted his knee in another one of his hotheaded moves, he was out for the rest of the season. America thus became an unattainable ideal. For the last few months, he limped around the corridors of the school deeply frustrated.

Settling for Toronto by default, he decided to study law, motivated primarily by the big money there was to be earned in that field. During his studies, he pursued the line of the Rednecks by establishing *Goliath,* a satirical journal that stood up for the "rights of the strongest" and waged battle against the "terror of the underdog." He vigorously defended the right of the forest industry to chop down the last bit of northern rainforest in British Columbia, and of the trappers to club baby seals to death in Newfoundland.

On the editorial board he got to know Susan MacPherson, a respectable Canadian girl from a rich family. They married young, as befitted Rednecks, and the parents of the bride organized a garden party of an unprecedented grandeur.

After graduating, he got a job in a big law firm, where he specialized in environmental issues. His big opportunity came when there was an accident in a Canadian-owned chemical plant in Rio de Janeiro, resulting in a cloud of poisonous gas spreading over a slum. Three people died and dozens were injured. With the help of various international environmental organizations, a local lawyer launched legal proceedings. In response, the company called in a small army of lawyers from Canada, among them the fledgling Mark Daalder. Largely thanks to his rock-hard but brilliant plea, all the claims for damages were swept aside. In the end, the company didn't have to pay a single cent to the victims.

Marcel's reputation was established, but the public outrage

was enormous, even more so in Canada than in the country where the accident took place. The Canadian Broadcasting Corporation's coverage of the trial left the average viewer seething with helpless anger. Emma was also shocked and asked her son for clarification. The film was a perfect example of "underdog propaganda," he explained to her. Of course it was horrible to see a critically ill child wasting away in a dingy hospital. But to show a laughing Mark Daalder in the next shot, toasting with a glass of champagne to the favorable outcome in the boardroom of the chemical concern, that was a matter of suggestive editing. As if the lawyers of the victims wouldn't have drunk a glass if they had won. And besides, at the meeting in question the cameraman of the CBC had drunk everyone under the table!

It hurt Emma to hear her son talk this way. But Joop hadn't expected anything else. As a baby, Marcel had already been a cad who mowed everything and everybody out of his way and delighted in drawing and quartering the Sorels' beautiful teddy bear.

Golden Years

Following his master's death, Joop withdrew increasingly into the chocolate shop. After all, outside was where all the nonsense, the big void, began. He considered his kitchen a bastion of refinement in a world of encroaching bad taste.

Meanwhile, haute cuisine was coming into fashion in Canada. One day he was phoned by a journalist from *The Art of Living,* one of the countless glossy lifestyle magazines that modern Canadian consumers liked to model themselves after, who asked him if he was interested in an interview.

Absolutely not! He refused to be put on display as the newest yuppie toy. But after throwing down the receiver, he realized he had missed an ideal opportunity to vent his anger about the current spirit of the times in public. Didn't he owe that to Sorel? He telephoned back right away, to say he was interested after all, on the condition that he could say whatever he liked.

Of course he could. All the better, in fact.

Three weeks later his comments were available in every news kiosk.

The article opened with a full-page portrait of Joop at work in the kitchen of the chocolate shop. The journalist had asked him to look nice and stern—that suited the tone of the story. In it he recounted that, when he came to Toronto, the situation regarding the availability of quality chocolates had been deplorable. Although his chocolate shop had come to fill that void, there was still no one who had followed his good example. After a difficult start, everything was now going as he had hoped. In addition to the inevitable fatsoes, anorectics, and chocoholics, a handful of genuine connoisseurs—it was no coincidence that they were mostly European immigrants—had found their way to his shop. Not that he would ever become rich. Most Canadians simply had a taste that was too infantile to appreciate his chocolates. Anything with a cacao content higher than that of M&Ms was already too much for them.

With his punishing tone, Joop touched a nerve. Young, trendy Canadians were more ashamed than ever of their country and did everything they could to appear as cosmopolitan as possible. Many a reader of *The Art of Living* thus came to the following conclusion: if Canadians are too infantile to appreciate Joop Daalder's chocolates, and if I do like his chocolates, then I am no longer Canadian!

That same week, there was a run on his store.

Poor Martha Simmons, perfectly happy with her quiet job as a saleswoman at Daalder's Chocolates, came apart at the seams. Emma had to drop everything and come and help out in the shop. Joop didn't know what had hit him, either. Normally, after closing time, he would collect all the perishable chocolates on a tray and with a tiny, elegant prod of his knife, let them slide into the garbage bin ("my most faithful customer"). Now every last one of them was sold.

Whereas Emma and Martha fell into each other's arms, exhausted but elated, Joop didn't feel any cheerier from the sudden success. With his tirade in *The Art of Living*, his goal had been to keep the trendy boys and trendy girls at arm's length. And now they had advanced into his shop three rows deep.

Emma laughed happily at his grumbling. He was finally getting the recognition he deserved and still it wasn't good enough. She became even happier when she did the book-keeping. After all those difficult years, after those many evenings at the kitchen table with her hands in her hair when she had wondered how in heaven's name they could continue, now for the first time the future looked bright.

Jerry Somerville awoke from the slumber mode that for many years had been enough to supply that plodding little business with financial advice. It was time for action. This was the ideal moment for Daalder's Chocolates to expand. Joop should quickly hire a new hand to help in the kitchen, maybe even two. It was also advisable and for the first time financially feasible to move the business to a more fashionable area, like Yorkville, where his up-market product would be more at home than on St. Clair Avenue.

Joop refused to be goaded. Moving was out of the question, and he continued working at his usual slow tempo without hiring any extra help. He refused orders that were too big, and if the chocolates were finished halfway through the afternoon, it was just too bad for the customers. He preferred a few dissatisfied faces in the shop to some baby face beside him in the kitchen.

Emma knew her husband and hadn't expected otherwise. Jerry Somerville, too, resigned himself to his client's quirki-ness. Only Marcel gnashed his teeth watching his father miss opportunity after opportunity.

Meanwhile, people poured into the shop in ever-growing numbers. Daalder's Chocolates was "the best-kept secret in all of Toronto," which people could boast about at parties. Joop was "the difficult little man" with whom they had never-theless managed to establish a personal bond. Unpredictable behavior was simply inherent to the artist. That the choco-lates were sometimes finished midafternoon and that you often found yourself standing in front of a closed door simply added to the shop's charm. Besides, there was no alternative. The competition stubbornly persisted in catering to the traditional Canadian taste, at which the newfangled connoisseurs now turned up their noses.

Against his will, Joop became their hero. He only had to show his face in the shop and he was bombarded with questions. One person couldn't wait to share with him that she had tasted such and such a chocolate in a famous Viennese chocolate shop. Had he ever been there? Another wanted to know what exactly the difference was between cacao beans from Venezuela and those from the Ivory Coast. A third asked which "grand crus" he normally worked with. And had he seen the film *Chocolat*? And did he ever give courses?

Sometimes he exploded. They wanted to know something about chocolate in general and chocolates in particular? Then why didn't they surf to dublyooh-dublyooh-dublyooh-dot-chocolate-dot-whatever. He sold chocolates, not information! Upon which he turned around and slammed the kitchen door behind him.

The customers loved every bit of it. That man's anger—it was so wonderfully real!

Meanwhile, on the other side of the ocean, Françoise Daalder died after a short sickbed, at the respectable age of ninety-four. Since Joop's scandalous behavior at his father's funeral, his mother had never been in touch with him again. If next-of-kin turned out not to be kindred spirits, she saw no reason at all for maintaining any contact. Her daughters had followed suit.

And so Joop learned the news of her death from an official letter sent by a certain Mr. Andriessen, LL.M., executor of the will. He would be informed at a later date about the inheritance. Unfortunately, some legal complications had arisen.

His cousin Nico, presently the proud owner of several vacation parks scattered throughout the country, had launched legal proceedings in which he claimed half of Swaanendal, referring to the fact that his father had been robbed of his legitimate inheritance.

"No hard feelings, old buddy," he wrote in a letter to Joop. "But I had to set something straight. And who knows, maybe I'll be doing the dirty work for you, too. Because it wouldn't surprise me at all if your sisters tried to make off with all the loot on the pretext of conserving Swaanendal, just like your father did in his day."

That is, if there was anything left to conserve—for the estate had been in poor shape for years. To maintain the house, with pain in her heart Françoise had been forced to sell a large piece of land to the eldest son of Farmer Evert and Auntie Riet, who as a successful pig farmer was now wealthier than the landowners from whom his family had leased the land for generations. The proceeds fell drastically short of covering the cost of the repairs. Charlotte and Rosalinde had then thought up a rescue plan, the Friends of Swaanendal Foundation, under the auspices of which promising young musicians, sponsored by the business community, could stay on the estate during the summer months. But because of a dispute about the best strategy to follow, the plan never got off the ground.

Nico's legal proceedings were the final blow. The sisters tried to strike a deal in which their cousin would get his portion but at the same time commit himself to investing in the maintenance of the house. He flatly rejected the proposal. He wanted to see the color of money, with no fuss and bother.

After a lengthy trial, the judge ruled in Nico's favor, although in the end he was granted only a quarter and not half of the estate. Because the sisters weren't in a position to buy him and Joop out, there was no alternative but to sell Swaanendal—for the tidy sum of three million guilders. The new owner, a stock jobber still in his twenties, recovered his costs in no time by refurbishing part of the stately home, including the music room, as a training center where burned-out senior executives could learn to laugh and cry again.

By this time the chocolate shop was doing so well that Emma almost found it a shame when an enormous sum of money from Holland was transferred to their bank account in Toronto. It lacked all proportion: as if Daalder's Chocolates, her husband's life's work, and to some degree hers as well, had been devalued to a nice little job on the side.

The financial reserves came in very handy, though, when, soon after, MegaDeli and The Three Chocolateers appeared on the stage.

Part 6

ONE LAST CHOCOLATE

A Press Clipping

J oop sat in his armchair staring gloomily in front of him, following his visit to the demolition site on St. Clair Avenue. Emma and the grandchildren could come charging in at any moment.

What now?

Sighing, he picked up the pile of mail that Emma had already gone through and had laid out for him on the end table.

Bills, advertising brochures, the usual rubbish. But among them was also a letter from Peter and Corinne. Gosh, that was the first time in a long time. Joop had finally convinced Emma to limit her correspondence with them to the obligatory New Year's wishes. For a while their friends had persisted in writing, even though their letters remained unanswered, but in the end they had also called it a day. So they didn't even know about the demise of Daalder's Chocolates. It was a good thing, too. Commentary from Peter was the last thing Joop could use at this moment.

In her letter, Corinne acted as if the long silence had been her fault. Alas, she too had been caught up in the spirit of the times ("busy, busy, busy"), which was why she hadn't written for so shamefully long! But she was going to do more than make up for that now, not only with a nice long letter as of old, but also with the announcement that she and Peter would like to come and visit them in Toronto this fall! They were planning to rent a camper and travel around the country for a few weeks during the Indian summer.

Well, well. So their super-refined Dutch friends wanted to honor humble Canada with a visit, after they had turned their noses up at that for years on end. Why the about-face? Had some influential intellectual written a favorable travel account in the *Nieuwe Rotterdamse Courant* or some other highbrow newspaper or periodical?

Perhaps Emma and Joop could join them for a while, Corinne suggested. Maybe they could show them some of their favorite beauty spots.

Beauty spots? Canada was made up of regions that Holland would fit into God knows how many times. And that famous Indian summer might very well end up being the first snowstorm. Joop chuckled at the thought of Peter in his shorts, scraping ice off the windshield of the camper.

"P.S. Enclosed, a press clipping from the *Nieuwe Rotterdamse Courant*. Don't be put off. That BvB is pretty foul-mouthed, the way the young people here in Holland think they have to be in order to be taken seriously by each other. Is it like that in Canada too? All the same, his comments reminded us of the things Joop was saying years ago. Justice at last?"

Press clipping? What press clipping?

Just to be sure, Joop ran his fingers along the inside of the envelope and went through the pile of mail a second time. He looked on the floor, under his armchair, and among the letters piled near the telephone, then upstairs in the bedroom on Emma's night table, and even between the pages of the novel that was lying there. Then he returned to the living room, where he looked through the pile a third time and peered into the envelope again.

In the meantime, the front door opened gently. Ever so quietly

Jessica and Tyler sneaked straight on to the kitchen. Emma had drilled them well. Grandpa was unhappy because of Daalder's Chocolates and was to be left alone in his armchair there in the living room. As a reward, they were always given a glass of pop and a dish of candy. That was a big treat for them. Their mother never gave them anything containing sugar, because according to the latest research it made children aggressive. After their snack, Emma usually sent them to the guest room upstairs, where the television had been moved recently so that it wouldn't disturb Grandpa as much. Often during these visits, the children never even saw their grandfather.

But today he came into the kitchen of his own accord.

"Hey, Grandpa!" cried Jessica.

"Hello," he said, without looking at her. "Say, Emma, do you know where that press clipping is?"

"Press clipping? Oh, you mean the one from Peter and Corinne? That's funny . . . Wasn't it in the envelope?"

"Emma . . .," he began, sternly.

She blushed.

"I was afraid it would make you feel even worse," she confessed. "But if you insist on reading it, it's with the old newspapers."

Cursing, he went down the basement stairs. After looking in vain in the box with old newspapers and magazines, he enlisted the help of Emma, who fished out the clipping right away. He had missed it each time because it was printed on glossy paper. So Dutch newspapers had also started publishing glossy supplements. There was something pathetic about it, like those old men in the park near their house who rode around on Rollerblades in an effort to still be a part of it.

He returned to his armchair, reading as he went. BvB turned out to stand for a certain Bas van Beuningen, purportedly the enfant terrible in the world of Dutch chocolatiers. A photograph showed a young man with a blue crew-cut and a ring in his ear, who was sticking up both his middle fingers. The caption under the photograph: "A fuck-you attitude."

According to BvB, dullness prevailed in Holland, where staid old chocolate shops like that of Erik Vermeulen still set the tone. And this dismal state of affairs was perpetuated by the Golden Chocolates, which a small group of old men stuck up each other's asses every year. Meanwhile, elsewhere in the world the coolest things were happening with chocolate, not only in the traditional trend-setting countries like Belgium or France but also in North America, of all places. Right now, Marty Finnegan in Chicago was the absolute top. And The Three Chocolateers, over in Canada somewhere—in Quebec or thereabouts. Now, those were real artists!

But, unfortunately, the Dutch national character was made up of an ass-licking cautiousness, a lack of confidence in one's own potential, and a tremendous awe for outmoded traditions.

"That way, things will never change," said BvB. "If you want to make your mark as a chocolatier, you have to break new ground and not give a damn about anything or anybody. In short, you have to have the guts to adopt a fuck-you attitude."

"Nice, eh?" Corinne had scribbled in the margin next to the part where The Three Chocolateers were mentioned. "Do you know them?"

Joop stood up and walked to the hallway to put on his jacket.

Emma tried to stop him, but for the second time that day he set out for St. Clair Avenue.

Angrier Than Angry

The automatic doors swung open and Joop entered the modern consumer's paradise.

He had sworn never to set foot in MegaDeli, but the Bas van Beuningen interview had been the last straw. It had now become a question of self-preservation. If he didn't want to literally die of irritation, he had to make a move. It was time for a direct confrontation, so that after all the years of repressed anger he could finally really explode. Even if they had to carry him off to a mental institution frothing at the mouth.

Food, as far as the eye could see. Total madness. But high up above all the delights, from various speakers in the ceiling, emanated the soothing voice of Louis Armstrong, singing what a wonderful world it was. If a poor black man like him already thought so, well, what could you, as a privileged white man, possibly say against it? That was very clever of MegaDeli.

It was the evening rush hour, the moment when, after a superinspiring day at work, hip young people popped in to score a few delicacies. It seemed they scored more than just delicacies. In a recent newspaper article the supermarket was lauded as the "hottest meat market in town," where hyperattractive singles eyed each other lasciviously from behind their shopping carts. And, of course, those weren't just ordinary carts they were pushing in front of them. They were tapered at the front and had three sturdy rubber wheels attached below, instead of four dumb little swiveling wheels. The design had been copied from those cool modern baby buggies like the one Marcel and Susan drove their little King Tyler around in. The unwieldy, somber perambulators of yesteryear over which admiring old ladies used to lean had made way for these battering rams. Here we come! Out of the way!

And now it was the turn of everyday shopping to be elevated to a dynamic statement.

Joop admonished himself to remain calm. Don't get wound up about those irritating carts. Don't look around too much. Don't use your ammunition too early. Hurry on past.

Up ahead, the aisle was blocked by a pretty young thing accosting passersby with crackers covered with foie gras. She really did look as sweet as could be, with her radiant smile and the freckles on her nose, but Joop gave her such a foul look that she left him alone. No foie gras. Not now.

It was all there, Joop observed, out of the corner of his eyes. The very best that French and Italian cuisines had to offer, all the exquisite products he often yearned for—and much, much more.

Venison steaks, for example—on sale, even.

They had a "spectacularly subtle flavor."

Spectacularly subtle. That's what it really said!

No, ignore it. Head straight for your target, and only explode there.

But to head straight for your target was easier said than done. The aisles made all kinds of so-called "playful," so-called "organic" turns and often ended in open spaces from which there was no other exit. The signposting had doubtless been contracted out to some hip design agency, judging by the many incomprehensible little symbols in fluorescent colors, and had probably intentionally been designed to scare off older people like him.

After having to walk past the goose-liver-girl twice, he more or less accidentally bumped into his goal.

You could walk right around their "chocolate studio," so that you could observe, from all sides, what a terrific time they were having.

Amid great public interest, the boy with the rings through his eyebrow held up a skewer with flaming chunks of papaya, which he extinguished with a thin spray of chocolate from a little can.

Yes, flambéing was always a crowd pleaser. The end result—pieces of fruit coated in chocolate—came horridly close to chocolate fondue, the dish to which his master had taken such offense that alone the thought of it had killed him. It could hardly be more obscene, but Joop looked on silently and did nothing.

"You look like someone who might enjoy a course in making chocolates," resounded a chirpy voice.

Like everyone around him, Joop had a folder pushed into his hands by the boy with the goatee. The same boy who, not long ago, had so brazenly come into Daalder's Chocolates seeking to buy kitchen equipment didn't even recognize him now. He, the proud chocolatier, was seen as just another sucker who might want to take a course. Well then! Wasn't this the ideal moment to explode? "Visit our Web site," it said on the back of the folder. Oh sure, why not.

Joop walked around the studio. There, the third one of The Three, the girl with the silver pimple on her lower lip, stood sculpting a head of chocolate. The model, a young woman from the public, looked rather plain, but she became almost beautiful the way she sat there posing, with a self-conscious, inward smile, gaped at by an admiring public, with her boyfriend proud as a peacock in the front row. When the portrait was finished, it was turned in all directions to loud applause. The boyfriend nodded enthusiastically and pulled out his wallet. And the spectators started walking off with their shopping carts in search of the next attraction.

While the artist washed her hands, she noticed that someone was still standing there. Did he perhaps want to pose too?

Joop was startled by the sudden attention and shook his head vigorously.

"Are you sure, sir? Because you do have a good head for it."

She looked at him with such an open, warm expression that he almost felt conscience-stricken. As if needing to make amends for something, he pointed to the shelf behind her, where a row of chocolate Venuses of Willendorf stood, the fertility figure she had spoken about in *The Art of Living*.

She wrapped one for him.

"Here you go, sir." The silver pimple on her lower lip bobbed as she spoke.

Instead of shouting his head off at The Three Chocolateers, Joop now bought back his freedom — for the sum of sixty-five Canadian dollars.

The box only just fit into the inside pocket of his jacket. Then off he raced — to the extent that the tortuous route allowed it — to the nearest exit.

Emma served dinner. Joop joined the others at the table, but avoided Emma's anxious look. It was the look of a damage expert inspecting a house after an earthquake. How much danger was there of a cave-in? Were we dealing with uninhabitable ruins here? As usual, little Tyler was stuffing himself and paying attention to nothing else, but Jessica secretively eyed her unhappy grandfather. He had already noticed on other occasions that his dark moods intrigued her, and this moved him deeply. But it was going too far for him to let this show. Each time he looked grumpily in her direction, she diligently started eating again or quickly struck up a conversation with her grandmother.

After dinner, he returned to his armchair.

The front door flew open and a heavy bag was dropped on the floor with a tired sigh. It was their daughter-in-law, Susan, on her way home from her fitness training, come to pick up her children. She stuck her head around the corner of the living-room door to greet her father-in-law, then continued to the kitchen. She always brought a whirlwind of unrest with her, so that within five minutes one or both of the children were in tears. Today it was Tyler, who made it known with a temper tantrum that he didn't want to go home yet. The children hadn't been given any sweets, had they, he heard Susan ask Emma. They had? Damn it, wasn't it obvious by now what a terrible state it put the poor little fellow in? How often did she have to explain? Come on, kids, we're leaving. Damn it.

After they were gone and the house was quiet again, Joop heard Emma wash the dishes, then knead the bread dough. She went upstairs earlier every evening, especially now that she no longer had to do the administration for Daalder's Chocolates. These days, she came downstairs in her nightgown only to take the bread out of the oven, and then was off to bed.

"Don't stay up too late, darling," she said.

"Yes, yes. I'll be up in a minute."

When the lights upstairs had gone out and it was completely quiet, Joop snuck into the hallway and pulled the box with the Venus of Willendorf out of his jacket. Back in his armchair, he turned the robust little figurine around and around in his hands. Where should he start? Should he shave off a layer from her bosom with his front teeth, or take a bite out of her buttocks first? In the end, he jammed her head between his jaws and broke off the rest of her body.

With his tongue, he rolled the head around in his mouth, which slowly filled with saliva and chocolate. He hoped she would taste bad, he was afraid she would taste good, but she tasted . . . Hmm, how did she really taste?

The Cruel Sense

Joop swallowed the chocolate and returned the beheaded primeval woman to the box. He had known it for some time now, although he didn't know for how long exactly.

He couldn't taste anymore.

Or ... no, it wasn't that. It was worse.

Because if he had really lost his sense of taste, he could at least be considered a tragic hero. Peter and Corinne had once sent him the Dutch translation of a Japanese novel about an aging chef who had lost his sense of taste, grabbed his boss's flirtatious daughter in desperation, and ended up on the street.

But Joop's tastebuds were fine. That wasn't the real problem.

He had to be honest with himself now. Daalder's Chocolates was passé, that much was clear. He had been overtaken on the left by The Three Chocolateers, and on the right by Bas van Beuningen. As a chocolatier he had nothing left to contribute, now that even his former archrival Erik Vermeulen had been jeered offstage by the new generation. Earlier today, he hadn't even been recognized in MegaDeli. He had been reduced to just another passerby with a folder pushed into his hands, to just another nobody who might like to pose and thereby lift himself out of the anonymity of the everyday, even if only for a moment. Once again he was as invisible as he had been in his childhood, when he wandered lonesomely around the estate. That was why it was important to be honest now, however painful that may be. It was the only chance left for him if he didn't want to dissolve into the void.

Well, then, how long had he had this problem? Since Sorel's death, when he had started to see chocolate making as a political act? Since he had wanted to pour chocolate sauce over Julia Shaw's breasts out of pure boredom? Or had it already begun when he was wasting away as a misunderstood genius in Otto and Erik Vermeulen's kitchen? Or even in heavenly France, when he had burst into tears at every moment of hyperharmony? Had it perhaps always been this way? From the very beginning?

I taste, therefore I am.

It had been a beautiful moment when, during that murderous walk in Provence, he had taken a bite out of that apricot. They were all beautiful moments, those moments of tasting that had made his life worthwhile.

But when I'm not tasting, I still am, and what then?

That's when the problems began, the nonsense, the big void.

Longing nostalgically for those overwhelming moments, clinging to them desperately, making everything depend on them, he had behaved more and more like a religious zealot or a terrified despot. To avoid acknowledging the void, he had worked himself into a frenzy, until he had begun to confuse his anger with the passion that was absent, and had gone into a trance. But it was a destructive sort of trance. To avoid collapse, he had had to rotate on his axis like a tornado and lash out around him like a madman.

There was a reason that the ultimate confrontation with The Three Chocolateers had come to nothing. At the eye of the storm, calm prevailed; at the heart of his faith, a total lack of faith prevailed. And that was where he found himself now.

It didn't matter anymore. He didn't need to form an opinion about the Venus of Willendorf anymore.

All his anger and his taste were spent.

His mouth had become a mausoleum, where his tongue lay embalmed like a dead despot.

la la la
he pinched the corpse and pulled at it
luh luh luh

The Cruel Sense. That was the name of the novel about the Japanese chef. "An intense and tragic story," according to the review Peter and Corinne had sent along with the book. Especially the gory final scene, in which the chef cuts off his tongue with a kitchen knife in a fit of madness, was lauded as a tranquil, almost abstract choreography.

But Joop, if he was honest—and he had to be honest now to avoid becoming invisible—had returned from MegaDeli anything but hopping mad. Instead, he was relieved that all his anger had been spent.

Was the world being ruined by bad taste? Well, the world was being ruined by so many things. To each his own, you might say. Even doom scenarios had become a commodity nowadays. So you might as well leave them on the shelf and just keep on walking.

It didn't matter anymore. Peace at last, the peace of the bay where he had canoed with Donald Wilson on the Thanksgiving weekend a few years ago. An almost mystic peace.

Joop suddenly blushed.

He remembered how the peace of the bay had been disturbed when Donald had pointed out a blue heron, and how he had laughed scornfully. And how he had gone on to ridicule Margaret because of her turkey. Had he ever ranted and raved that evening!

In the end, he hadn't shed a single tear about the demise of Daalder's Chocolates. But now he did cry—about the havoc that his tyrannical tongue had wreaked over the years. He wasn't only thinking of the infamous Thanksgiving dinner, but of all the decent customers he had abused, and of Emma, how for thirty years she had stood dead tired every evening, kneading bread because the store-bought stuff wasn't good enough for him, and of how, by way of thanks, he had deceived her with Julie Shaw. And of how, since Marcel's birth, he had never given him a fair chance, and of how he had already started to find him repulsive because he drank breast milk. He cried about all of this—and about much, much more.

Now that all his anger and taste were spent, he wouldn't act like a proud samurai and cut off his tongue. Rather, he would live out his days as a tearful old man, as the lead actor in the kind of sickly-sweet family film that Hollywood secreted every year around Christmas, as the miser who sees the error of his ways and turns out to have a heart of gold. Too good to be true? Perhaps. But at least he could give it a try. Perhaps it wasn't too late to make amends here and there.

Now that all his anger and taste were spent, and his energy and tears as well, Joop walked upstairs to bed. After brushing his teeth, he looked at himself in the bathroom mirror. What an ugly old head he had now.

He stuck his tongue out—at himself, but, more specifically, at his tongue.

A Small Gesture of Reconciliation

Emma noticed a change in Joop. He no longer went to look at the demolition site every day. Sometimes when she came home from shopping, he would be on the phone, but he never wanted to say with whom. He bought the Saturday editions of various newspapers, something he had always detested, and sifted through the classified ads without saying what he was looking for. He went off in the car and stayed away all day, only to return home by evening. If she asked him where he had been, he said he had gone for a ride to calm down. A strange reply. He had never been that kind of a man.

One morning, smiling secretively, he invited her to come with him. In the car. He didn't want to say where. It had to remain a surprise.

They drove out of the city, heading north. The spring green gradually crawled back into the buds, and there was still some snow in the fields. Soon they were driving through a forest. Joop now even wanted her to close her eyes. She felt the car turn off the road and heard the tires crunch on gravel. They stopped.

"Don't look yet," said Joop.

He got out, opened her door, and supported her by the elbow to help her out of the car.

"Yes, now!"

They were standing in the forest on a muddy driveway in front of a wooden cabin. A FOR SALE sign was nailed to a tree.

"And?" asked Joop.

"You don't mean . . . But surely this is nothing for you, such a cabin?"

"A person is never too old to change."

He led her by the hand over the path that ran behind the house. After walking a few dozen yards through the bushes, they arrived at a lake. Along the shore, a few other cottages were visible among the trees.

"Shallow Lake," said Joop, beaming.

As they stood there together looking out over the tranquil black water on which large, white chunks of ice still floated, he told her about his visit to The Three Chocolateers, how he hadn't exploded but had instead seen the error of his ways, and how his dictatorial tongue had come to rest, and how, in a vision, he had seen himself canoeing with Donald Wilson through that calm bay. This was how the idea had come to him of going to look for a cottage of his own.

They walked back along the path to take a look at the inside of the cabin. It smelled musty, the floorboards creaked, and the doors sagged on their hinges. Joop told her it had belonged to an elderly couple. After their deaths, it had taken a few years before the heirs had decided to sell.

"Talking about elderly couples, aren't we much too old to start on something like this?"

"It's not only for us, but especially for Marcel, Susan, and the grandchildren."

"But all the work . . ."

"We don't have to do it. The real-estate agent has recommended a handyman who lives just down the road from here. Very reliable and not expensive."

"I don't know, darling."

"Come," said Joop, taking her hand and leading her out-side, back to the car.

"Where are we going now?"

"To the real-estate agent's, to complete the last formalities."

Emma looked at him incredulously. The last formalities? Joop, who in his long career as a chocolatier had never had to add more than a scribble to forms or invoices because she had always taken care of everything, that same Joop had now arranged everything on his own initiative. Now she was the one who had to do nothing but cosign the papers, as the lawful wife.

It made her anxious, and excited, and giggly. It was absurd. But at the same time this was the dream Marcel had already had as a young boy—a cottage of their own. And with that, perhaps her dream would also be realized, the dream of a reconciliation between father and son.

"I'll have to sleep on it for a few nights at least," she said. "I can't oversee it yet."

"You can never oversee a leap in the dark. Even if you sleep on it for a few nights. And we have to decide quickly. There seem to be other candidates, too."

"According to the real-estate agent."

"Do you remember what Nico said once? Sometimes you have to say 'Wow!' instead of 'Well . . .'"

Emma still had her reservations, but she couldn't deny that the sullen lines between Joop's eyebrows had disappeared for the first time in years.

They stopped in a tiny village comprising a grocery shop, a gas station, a fake wigwam where Indian souvenirs were sold during the summer, and a cluster of wooden houses. They walked toward the mint-green house of Vivian LaRue, the real-estate agent. She was wearing equally mint-green nail polish and eye shadow, her living room was filled with little porcelain frogs, and she called Joop "honey" and Emma "darling."

Hoping for the best, Emma signed the papers.

To celebrate the transaction, Vivian appeared with a pot of tea and a cream-filled cake covered with a soft-green frosting that turned out to taste like peppermint. Glancing defiantly in Emma's direction, Joop ate every last bit of his piece. Fortunately, he declined a second one, otherwise she really would have started to worry about his mental state.

The handyman set to work almost immediately. His name was Lenny McIntyre and he lived a few miles farther down on Shallow Lake. He drove up early one morning in a pickup truck filled with tools and building materials. He was a taciturn man with an expressionless face half hidden behind a baseball cap. He never laughed but he also never complained, and he worked like a horse. Occasionally, his son Kirk came along and helped too.

Whenever he could, Joop drove to Shallow Lake so he could follow the progress. Sometimes he even stayed overnight. He helped where possible, although he realized Lenny was a hundred times handier and stronger, and that he only got in his way. One day, Lenny had felled a pine tree that was growing too close to the cabin. Joop thought it would be an ideal task for him to remove the many little side branches from the trunk with a hand saw. As he worked, it struck him how simple his thoughts were, how straightforward, like the sawing itself, without all the little detours and hidden meanings that had always bothered him when he was fiddling away at a chocolate. But his salutary work meditations came to an end when Lenny saw him slaving away and thought he would do him a favor by whizzing over the trunk with a chainsaw.

In the evenings, Joop reported on the progress at Shallow Lake. He proudly let Emma smell the black patches of resin on the palms of his hands and feel the rough calluses on his once-so-velvety fingers.

To his disappointment, his wife seldom went with him. She preferred to stay in Toronto to take care of the grandchildren. Marcel had to go to the United States more and more often lately, and with Susan's busy job and various other activities, the threat of a nanny loomed. Not that Emma had any objection on principle to a paid babysitter—she had, after all, been an au pair herself. But Susan was so quickly dissatisfied. It had happened several times in the past that such a girl had been fired over some trifle or other, just when the children were starting to become attached to her.

One warm day in May, Joop was sitting on the brand-new sundeck leafing through a thick motorboat catalogue. He asked Lenny for advice. He wanted to buy a boat that didn't make too much noise but that was powerful enough for water skiing— not that he would ski himself, of course, but his son and daughter-in-law would, and before long, their children, too.

Lenny took off his baseball cap, a habit of his whenever he had to throw cold water on the plans of an overly enthusiastic customer. There was a reason why the lake was called Shallow Lake, he explained. There were such shallows here, and right out to the middle of the lake, that at the very best it was suited for a flat-bottomed boat with a light outboard motor.

Somewhat disappointed, Joop now skipped the pages with speedboats and asked advice on the lighter boats. They chose one together, and Joop asked Lenny to go and fetch it with his pickup truck.

After the motorboat had been bought, it was time to buy a lawn mower.

Again, the baseball cap was taken off. A lawn mower? But there was no grass here, was there?

"Not yet, but between the deck and the lake I want to plant a lawn where I can play ball with my grandchildren."

"Play ball? So it has to be leveled, too?"

Lenny calculated how many cubic meters the ground would have to be raised, and how many truckloads were needed for that. Moreover, because of the poor drainage, big ditches would have to be dug on both sides of the lawn. And then there was the question of whether the grass would even grow on this marshy soil.

"As long as we leave a wide strip at the sides for flower beds," mused Joop. "My wife loves gardening."

"No problem," said Lenny, sighing. He put on his baseball cap and went back to work.

In addition, Joop wanted a canoe, a gas barbecue, and, in time, a snowmobile.

Meanwhile, the costs were skyrocketing.

For years, Emma had managed to keep Daalder's Chocolates afloat by being tight-fisted. Thriftiness had become second nature to her, a habit she could no longer unlearn, not even after the money from Swaanendal was transferred to their account. But Joop, who as a chocolatier had never worried about money because his wife had done that for him, now encountered a fat bank account and dipped into it at will. In the beginning, Emma had the greatest difficulty not to interfere with his exorbitant spending, but in the end, sighing happily, she forced herself to let go of her worries. What did money really matter? What was important in life, anyway? Joop was so much happier now that he had definitively said good-bye to Daalder's Chocolates. Across the board, he had become a more positive, nicer person. Recently, for example, she was in the kitchen kneading bread when he had come up to her and said, with a soft, almost shy voice, that she no longer needed to bake bread for him if she didn't feel like it. She thought it was so considerate of him, so sweet, that she had promptly carried on with the routine.

Marcel was less charmed by his father's miraculous

transformation. They were barely rid of Daalder's Chocolates and now that stupid cabin was soaking up all the
money. And there was his mother thinking he would jump
for joy—because it had been his dream, a real cottage! Yes,
a long time ago, maybe, but not any more. He had had
trouble finding Shallow Lake on the map. Just what he
thought, anything but a top location. He had raced there
with the car to view the damage with his own eyes.
Swearing, he drove over the gravel road that led around the
lake. His suspicions were confirmed by the ramshackle
houses, the caved-in sheds, the lots full of car wrecks that,
according to the DANGER SIGNS, were guarded by blood-
thirsty dogs. Shallow Lake was a refuge for weird odd-jobbers,
for dimwits who decorated their houses with hubcaps and
who would stick their heads in a bucket of shit for as long
as possible if that would get them into *The Guinness Book of
World Records*. Losers' Lake it should be called. And now his
father had bought a cottage there.

He turned around and drove full-speed back to Toronto.

A bad buy, he told his father. He could just as well withdraw all of his money from the bank and throw it straight into
the water.

Joop underwent Marcel's anger stoically. He had allowed
for that risk. Reconciliations were simply less spectacular and
complete than Hollywood films suggested. Perhaps a generation would have to pass to undo the damage his dictatorial
tongue had done. That was why he concentrated on Jessica
and Tyler. In the meantime of course, he hoped that Marcel
would come round when he saw how much his children liked
the cottage.

As soon as the rougher work was finished, Joop and
Emma took the grandchildren with them for a day. From the
brand-new dock, they chugged off over the lake in the newly

purchased motorboat. At the last moment, Joop had thought of lifejackets—because you never knew—and Emma had thought of suntan lotion—because Susan insisted the children's tender skin be covered with factor 30, even in the scantiest rays of sun. The four of them enjoyed themselves to the hilt, even though the boat ran aground a few times and they had to row back quite some distance after the motor shut off and Joop couldn't get it started again. After that, the children spent hours by the dock, catching tadpoles and water bugs with hand nets. At Grandpa's request, Grandma kept the day completely sugar-free. There had to be as little reason as possible for Susan to complain. As exemplary grandparents, they would deliver two radiant grandchildren to their grateful parents after a lovely day in the great outdoors.

There was something, though, they hadn't reckoned with. It was June, the season when the infamous black flies were at their worst. Scarcely larger than fruit flies, they were more dastardly than mosquitoes. Unnoticed, they would take a small bite out of your body, and instead of a bump, leave a red hole in your skin that itched like mad for days on end.

Susan was livid. Tyler in particular was completely covered. There were seven spots on his darling little face alone. And were they aware of the fact that black fly bites could leave scars?

That same evening, Marcel phoned a former fellow student to ask what legal steps were necessary to declare someone a ward of the court owing to senility.

Word of Thanks

The cottage was ready by the beginning of October, in time for Thanksgiving. Now, in their own cottage, they would have another go at the ultimate Canadian experience, which Joop had once spoiled so completely for the others.

Joop invited Donald and Margaret as well. Regrettably, they were unable to come. They had other plans, resulting indirectly from Joop's behavior during the Thanksgiving dinner at their cottage. Margaret had taken his criticism to heart and, immediately upon her return to Toronto, had registered for a course in French cooking. She had liked it so much that since then, she had worked her way up through all kinds of follow-up courses to become an amateur chef of some distinction and a discerning connoisseur. She and Donald were flying to France now, right on the Thanksgiving weekend. A specialized travel agency had mapped out a *route culinaire* for them in the Loire valley.

Marcel would have preferred to call it off, too, but under pressure from his daughter, who had been primed for weeks by her grandparents, he couldn't get out of it. The closer they came to Shallow Lake, the angrier he was that he had succumbed.

"Father's latest chocolate," he growled, when the cottage came into sight after the next curve. "And we have to play the filling."

Joop was outside raking leaves and waved to them.

"Grandpa!" cried Jessica. She threw the door open, rushed over to him, and jumped into his arms. "Grandpa!"

Still hugging, they did a pirouette together. Then he put her down to shake his son's hand.

"Hello, Mark!"

That was his newest thing. After all those years, he had suddenly decided to drop "Marcel."

While Marcel and Susan went inside to greet Emma, Joop began to horse around with his grandchildren on the lawn.

An hour later, they sat down to dinner. All the ingredients for a traditional Thanksgiving meal were present: turkey with cranberry sauce, sweet potatoes, pumpkin, corn.

Marcel was astonished. What was it his father had said? Meat with jam? Baby food? Pig feed? There was even a bottle of Canadian wine on the table, would you believe it!

Joop then gave a speech in which he delved deeply into his own conscience, before delving into the turkey with the knife. He addressed himself to his grandchildren, to Jessica in particular, because Tyler, of course, didn't understand any of it. He told her about long, long ago, when Grandpa was still a little boy, and a Canadian soldier had kneeled down in front of him and said, "Here you go, sonny," and handed him a bar of chocolate. And that he had thought the chocolate tasted awful and had spat it out on the street. And that his eldest sister Charlotte had smacked him, and called him an ungrateful wretch. And that not long ago, another Canadian had handed him chocolate with a "Here you go, sir." A woman chocolatier. No spitting out this time, and no slap from an older sister, and still this chocolate made him realize for the first time that he had indeed been an ungrateful wretch—in fact, all his life.

So, on this day of giving thanks, he, the ungrateful wretch of yesteryear, wanted to thank everyone after all: Canada and the

Canadians, who had made Daalder's Chocolates possible; Margaret and Donald Wilson, who unfortunately couldn't be with them that evening, for their unremitting support, even in difficult times; his wife, who had stood by him so faithfully all these years and borne him a son; his son, who, with his candid criticism over the years, had kept him alert; his daughter-in-law, who had given him two beautiful grandchildren. And lastly, he wanted to thank his grandchildren, for not having beaten him too badly at soccer just now. Everyone had to laugh except Marcel.

Ha, ha, ha, he thought. A final joke to wash away the sweetness, surging music, end of film. No way.

While the smiling paterfamilias sank the knife into the turkey, the son now stood up.

"I also have an important announcement to make. I've accepted a job with Merson, Prim & Gilmore. We're moving to Texas."

Joop looked up from his slicing. "Are you? Really?"

"When?" asked Emma.

"At the end of the month. We already have a house."

"And I've found a terrific job as well," added Susan. "In the marketing department of one of Mark's clients. We only wanted to tell you when everything was settled. And now it is."

Marcel saw it was the wrong person who was affected by the news. It was his mother who had turned pale, not his father, who had returned to carving the turkey with a fury.

"And how will you manage things with the children?" she asked.

"Oh," said Susan. "We'll find a nanny. We're close to Mexico, so there's plenty of choice."

"What in heaven's name is going on, that all you young people want to leave this wonderful country?" asked Emma angrily. "You have a good life here, don't you? What does the United States have to offer that you don't have here?"

"More money," said Marcel, chuckling. "And the death penalty."

Joop usually didn't have a good word to say about the United States, the country that had brought forth Graham Kelso and MegaDeli, but this time he didn't respond to Marcel's provocations.

"You're always welcome here," he said. "In the summer holidays, at Christmas, and anytime in between. Even when we're not here."

"Well, thanks, Pa, but I think there's enough for us to see down there for the time being. We're only a one-day drive from the Grand Canyon. A teeny-weeny bit more spectacular, I would think, than Shallow Lake, with all due respect."

"No problem," said Joop. "Jessica, what shall I slice for you?"

No problem? You just couldn't break this man. Marcel had had it.

"Come on, Susan. Come on, children. We're going home."

Susan looked at her husband for a moment, baffled. But when she saw he meant it, she stood up too.

"Hey, people, what kind of weird game are you playing at?" cried Emma.

"This," said Marcel, gesturing to the Thanksgiving table, "this is the weird game. And we're not playing anymore."

"Come along, children," said Susan. "You heard your father. We're leaving."

"But we haven't eaten yet!" protested Jessica. "And we were going to sleep here!"

"Quiet now. When you're older you'll understand this much better."

Jessica began to cry. Emma began to shout. But Marcel and Susan were implacable. They got into the car with the children and drove off.

"Self-inflated old bastard," muttered Marcel, as he tore off over the gravel road at a considerable speed.

Susan patted him on the thigh. "First rate, darling."

But Jessica was crying in the backseat. Tyler looked at his big sister and began to whimper too.

"Listen here, Jessie," said Marcel, looking at his daughter in the rearview mirror. "Thanksgiving is originally an American celebration. You're supposed to celebrate it on a Thursday in November, not a Sunday in October. What they celebrate here in Canada is a fake Thanksgiving. It's much cooler to eat turkey in November, the way the Americans do it. And shall I tell you both something? In two weeks we'll be living in Texas, so we're in plenty of time for the real celebration! Okay? And Daddy and Mommy will open a bottle of California wine then, which will be just a teeny-weeny bit tastier than Grandpa's Canadian wine, right, Susan?"

When Jessica noticed that her mother was laughing, she began to cry even harder.

"And now shut up!" shouted Marcel.

In the miles that followed, a tense silence reigned in the car.

"I have a good idea," said Susan finally. "When we get to Orillia, we'll go to McDonald's!"

"To McDonald's!" cried Tyler happily.

Jessica didn't react. A dark look had come into her eyes, exactly like her grandfather's when he had been so sad about Daalder's Chocolates.

Old Man with Ax

N o-o-o . . . problem!

Joop was chopping wood.

Lenny had cut down a dead birch tree and sawed the trunk into pieces, which still had to be split to fit into the wood-burning stove. "Let the ax do the work," he had said. "Don't tense up, don't hesitate, but do pay attention that you don't chop your own foot in two." Joop had almost mastered the stroke. Relaxed concentration, that was the secret. Like when he had chopped almonds for Sorel.

Chopping wood near the cottage on a cold October morning: it couldn't be more Canadian. There was still some mist, but it was going to be another sunny day. The fall colors were at their peak now. Crazy to have called them vulgar, the way he had that time when they were driving up to the Wilsons. They were simply exquisite! Too bad Peter and Corinne had decided to go to Crete at the last moment (Peter had been suffering from sinusitis for months, and after the miserable summer in Holland, they wanted to catch some sunlight before the dark days arrived. Next year perhaps?).

By this time, Joop was rather hot.

The dictator in his mouth was stirring and licked the perspiration off his upper lip. And sure enough, he tasted the salt. His taste buds were perfectly fine. But now it was an ex-dictator who was tasting, who, in the quiet of his dacha, was reflecting back on a turbulent life. He tasted, but without attaching any consequences to it, without bothering anyone with it. Such experiences of joy were the purest of all, like the ones he knew from his childhood when he had wandered around the estate on his own, chewing on a sorrel leaf, feeling the space around him — space he felt now, too. Strange, though, to move to a vast country like Canada, then spend all your time obsessed with the inside of a chocolate.

He lifted the ax high above his head.

No-o-o . . . problem!

But now there really was a problem, albeit a small one. The ax had become lodged in the wood. Perhaps he had held himself back at the last moment. By placing a foot on the block of wood, he managed to dislodge the blade from the crack.

Then he lifted the ax high above his head again.

No-o-o . . . problem!

This time he went right through the wood.

But the effort had made Joop dizzy. The blood left his head, the fall colors became paler, more European. Staggering as if drunk, he let the ax fall out of his hands. Easy does it, he thought, panting, as he tasted iron in the back of his throat, easy does it, easy does it . . .

The colors slowly returned.

Oof! Mustn't overdo it.

Just three more blocks of wood, then an invigorating dive into the lake. As a manner of speaking, then, because the water was too shallow for diving. Two blocks of wood would do. Or maybe even one. You know what, fellow, you don't have to prove a thing, you've already done more than enough.

His arms filled with wood, he walked to the side of the cottage, where Lenny had recently built a lean-to to keep the woodpile dry. It was a nice job, stocking the pile with freshly chopped wood.

He stamped the mud off his shoes and went inside. Emma was sitting in the chair staring in front of her.

"Whenever you want," he said. "I'll go with you, too. And if they don't want us to stay with them, we'll take a motel close to where they live."

Poor Emma. She was completely out of sorts because of the Texas business. She had cried, at length, which she never did normally. The grandchildren meant everything to her. But he would help her through this dip.

"I'm going for a swim. Do you want to come?"

Emma shook her head.

In his white bathrobe, Joop walked down the path to the lake. He dropped the robe on the dock. Now he was naked. That was no problem here. No one saw him. It had been a cold night, and because the water was warmer now than the air, steam rose up off it. His perspiring body gave off steam, too. He climbed down from the dock. For a moment, he had the illusion of stepping into a warm bath. But it was just an illusion. The water was only slightly less icy than the air. That was all.

An ambitious son who had moved to the United States with his young family to make more money? It couldn't be more Canadian. No problem.

He looked over his shoulder and saw Emma standing in front of the window. He waved to her. At first nothing happened, but then she raised her hand hesitantly. A good sign. She was doing a bit better already. Suddenly he had to think of Emma rising up like a wood nymph out of the black water in the Morvan. Now the roles were reversed. Well, not exactly: naturally there was a difference between an old man with a fat belly and pale spindly legs, and a young woman in the prime of her life. God, was she ever beautiful that day!

Holding on to the dock with one hand, he inched his way over the slippery bottom. Beyond the last reeds, the ground under his feet became more solid again. The water was so misty now that he couldn't even see the other side of the lake. He waded a bit deeper till the water reached halfway up his thighs. Hands folded devoutly, he stood there for a moment. Then he let himself fall forward. The moment the icy water enveloped his body, he felt a severe pain in his chest. His breath caught in his throat.